Tales of the Strange and Sinister

Gregory Holden

Order this book online at www.trafford.com/03-2188
or email orders@trafford.com

Most Trafford titles are also available at major online book retailers.

Note for Librarians: A cataloguing record for this book is available from Library and Archives Canada at www.collectionscanada.ca/amicus/index-e.html

ISBN: 978-1-4120-1811-1

We at Trafford believe that it is the responsibility of us all, as both individuals and corporations, to make choices that are environmentally and socially sound. You, in turn, are supporting this responsible conduct each time you purchase a Trafford book, or make use of our publishing services. To find out how you are helping, please visit www.trafford.com/responsiblepublishing.html

Our mission is to efficiently provide the world's finest, most comprehensive book publishing service, enabling every author to experience success. To find out how to publish your book, your way, and have it available worldwide, visit us online at www.trafford.com/10510

www.trafford.com

North America & international
toll-free: 1 888 232 4444 (USA & Canada)
phone: 250 383 6864 • fax: 250 383 6804
email: info@trafford.com

The United Kingdom & Europe
phone: +44 (0)1865 722 113 • local rate: 0845 230 9601
facsimile: +44 (0)1865 722 868 • email: info.uk@trafford.com

10 9 8 7 6 5 4

Contents

Carlos Monroe drove along a desolate stretch of country road. He cast a sleepy glance at the speedometer and eased some pressure off the accelerator.

It was hot, the time of year when days were stifling but nights could turn chilly. Although it was early, the sun seemed to have reached its meridian. The warm rays beamed through the windshield. Needlessly, he fumbled with the air conditioner controls. He'd been meaning to have a repairman take a look at it. Somehow, though, there was always something that took priority or preference, usually the latter.

Swearing, he pressed the window control button. A low click followed, and then the window rolled down smoothly. Thank God that was working, he thought.

Drowsiness rode with him, a silent but deadly companion. Under the circumstance, a momentary lapse into sleep could very well prove fatal.

The road was like a tar serpent, winding its way off into the distance. Deep declines ran along each side of it. To say the least, the route was one of definite distaste. But for one fighting against the pull of sleep, it was more than merely distasteful. It was a veritable death trap.

There were protective railings alongside the road. But they were not placed in a continuous stretch, only at the sharpest curves.

Carlos' job paid well, but at times he wished it had been closer. Considering the money he made, the distance wasn't so bad. It was just the route he chose that he had qualms about. It was the most timesaving, but also the most dangerous.

Many times he'd considered going to a less dangerous but longer route. He saved about an hour off his trek by using the road he'd chosen. But he had begun to ask himself was it worth the risk. There'd been times in the past when he would've answered with a definite yes. But now, he couldn't even come up with a tentative one. That was largely due to the fact that his wife, Sarah, had changed.

In the past he used to rush home, glad to get into her embrace. The risks that his route involved didn't really matter then. But now things were different. Sarah was different. Yet, he still rushed and continued his chosen route. It was mostly due to habit now though.

Most of the time Sarah would not treat him bad. But she rarely gave him any attention. And she was gone frequently. She would occasionally surprise him by doing something kind. Still – things were different. He just could not put his finger on what the problem was.

Normally Carlos smiled often. But now, his troublous thoughts made him frown, a look not fitting his dark face.

Questions rambled through his sleep-dulled mind, questions he could not answer. Why had she changed? When did she first start acting different? How long since we've made love?

Carlos yawned and shook his head, a futile gesture. His body's yearning for sleep refused to be satisfied by just yawning. His troubled thoughts, too, were relentless. Must be something I'm doing wrong. Maybe I could be more . . . what? What do I change? Must be another man . . . would she . . . after so long together?

His troubled thoughts did not keep the fog of sleepiness from creeping over him. The warm air whispered through the open window. It rushed over his face lulling him further toward sleep.

Slowly, very slowly his head drifted toward the steering wheel. He jerked it upright again. An intense yawn escaped his lungs. The feel of moisture came quickly to his eyes. He did not know how much of the water was caused by his thoughts.

A hint of danger penetrated his dull mind, prodded his conscience. Without doubt, he needed to pull over and stretch. But his thoughts were the same as most people who found themselves in such a plight. I can make it. Get home, take a shower then rest for a while. Might even go to bed for a few hours. Staying up late is really getting…

Carlos' eyelids drooped. His eyes closed. The car swerved slowly toward the centerline. It remained on the centerline for an instant, and then it crossed over. Gradually his body eased forward. It was easy, because he didn't have his seatbelt on. Seldom did he use it.

Coming from the opposite direction, an eighteen-wheeler topped a hill. The truck driver, Mack Dearborn, was temporarily distracted. With one hand he fumbled with a knob on the radio.

Suddenly realizing he'd been preoccupied for too long, he looked up quickly. Instantly his eyes widened in shock. Carlos' car was heading straight for the truck! Mack was too shocked to shout audibly but in his mind he shouted, "Oh, God!"

Mack downshifted frantically. And in desperation, he honked the horn. Heart thumping rapidly, pulse pounding, he yelled a useless plea. "Wake up! Wake up! Please man, wake up!"

The brakes on the truck squalled. The sound ripped through the still air. No other sound prevailed. Time sped past. Mack's mumbled prayer was drowned out. Sweat glistened on his forehead. The two vehicles seemed to be pulled together as if they'd been magnetized.

Hot sweat crawled over Mack's body. His lips worked faster, emitting an unheard and futile prayer. Deep down, he knew that prayer wouldn't help. His truck was too close. Still, he honked the horn and braked without let-up.

Miraculously, the sharp peal of the horn cut into Carlos' sleep. His eyes sprang open. All traces of sleep vanished in the briefest of instances. Everything rushed at an impossible speed. His racing mind quickly assessed the situation.

Mere seconds from impact, Carlos jerked the steering wheel. The truck squealed past. Plumes of smoke, fueled by hot rubber, drifted on the hot air. The wind strung the smoke out from the tires. It trailed away, gray-white, riding the air like material attachments.

Carlos had barely missed a crash with the truck. But now, a new danger…. He was headed directly for the edge of the road, aware that a steep decline awaited, death for certain. His sweaty hands tightened on the steering wheel. He snatched the steering wheel in the opposite direction. At the same moment, he jammed his foot down on the brake. The sudden braking jerked him violently forward. His head slammed into the steering wheel.

Out of control, the car went into a spin. Darkness swallowed Carlos. The car spun several times before it was pointed back toward the wrong side of the road.

When the car ran off the side of the road it was no longer traveling at a dangerous speed. It tilted just over the brink of the roadside decline. Then slowly it rolled down the hillside. Gravel crunched under the turning tires. There was an abrupt thump, the crunch of metal, and the car halted.

The motor still continued to hum, but the car couldn't go any further. The front was crunched against a tree.

Carlos swam amid a dense darkness, slowly coming around to consciousness. He opened his eyes slowly. A groan escaped his lips. His hand went to his forehead where it had impacted the steering wheel. Lowering his hand, he was amazed that there wasn't any blood on it. Somehow, the impact had not broken the skin. But, he could feel the ponderous weight of a swelling.

He leaned back, closing his eyes against the throb in his head. Behind his closed eyelids, a picture flashed suddenly. It was a picture of his wife. He saw her smiling, naked in the arms of another man. The images began to fade. But not before a glimpse of the man's face presented itself. Though the image of the guy's face was fleeting, he thought he recognized it. It had looked like the face of his best friend! His eyes snapped open.

A single word formed in his mind. He said it without much force, not much more than an exhalation. "Jay..."

The truck driver pulled his truck to the side of the road. He ran back until he got to where Carlos' car had gone over the edge of the decline.

Mack stood at the top of the hill, sucking in huge gulps of air. He stared down the hillside. He could see Carlos' head lying against the seat. Quickly, he started scrambling down the graveled declivity, his thoughts awhirl. Man, please don't be dead? I'm sorry…so sorry. It was my fault.

Carlos turned his head to assure Mack that it wasn't his fault. He opened his mouth to speak. Nothing came out. His eyes widened. No one was near the door. He could have sworn that he'd heard the man's voice right at the side of his window. He looked quickly out the passenger's side window. No one was there either! "What the devil?"

He turned in his seat to see where Mack was. Mack was still too far up the hill for Carlos to have heard him!

Carlos' head was throbbing madly. The pain seemed to be concentrated where his head had swollen. But it pounded all over, making his vision alternate between hazy and clear.

The figure of the truck driver blurred in and out of focus as Carlos watched him descend the hillside. Mack slipped, caught himself, and then looked directly at Carlos. A smile spread across his face. And then Carlos heard the voice again. "Whew! Fellow, I'm glad that you're a quick thinker. Wasn't for that, you wouldn't be alive now."

Carlos gaped. Mack was still smiling. He hadn't even opened his mouth. What had the accident done to him? His vision blurred again. He felt extremely feverish. Blackness sucked at the fringes of his consciousness, then engulfed him.

After numerous observations and various tests, Carlos was released from the hospital the following morning. The doctor gave him a pain-reliever and a medicine to help reduce swelling.

Upon his release, his best friend, James Halden came to pick him up. The ride to Carlos' house was not what one would expect. The conversation was awkward and broken by stretches of silence.

"Jay," Carlos said, "you know, I had the strangest..." He stopped, not knowing how to complete what he was about to say.

When Carlos paused, James glanced over at him. "What's wrong, man?"

Carlos looked at James. He opened his mouth to speak but changed his mind. He shook his head slowly. "Nothing, just thinking." His mind kept replaying what had happened to him after his accident. The picture of James and his wife together, the truck driver's, unspoken words...what did it all mean? What he'd seen scared and confused him.

To himself, he could explain those things away as hallucinatory. He tried not to be disturbed by them. Something else, too, had been disturbing him long before the accident. That, he couldn't explain away. Was it coincidence that both James and Sarah had been acting differently toward him? Maybe the two changes in attitudes had something in common. Maybe James and Sarah had... He pushed the thought from his mind.

Again, he looked at the big, blocky man behind the steering wheel. He scrutinized the square jaw, the smooth, almond-colored skin, wondering… What's happened to you, Jay? We used to talk so easily. We used to share a lot of laughs. Now…you seem like a stranger.

Very little was said during the rest of the ride home. When the car pulled into the driveway, Carlos invited James in for a beer.

"What do you say to drinking a cold beer with me?"

"Uh, I would but…, I…I promised Elaine that I'd run an errand for her."

Carlos noticed the way James had avoided his eyes. He knew that James had lied. He fought down the urge to shout and demand an explanation. Long time friends didn't just change attitudes toward each other. Something was not right.

"Well," Carlos said, "maybe you can come over and watch the game with me tomorrow."

Uncomfortable, he reached for the car door before James replied. He wanted to get away suddenly, escape the tension.

"I'll do that." James replied. "I'll take you to get your car too."

"Alright then," Carlos said, "later."

He didn't hear if James said anything else. He was too consumed by his thoughts.

Carlos still didn't look back, but he nodded. It was a doubtful nod. Would things be alright? He wondered. Something had changed…

When he heard James' car start up, he turned. He watched James pull out of the driveway. His dark, handsome face wore a frown.

Even after the car had gone, he stood there, staring at the driveway. Six-one, one hundred and ninety five pounds of muscle, he stood, unmoving, like a statue.

The next day, Carlos and James sat on Carlos' broad, high-back couch. They faced a blaring big screen television.

An exciting game was being aired. Loud, constant cheers erupted from the speakers. But James noticed that Carlos seemed to be distracted. Instead of paying attention to the game, Carlos was staring at the floor. James called to him, but he gave no indication of having heard. James spoke louder. "Carlos. Hey, Carlos, what's wrong?"

"What? Oh, I must've been daydreaming," Carlos said. "Sorry."

He flashed his almost ever-present smile. The darkness of his face made his smile appear illuminating.

"Hey, man, I…" Carlos paused. For a moment he didn't know what else to say.

"What?" James asked.

"Nothing," Carlos replied. "It was silly—I mean, more like weird. Nothing worth discussing."

There was a brief silence before James spoke again. "Okay, if you say so. But, man, a minute ago you looked really strange. And even now you look kind of pale, like a ghost or something."

"Yeah, right. Humph, I didn't know that ghosts come in this shade." Carlos smiled, and they both began to laugh.

James turned toward the television. A trace of a frown creased his forehead. "Got any beer in there?" he asked.

Carlos got up slowly; he didn't speak. James watched as his friend went toward the kitchen. This time, his frown was more than just a trace.

Carlos was in the kitchen only for a moment. He came back carrying two beers, one in each hand. He gave James one of the beers, noticing that when James took it he wouldn't look at him.

James pulled the tab on his beer then took two huge swallows. He did not notice that Carlos was staring at the floor again.

"Yea-a-ah!" James shouted. "You see that? That boy's bad. Thirty-five and still slamming the ball like that. Carlos?"

Carlos didn't reply; he seemed to be unaware of anything around him. James slid closer, placing one hand on Carlos' shoulder. He shook it gently. Still, Carlos showed no sign that he was aware of anything. It was like he was sleeping, but his eyes were open and unblinking.

Suddenly, he gasped, "No!" in a whispery voice. His breath started coming heavily. Slowly, he turned to look at James whose mouth was agape, confusion plain on his face.

James spoke pleadingly. "Listen, man, you need to talk to me, tell me what's going on. Something is most definitely not…"

Carlos interrupted. His sentences were broken. It seemed he had a hard time getting his thoughts to form into words. "I…don't, don't know. I…had a…something like a vision. You…you were there…with…with Sarah. You two were…were…" It seemed he couldn't go on with his sentence. The mere thought of voicing what he'd seen made him swallow. It caused an uncomfortable lump to form in his throat.

James waited, staring intently at Carlos. He shook Carlos' shoulder again, prompting him to continue.

Carlos' gaze was wild as he searched James' face before going on. "You and Sarah, I saw you two have…having sex."

His voice dropped so low on the last few words that James leaned closer. "What? You couldn't have said what I thought you did. Me and your wife! Me and Sarah having sex? Carlos, that's ludicrous! I hope I didn't hear you right. What in the world…"

Carlos interrupted James' exclamations. "I know…you're right, it is ridiculous." Some of the wild look was now vanishing from his eyes.

For a moment everything was quiet, except for the blaring television. The two men were at a loss for words.

Dropping his head into his palms, Carlos muttered, "What's going on? What's wrong with me?"

James patted his shoulder reassuringly. "It's alright, man. Nothing's wrong. Sometimes the unexplainable happens. Try to forget it."

Carlos raised his head and gave James a half-hearted smile. "Yeah, you're right," he said. "Thanks." Verbally he agreed with James, but inwardly it was different. The vivid images he'd seen wouldn't let him forget. Seemed so weird, so real, he thought.

Suddenly loud cheers dissected his reflecting. "Man!" he shouted, "look at that replay. You're right, that boy is bad. He just slammed again."

Carlos noticed that James didn't respond, so he spoke a little louder. He used James' nickname. "Jay. Jay, what's wrong?"

"Huh?" James asked, casting a quick, nervous glance in Carlos' direction.

Carlos saw that James' hands were trembling and that James did not look directly at him. He pretended that he hadn't noticed. "I was just asking you what's wrong, that's all."

James kept his face turned away when he replied. "Oh, uh, nothing. I'm alright."

It wasn't hard to tell that James was lying. However, Carlos didn't question him any further. What could he say?

Trying to smooth out the mounting tension, James patted Carlos' back. "Hey, man, you act like you didn't believe me. Really though, I'm alright." This time he forced himself to look Carlos in the eyes, but it didn't last long.

Again, there seemed to be nothing appropriate to say. In Carlos' mind though, he said something that made his heart thump faster. He's done something...he looks guilty. God, could it be?

It took a lot of effort to dismiss the thought his mind was formulating. Leaning back, he let out an audible sigh.

"You know," he said, "maybe I've got an explanation." Without seeing if James was listening, he went on. "I've never been a coffee drinker until recently. So maybe the caffeine is doing something strange to me. I mean, since caffeine is a drug, who's to say exactly how it affects the brain? Who's to say how it's affecting my brain?"

His questions were not ones he really wanted answers to. He was really trying to convince himself. Carlos wanted to attribute what he'd seen to anything. He did not want to think that he had actually had a veritable vision. Those things do not really happen in real life. Do they? Yet, what he had seen was real to him, at least in a sense.

"Jay," he said, "have you ever heard of caffeine doing anything strange to someone?"

"No," James said. "Can't say I've ever heard anything like that."

James changed the subject quickly. "Hey, how about another beer, huh?"

"Yeah," Carlos responded, getting up hurriedly. He was glad to get away, even if only for a moment. Suspicion was crowding into his mind despite his struggle against it. Heading for the kitchen, he queried over his shoulder, "Bud or Natural Lite?" Carlos was almost at the kitchen before James replied, "Either one'll be alright." It was obvious that James had been distracted again.

The tension, thick now, unrelenting, inclined Carlos to believe that something really was amiss. In spite of the feeling, he forced a smile when he came back.

Giving James the Natural Lite, he sat down heavily. Wanting to dissolve the uneasiness between them, he made an attempt at humor. "You know," he said, "when I was in the kitchen, I heard something really strange."

James gave Carlos a quick apprehensive look. He took a huge gulp from his can of beer, unable to keep his hand from shaking. His voice was shaky too, when he spoke. "Yeah? What'd you hear?"

"Well," Carlos replied, "I'd just made my mind up to give you the Budweiser when a voice said, 'Don't.' For a minute, I was confused. I looked around slowly, and then I heard it again. It seemed to come from somewhere above my head. So I thought back to what my mother used to say a long time ago. She said, 'The Lord works in mysterious ways, son.' Now that I knew whom the voice belonged to, I asked, 'Why, Lord? Why can't I give James the Budweiser?' Then the voice said, 'O my son, if you would only look at that person's waistline, you would see that he is already affected by done lapped.' 'Done lapped?' I asked. 'Yes, my son,' the voice said, 'his stomach done lapped over his belt.'"

Carlos started to laugh. The look on James' face stopped him. James was trying to smile, but he failed.

"Carlos, that was pretty good. One thing though, for a minute I thought you were serious. Man, you had me worried." He looked down at his thick middle. Although he was not fat, his waistline was beginning to thicken with the passage of years.

"Humph," he said, "I guess that voice had a point. I really don't need the extra calories. Done lapped," he said as he started to smile. "Pretty good. Yeah, that was a good one. I guess maybe I will start drinking this stuff more often." He raised the Natural Lite can, paused, and then took another swallow.

"And speaking of drinking, didn't you tell me you had two whole pots of coffee both Monday and Tuesday nights?"

Carlos nodded. "Yeah, that's an awful lot, huh?"

"Shoot, yeah, that's a lot," James said. "Especially considering that it tastes about like used oil."

Replying, Carlos frowned as if he could taste the bitter bite of coffee at that instant. "Well, I've got to agree, it doesn't taste all that great. I have got to do something to stay awake though. My last assignment called for quite a few extra hours. My supervisor said he needs it completed by Friday. So I guess I don't have much choice, but to date Mister Coffee every night."

Carlos stopped talking for a moment. He saw that James was staring at the floor; it did not seem that he had heard Carlos at all. Even when another cheer erupted from the television, he did not lift his head to look.

Carlos called to him twice before getting his attention. "Jay. Jay, did you see that?"

James brought his head up sharply. "Oh. I…man. I…I don't know what's wrong with me. I've got to go. Anyway, I need to pick up some…"

Carlos cut in before James could finish what he had started to say. "You have to pick up some cold medicine for Elaine."

James stood up quickly. His eyes were wide in surprise. "What the devil! How'd you know what I was going to say?"

Again, a lump caught in Carlos' throat. His thoughts whirled; his pulse began to hammer. What was going on here? "Man," he answered, "I really don't know. It…it was like I heard you even though…"

"Wait a minute," James said. "People don't really read minds. I mean, for sure…"

"Oh, God!" Carlos exclaimed, "I know what you're about to say. You were about to say, for sure there's got to be some logical explanation."

James' mouth fell open. He took two hurried steps backward while his eyes searched Carlos' face wildly.

The thud of Carlos' heart and the pounding cadence of his pulse were furious now. He had begun to think that maybe, through some inexplicable way, he was developing a strange ability. Twice is more than coincidence.

For some reason, Carlos felt an incredible surge of energy, the feeling that often occurs when one is in danger. He stood suddenly, causing James to back up another step.

Instinctively, Carlos reached toward James. Carlos had seen the look of fear before; it was plain upon James' visage now.

When Carlos reached toward him, James put another step between them. Suddenly, without a word, he turned. In a few long strides, he was at the door.

Momentarily, Carlos was motionless and speechless. When he was able to utter a few words, it was too late. "Jay, Jay wait! I…" The door closed, chopping off his utterance.

Staring after the closed door, he felt a detachment creep over him. "I'm dreaming," he muttered. "This is a dream."

Slowly he lifted both hands, staring at his palms. He brought his hands to his face and rubbed them roughly against his skin. I'm not sleeping. God, this is real, he thought. This is real.

Carlos turned slowly. Each movement seemed to take an awful effort. The rush of energy he'd felt had vanished. He now felt weak and numb.

He went into the kitchen, his thoughts awhirl. Jumbled and rapid questions rushed through his mind. No sooner had one reached completion, than another forced its way upon him. Torture. The questions were torment because he did not want to accept what his answers were. Why had Jay lied about having to get cold medicine? Was it because of a feeling of guilt? Was Jay actually capable of having sex with Sarah?

His shadow cast a fuzzy replica, the contour of his body, upon the shiny tile floor. Temporarily he'd forgotten why he'd come into the kitchen. Just standing there, he was wrestling with the constant barrage of questions. Did I imagine seeing Sarah with Jay? I could not have really read his mind, could I?

A picture of James' reaction flashed through his mind. Along with the picture, he heard a vague echo of James' words. "How'd you know what I was going to say?"

So lost in thought was he that he did not hear his wife come into the house. Partly though, that was due to the blaring television. However, he still did not hear her even as she approached the kitchen.

Sarah was tall for a woman. Yet, at six-foot even, she was very well proportioned. She was not quite pretty, but she exuded a certain intrinsic attractiveness.

She leaned against the doorjamb, studying her husband briefly before she spoke. "You alright?"

Carlos' head was down. A frown of deep concentration was on his face. At the sound of Sarah's voice, he jerked his head around, startled. His first replication followed, sounding much like an exhalation. "Huh? Oh, I didn't hear you come in."

For a moment he did not know what else to say, neither did Sarah. Even though Carlos expressed nothing verbally, his mind was saying all sorts of things about Sarah. They were the sorts of things that no man wants to think about his wife.

Sarah started toward him with a hint of a smile. However, when she saw the look in his eyes, all traces of the smile vanished. When she approached Carlos, she reached out to embrace him. All the while, she avoided his eyes. Something she'd felt in her husband's gaze did not feel right.

Forcing himself, Carlos embraced her in return. In an attempt to ignore some of the tension, he said the first thing he could think of. "Sarah, how's Elaine been feeling?"

Sarah stopped embracing Carlos; she looked at him quizzically. "She's fine. But where did that question come from?"

Carlos did not answer her directly. "Well I was just wondering. Does she have a cold?"

Raising her brows questioningly, Sarah replied, "No, like I said, she's fine."

Therefore, James had indeed lied about having to buy Elaine some cold medicine. The thought made Carlos feel a deep, gnawing emptiness. He could think of only one reason why his long-time friend had lied to him. James was afraid! He obviously had something to hide.

"No," Carlos said. His voice was not much above the sound of a whisper.

"What?" Sarah asked.

"So," Carlos said. "I said so, did you and Elaine have much fun?" Somehow he managed to affect a strained smile.

Sarah was not quite satisfied with his response; it showed in her eyes. She responded though, despite Carlos' answer. "Well, Elaine was in such a God awful hurry to get back to James. If it weren't for her constant rushing, I guess we could have had some fun."

It wasn't hard for Carlos to detect the envy in his wife's voice. What he'd heard in her voice was unmistakable. It snatched his mind back into a whirlwind of tormentful questions all over again.

Sarah went on speaking. "So, aren't you going to tell me how your day…" Carlos turned away from her quickly. She frowned. "Carlos, honey, what's wrong? Why're you acting like that?"

Carlos wanted to scream, "You slut! What's wrong! What's wrong! You're cheating on me, that's what's wrong." However, he did not say anything even remotely similar. "No reason. Nothing's wrong, nothing at all."

He went swiftly over to one of the kitchen cabinets. "I need a drink," he said. It was hard for him to keep the water from his eyes.

A flicker of anger flashed behind Sarah's golden brown eyes. She made no attempt at keeping it from her voice. "Carlos Monroe, you're acting strange, and I most certainly want to know why."

Before making a reply, Carlos reached into the cabinet. He took down a bottle of liquor. Then he turned quickly, his eyes alight by a commixture of powerful emotions. "Betrayal! Cheating, that's why!" he shouted. However, the shout was only in his mind. He could not bring himself to say those things aloud.

Carlos bit down hard on his teeth, attempting to keep his anger under control. An icy stare emanated from his eyes though, conveying how he felt.

Not making a reply to Sarah's demand, he spoke. It was only a repeat of what he had said earlier. "I need a drink."

Turning his back on his wife, he went over to another cabinet. He set the bottle down and took down a glass.

Sarah's gaze followed his every move. She watched quietly. Her anger was slowly turning into something else, something like fear. Her thoughts went back to when she had ridden past James. She pictured the look in his eyes when he had driven past. Sarah had tried to wave him down, but he was hurrying undeterred. Fear was in his eyes.

James had shouted something out his window. However, the wind had muffled some of his words. She thought back to what she had been able to hear. "…at Hill Road Park…8:30. Trouble…he knows."

James had shouted for her to meet him at one of their frequent hideouts. However, what was the last thing he'd shouted? It sounded like, "he knows."

Sarah's thoughts were rushing now. She was struggling to think clearly. In her mind she went back to some of the places she and James had been meeting. They had been very careful. He can't know, she thought. We have been so careful. How could he possibly…?

Carlos turned so quickly that it made Sarah inhale sharply. The inhalation disrupted her breathing pattern; she struggled to get it under control again.

The stare Carlos gave her was unnerving. She smiled weakly. However, Carlos did not return the smile.

Sarah felt herself stiffen as Carlos started toward her. His gaze remained fixed on her, boring into her eyes. She lowered her head, avoiding Carlos' stare. Her mind fumbled for words, but then Carlos was past her.

Carlos took the bottle of liquor and the empty glass into the living room. He placed the bottle and the glass upon the coffee table. His head fell weakly, falling into his hands.

I must actually be losing it. Is this what it feels like to go crazy? he thought. Then, as in answer to what he had thought, he heard James' words. "How'd you know what I was going to say?" There it was then, some comfort. He did not know how to explain what was happening, but he was not crazy. He could actually read James' thoughts.

With hesitant steps, Sarah made her way into the living room. She approached to within a few steps away from the couch where Carlos was sitting. Placing her hands on the curvature of her hips, she spoke. However, she tried to sound thoroughly irate, her voice came out tremulously. "Sometimes you…you can act so…so damn weird, mister! Mind telling me what's on your mind?"

Carlos raised his head slowly. His eyes were squinted down to mere slits. He did not bother to acknowledge his wife's query. Instead, he reached for the bottle of liquor.

While continuing to ignore his wife, Carlos removed the top from the bottle. He swung it up, taking a long, loud swallow.

Picking up the remote, he clicked the television off. The quietness that settled seemed to Sarah that it could actually be felt. When Carlos swung the bottle up again, the sloshing of the liquor sounded loud. In contrast to the quiet, it might have been crashing waves.

Sarah's next words were no longer demanding; they were almost pleading. "Carlos? Carlos Monroe, do…do you hear me? Well…since you, um…since you're not going to…" she swallowed loudly and then continued, "talk, I guess I will. You will never guess what Elaine and I did. We…"

Carlos interrupted her. "You bought the two men in your lives surprise gifts." In response to Carlos' statement, Sarah raised her brows in surprise.

"Carlos! That's what I was going to say," Sarah said. "How did you …?"

"My God," Carlos uttered, "this really is happening. This is real…"

"What are you talking about?" Sarah asked. "What is real?" She waited, watching Carlos; her fear was temporarily suppressed by the curiosity she was feeling.

Reaching for the bottle again, Carlos tried to respond. However, at first, his words did not come out right. They massed together in his mind, becoming a conglomeration of tangled syllables and half-formed sentences. "I, I don't…when I…at first I thought I was going crazy."

His voice dropped down to a whisper. Sarah could scarcely hear him.

"I can actually hear thoughts," he said. Excitement started to overwhelm him. For the moment he had even forgotten about being angry with Sarah.

He set the bottle down with a shaky hand. His words poured out rapidly and loud. "I mean, man … that's got to be the craziest thing I've ever said. But..."

Sarah sat down beside him, placing one hand on his shoulder. Until then he'd been talking without even looking in her direction. Now he turned and looked at her; his eyes gleamed excitedly.

He went on at a fast rate. "Listen, Sarah, I know it sounds really absurd, but really…I don't…people's thoughts just come to me, just pop into my head."

Sarah didn't say anything; she only stared. She too, was getting very excited. She was thinking that Carlos' knowing about the gifts had to be more than coincidence. Although, mind readers, in Sarah's opinion, had belonged to the sphere of fairies and goblins, her opinion was rapidly changing.

"Wait a minute," Sarah said, "what if there's some other kind of explanation? What if what you just did was just coincidence? What if …"

"Let's…try…something," Carlos interrupted. "Think up a number between, well, think of any number?"

"Okay," Sarah agreed. "Well" she said. "I'm ready for you to make a…"

Even before she could complete her sentence, Carlos blurted out "Three thousand-four hundred and fifty-six."

He smiled at Sarah in confidence. She did not need to tell him that he'd gotten every number correct. Her expression was revelatory enough.

Sarah blinked rapidly several times. She stood quietly. The fear had returned. Two of James' words echoed through her mind. "He knows."

She now understood why James looked so afraid. In addition, she knew now how Carlos must have come to know about her liaison with James.

Her breasts began to heave; she felt unsteady on her feet. "I don't feel so good," she said. "I think I…I'll go outside. I need a little fresh…"

Carlos stood up quickly; Sarah backed up a step. Her eyes watched Carlos like an animal, cornered and desperate.

A hard stare was the only means of communication Carlos used. His eyes were a ponderous weight upon Sarah. She fumbled with her hands. Then she turned quickly, only to be halted by Carlos' sudden grip on her wrist.

Sarah stiffened and winced. She turned slowly. Carlos attempted to look into her eyes, but Sarah hung her head quickly.

Carlos' next words were spoken quietly. It was clear though, that they left no option for Sarah. "Sit down," he said, and let go of her wrist.

She sat down watching Carlos with wary eyes. He neither looked in her direction nor said anything. She watched mutely as his shoulders rose and fell with several loud sighs.

Shifting uncomfortably she mustered up enough courage to speak. "Carlo…Carlos, what…"

Carlos brought his head up quickly. He pointed a shaking finger at her, almost touching her face. "Shut up!" he shouted. "Shut the hell up!"

She was stunned. She opened her mouth to protest, but words eluded her.

Carlos dropped his head into his palms. An audible groan escaped his lips. Then he muttered without raising his head. "Why? Why, Sarah? Why'd you do it?"

Sarah turned her head to look at the door. At the same instant, she jumped up. In the split second that she straightened up, Carlos' hand shot out. He grabbed her wrist again. "Ow!" she expelled. "Carlos, let go. You're hurting my wrist."

Flinging her wrist away from him, he spat out angry words. "Yeah, yeah, I'll let go! However, I know Sarah. Trust me; I know your little nasty secret."

Sarah could feel herself cringe on the inside. She tried in vain to quell the merciless fear that knotted her insides. Its effect was discernable in the quaver of her next words. "Secret, what kind of...what kind of secret? I don't know..."

"Stop! Just stop it, Sarah," Carlos said. His voice was hoarse, choked with fury. "I know about you and Jay!"

"What?" Sarah shouted. "You know about me and..." Sarah tried to giggle, but it sounded forced. "Pl...ease! Don't make me laugh."

Backing toward the door, Sarah continued, "You...you've lost it! You're crazy. I..."

Carlos started toward her. In a few long strides he had overtaken her retreat. He raised his hand as if to strike her a back handed blow.

Sarah threw both hands up in front of her face protectively. "Stay back! Stay away from me!"

Carlos halted, his hand still poised. For an instant he remained in that position even after the door slammed. Sarah was gone.

Instinctually, Carlos reached for the doorknob, but then he dropped his hand and turned away. He ambled listlessly to the couch, wondering where his wife had gone.

Sitting down, he dropped his head. Suddenly though, he brought his head back up. He wondered what would happen if he concentrated? If he'd seen things that he did not want to see, why couldn't he see things that he did want to see? He closed his eyes. Perchance he could see where Sarah was headed, perchance.

After a moment, Carlos opened his eyes. Nothing! he thought. Maybe she's right. What if I am going crazy?

Unmerciful questions bombarded him, resonating inside his mind. Is she really having an affair? God, if she is...what can I do about it? What will I do? Murder? Could I actually mur…? He shook his head vigorously. However, the action failed to clear his thinking. The liquor he'd been drinking was fusing with the turmoil his mind was undergoing.

Not knowing what else to do, he reached for the liquor again. At the least, he hoped it would serve as a suppressant, drown the pain. It hurt him deep down on the inside, a consuming, relentless pain.

The vacuity, the emptiness inside was intense. For some strange reason it caused him to think of the universe. Vast, miles and miles of space.

Turning the bottle up, he took several hard swallows. When he brought it down, something else came down also. Nevertheless, he did not seem to take note. He did not bother to wipe at the warm liquid that crawled slowly down his cheeks.

Carlos turned the bottle up again. When he brought it down, it was nearly empty. He stood up slowly, hesitated and then walked determinedly into his bedroom.

In the bedroom, Carlos paused when he gripped the knob on the closet door. The metal seemed cold against the warm sweat permeating his sticky palm.

His surroundings became like things in a dream. He saw his hand turn the knob. He heard the creak of the door. And, he was aware of standing on his toes, raking things off the shelf. Nevertheless, it all felt like he was merely watching, not doing.

Finally, he pulled a shoebox forward. The box felt heavier than what he remembered. Carlos never realized that a gun could be so heavy.

He saw himself remove the top, felt his hand close upon the chill metal. Carlos thought he felt his heart actually leap. The thud of it seemed loud in his eardrums.

He was hardly aware of dropping the box and heading for the living room. When he went out the door, he didn't bother closing it. Carlos did not know if he would ever make it back, so it did not matter that the door was left open.

Elaine Halden stood peering eagerly out her living room window. She was waiting for James to come home. She wondered if he would like what Sarah'd help her pick out to buy for him.

After standing at the window for several minutes, she walked restlessly over to the couch to wait.

Elaine was short and thick, beginning to show signs of obesity. Still, it was very easy to see that her body had once been very enticing. Elaine's face was rounded, pleasant to look at, but not pretty.

She had hands that were small, better suited for a child it seemed. They lay on her lap, changing in position every few seconds.

Elaine seemed not to notice; her attention was drawn to the window. She had left the curtains pulled back, wanting to see when her husband would pull into the driveway.

She'd always thought that she and James had a good marriage. But, for the last nine months or so, things had been really different. James had begun acting cold toward her. Worry had pushed her to the point of questioning him on several occasions. This only served as a fuel, usually igniting James' temper.

The thought of James having an affair entered her mind constantly. Yet, she always fought valiantly against such thoughts.

Often she would attribute his coldness to her figure having become less attractive. Nevertheless, would he actually cheat?

Elaine sighed, and getting up off the couch, her face took on a somber look.

Her face brightened though, when glancing toward the window, she saw James' car pull into the driveway. The car rolled into the driveway with more speed than was necessary. Why was James in a hurry?

Walking to the door, she opened it hurriedly. Something's wrong, she thought.

James was hurrying toward the steps; it was obvious by his manner that something was indeed wrong.

He was walking at a fast pace and, he kept glancing to where the driveway met the street.

Elaine's forehead wrinkled in a frown that held for a moment. She stared hard at James as he ascended the steps. On the top step, he paused long enough to take another quick look toward the street. He brushed past her without speaking, hardly even giving her a glance.

Hurt was in Elaine's eyes. She turned slowly, watching James walk into the hallway.

Her mouth opened; she meant to say something, but nothing came out.

Biting down on her lip, she stared in the direction James had taken. Then she started walking in that direction. Her steps faltered, but then she went on.

The bathroom door in the hallway was closed. However, Elaine could hear vague shuffling.

She raised her hand and knocked hard several times. It did not escape her notice that she'd knocked harder than was necessary. At the moment though, she did not care; she was beginning to get angry. She felt that James' frigidity was unwarranted; she did not deserve such coldness.

After she knocked, there was a pause and then James mumbled, "Yeah?"

Suddenly Elaine was at a loss of words; she opened her mouth to speak. Nevertheless, for a moment she did not know how to start. Then finally, she said, "James, I…I want you to see something." She was thinking of the gift she had bought while she and Sarah were shopping.

There was a pause; the commode flushed, and then she heard James mumbling again.

The door opened. James remained in the doorway briefly, his large frame limned against the bathroom's beige interior.

Elaine started to tell him about the present she had bought for him. Nevertheless, the look in James' eyes stopped her. She had seen that look before, seen it on the faces of other people. But James? She could not recall ever seeing fear on his face.

James averted his eyes away from hers and started forward without speaking. She sidestepped allowing him room to pass. When he had barely gotten past her, Elaine reached for his shoulder.

"James, honey," she said, "please tell me what, what's…" He turned swiftly, causing her to jerk her hand away.

James ran one hand over his coarse hair. The rough texture massaged his palm lightly.

"I suppose you want to know what it is that's bothering me, huh?" A brief quiet fell before he went on. "A friend…a friend of ours is in serious trouble. We have to…"

"A…friend?" Elaine interrupted. "Trouble? Who?" She grabbed ahold of James by both arms.

"Sarah," James answered. "Sarah is in real serious trouble. Carlos is acting really weird. He's going into…into shock, or…or dazes. I do not know how to explain it, but he's definitely not himself. He's…I think Carlos is actually going crazy. He even thinks I've been sleeping with Sarah! He says that he…"

The doorbell rang several times in rapid succession. The sounds cut him off in his narration. He turned quickly, heading for the door in long, hurried steps.

Elaine was caught off guard. She was shocked by what James had just divulged. Not Carlos! She had known him for so long. It had to be something wrong with what James had said. Nevertheless, would he tell her such a horrible lie?

She finally moved from the spot she'd felt glued to. By that time, James was almost at the front door.

When she got into the front room, she saw that Sarah was their visitant. Sarah was standing in the doorway talking to James in rapid, whispery words.

Approaching, Elaine caught a glimpse of the fear in Sarah's eyes. She noted too, that Sarah kept looking over her shoulder toward the driveway.

Sarah was in the middle of a sentence when she saw Elaine approaching. Her words came to a halt; something like confusion, anger and worry flickered behind her eyes. But, the look vanished quickly.

James saw that Sarah had been distracted by something behind him. He turned quickly. A temporary look of surprise and agitation surfaced upon his face. It was as if he had forgotten that Elaine was there.

What Elaine had seen on both James and Sarah's face was puzzling. What was going on here? Elaine could feel the weight of a heavy unease coming upon her. She suppressed it when she spoke. "Sarah, come in."

James remained at the door after Sarah had entered. He peeked outside quickly before closing the door. He half expected to see Carlos pull up at any minute. He wondered what would happen if that did occur. How would Carlos react?

His hand went out toward the lock, but he changed his mind and walked away. James wanted to stop and yank the door open again. But, he knew he would feel silly if he did.

Elaine and Sarah were sitting on the couch. Elaine was hugging Sarah and speaking words of consolation to her that did not appear to be working. Sarah did not seem to hear her. Her head was down, cupped in her hands.

James stopped when he got near the two women. Elaine looked up into his eyes. There was concern on his face, and something else, something Elaine could not discern.

James spoke in hesitation. "I…I'm going in the back." He started to walk away, stopped, half turned, but then continued.

Immediately upon entering the bedroom, a vehement stream of curse words came out under his breath. He started pacing back and forth. After a moment, he went back to the living room.

Sarah had her head up now. She had told Elaine all that had transpired.

"Is…everything…alright?" James questioned. Elaine looked over at Sarah; her eyes were questioning. Sarah saw what Elaine's eyes asked. She nodded.

James said something else, but it was unclear. He was heading for the door as he spoke. When his hand reached out and gripped the knob, Elaine's voice stopped him. "James, what are you…we going to do?"

He half-turned. "Right now, to tell you the truth, I really don't know."

Elaine prepared to question him further. "But where are you

go…" The door closed and James descended the steps at a brisk pace.

As he walked to his car, he couldn't help but watch the entrance to the driveway.

Elaine stared for a moment, at the closed door. She frowned. It was apparent to her that James was very confused. Why had he left so suddenly if he thought that Sarah was in danger? Moreover, what about her? Am I being left out? she thought. Somebody is not telling me something. I just can't believe that Carlos…

Elaine looked at Sarah, looked away quickly, then looked at her again. "Sarah," she said, "I want you to tell…" A car slid to a halt in the driveway. The rough grind of the tires on the gravel cut into Elaine's statement. She glanced at Sarah as she stood up; she saw that Sarah's eyes had widened. It was obvious to Elaine that Sarah had guessed who had pulled into the driveway. Elaine too had a good idea who had driven up.

Elaine went to the door. She opened it and her guess proved correct. It was Carlos. He was hurrying toward the steps, teeth clenched, eyes squinting. He was looking at Elaine straight on. His eyes did not waver.

Reflexively Elaine's hand tightened on the doorknob. She started to close the door but just as Carlos reached the bottom step, she changed her mind. For some reason, she was not afraid. But still, for Sarah's sake she decided to be cautious.

Elaine opened the door a little wider, but she stood directly in Carlos' path, effectively blocking the entrance. She held one hand up in Carlos' direction, palm outward. For an instant, it seemed that Carlos was not going to stop.

He did stop though, mere inches from her hand. His chest was heaving heavily, and his gaze still remained unwavering. There was not even a hint of their long, amiable friendship in those eyes.

Carlos shifted his feet roughly. He could feel the slight tremble that accompanied a surge of adrenaline. Nevertheless, he struggled to maintain control.

Despite his efforts, when he spoke, his voice betrayed him. It quaked with emotion. "Listen…Elaine, I…I need to see my wife."

Elaine looked back at Sarah quickly. It took only an instant for her to see the look Sarah returned.

In reply to Carlos' statement, Elaine said, "Sorry, Carlos, I…she doesn't want to see you."

A moment of quiet hung in the air. This time, Elaine couldn't bring herself to look Carlos in the eyes. Hesitantly, amid the ponderous silence, Elaine began pushing the door closed.

Carlos reached out quickly, grabbing hold of the doorknob. "Wait! Wait a minute, Elaine, please? What did she…did they tell you?"

Elaine hesitated before she replied. "They, well…"

Carlos brought his hand up to silence her. "You were going to say that they told you that I need help. But the exact words you were going to say were…"

Carlos stopped. He had looked over Elaine's shoulder. The spot where Sarah had been sitting was now empty!

"Where'd she go?" Carlos asked. Elaine glanced behind her, and then she suddenly turned completely around. "Sarah! Sarah?" she said.

She started toward the couch and prepared to call out to Sarah again. "Sar…" She never got the other syllable out. Carlos had suddenly gripped her wrist. He stepped just beyond the entrance.

Elaine turned quickly, leveling a pointed stare at Carlos. He understood. He let her wrist fall from his grasp.

Elaine's next words shocked Carlos. "I don't believe you're crazy," she said. "But something very strange is…"

They heard a car start up. It was obvious that Sarah had sneaked out the back door to her car.

Elaine started toward the door. She stopped short when Carlos said, "Wait. No need to go after her. I need to talk to you." He waited for Elaine to reply. She did not, but she moved back away from the door.

Carlos went on. "So…they told you I was crazy, huh?" She nodded.

"I'm glad that you don't believe that garbage," Carlos said. He sighed heavily. "Because I'm really going to need somebody to lean on. Actually, before this is all over, you're going to need me too…we're going to need each other."

He saw the questioning look come over Elaine's face. He stopped then, trying to figure an easy way to tell her what he had found out. There was no easy way though.

"I don't know of any way to make this easy, Elaine," Carlos said. "They've been cheating on us…with each other…."

The mélange of emotions on Elaine's face caused him to pause. It was clear that she was hurt and confused. Nevertheless, other than her expression, she gave no indication that she had heard him. Carlos might have been a transparent entity, for her gaze seemed to pass right through him.

A battle was raging within, to the very core of her soul. She really did not want to believe what she had heard. Nevertheless, wouldn't James' inexplicable behavior suggest that what Carlos had said was true? With Sarah, though, her best friend….

Elaine felt as if she had been slammed in the chest by a massive hand. She turned away from Carlos slowly. She felt numb as she walked to the couch. Suddenly her world had turned into a dream, a horrible dream. Surely, such betrayal did not happen in the real world. This just could not be.

Carlos remained just beyond the entrance a moment longer. He regretted having to be the bearer of such news. However, what else could he do?

He walked slowly to the couch and sat down next to Elaine. She did not acknowledge his presence, did not even seem to realize that he was beside her.

She stared vacantly at her hands, fingers entwined upon her lap. Without looking at Carlos, she began a question. Her voice was weak though, enervated by the turmoil inside.

"Carlos," she said, "how do you know…?"

Carlos reached for her shoulder. Elaine leaned against his shoulder. Trickles of tepid tears slid down her cheeks.

Carlos felt, rather than heard, a long sign issue from within himself. He was trying to figure the best way of telling Elaine about his strange and sudden ability. He thought of several ways of approaching the subject. He dismissed them all, suddenly deciding there was not a best way. Therefore, he said simply, "Elaine, I can read people's thoughts. "

Elaine lifted her head off his shoulder. Carlos expected her to pull away from him, but she did not, she only stared at him. Carlos thought he detected a flicker of fear in her moist stare; she laid her head upon his shoulder again. He was a little surprised that she had shown no more reaction than she did. He figured that maybe what he had told her about James had already numbed her feelings. Maybe dealing with that was so much, for the moment, that nothing else mattered.

"I realize all this sounds…I know it is all so overwhelming, but all I've said is true." Though Carlos knew he was not the blame, his tone was apologetic.

"Elaine," he said, "think of your social security number?"

She lifted her head slightly, just for an instant. "Okay," she said.

Barely had she assented before Carlos responded, "Two-four-one-seventy-five-three-four-one-five."

Elaine brought her head up again, this time more quickly. Remnants of tears shined on her cheeks and made her wide eyes gleam. She smiled for the first time since Carlos had come. "My God, that was amazing," she said. "But…but how did you…what caused you to…I mean…"

Carlos smiled at her inability to express herself. Evidently she was in more wonderment than she had made apparent.

"God," she said, "can't even get my thought together."

"It's alright," Carlos responded.

For some reason, on impulse, he suddenly reached for Elaine's face. He placed one hand tenderly on each side. He brought her face up slowly so that their gazes met. Elaine's lips parted ever so slightly. Carlos thought that maybe she was about to say something. However, she did not; instead, she began to inch her face toward his.

Elaine felt her heart begin a rapid cadence, her breasts rose and fell heavily. A part of her mind shouted, This is wrong! Don't do it. But, hadn't her own husband done wrong? Still…

Her lips mashed against Carlos', feeling the warm softness. Then she felt their tongues seek out and find each other's. Elaine moaned softly. It had been far too long since she and James had done anything similar.

Again, the thought that this was wrong surfaced in her mind. Nevertheless, Carlos pulled her to him tightly; all the while, his tongue wrestled hers hungrily. Suddenly it was no longer a question of right or wrong. The question was, wasn't she entitled to love from a man?

Carlos too, was losing his battle with the issue of right and wrong. Hadn't Sarah wronged him, cheating with his best friend? Hadn't he been deprived of intimacy for longer than any married man should?

He thought of pulling back, stopping before they went any further. But, Elaine's tongue was so wet and hot. It slid across his furiously, working like the influence of an aphrodisiac.

Simultaneously they both pulled away, sucking in quick breaths of air. They still clung to each other, desire alight in their eyes.

Carlos broke the spell. He asked, "Elaine…do…do you feel guilty?"

She supplied him with a blunt answer. "No," she said. She stood, paused, cast Carlos a strange look, and then started for the door. Carlos thought he had seen the beginning of a smile play at the corners of her lips.

Neither Elaine nor Carlos had bothered to close the door earlier. Elaine reached out for the knob. Suddenly though, she turned facing Carlos. She had turned unexpectedly, catching Carlos off guard. He had been admiring the way her hips swayed when she'd walked away. He smiled guiltily.

The fact that Carlos had been watching her pleasured her deeply, but she did not reveal it. She said, "What in the world am I thinking? Suppose they come back and catch…"

"They won't," Carlos said, with aplomb. Elaine raised her brows in puzzlement. He decided to explain. "I saw where they are."

For a moment Elaine was still puzzled. "You saw…" she started, but then the realization of what Carlos had meant came to her.

She stared for a moment, without saying anything. She did not know what to say at first. "Gosh! Carlos, you mean you can actually see things too? Isn't that…that scary or…"

"Shh," Carlos said, bringing one finger up in front of his lips. "If you don't mind, missy pooh, what about saving those questions for a little later." He flashed his white teeth. "Right now," he said, "I want to use my energy in another way."

Elaine smiled back, and then she turned to close the door. After shutting the door, she leaned her back against it, fixing Carlos with a mischievous stare.

She spoke again, seemingly as if conversation had never lapsed. "After what they did to…after the way they did us, I don't think I can feel guilty." She paused. "No matter what."

While not taking her eyes off Carlos, she came toward him. The added swing of her ample hips did not escape Carlos' notice.

Elaine stopped in front of him, purposely letting her pelvic area remain only inches from his face. Carlos' eyes roamed over the rondure of her hips, the curvature of her thighs.

She reached for Carlos' hands. When he stood, she spoke softly. "James and I…we haven't made love in a long time." She paused and then said, "He has not even been paying me any attention. Bastard! Now I know why. I don't even…"

Carlos said, "Shh"…and lifted her chin with one finger. Their lips met. They embraced tightly as their tongues intertwined, conveying their lust.

Elaine pulled back first, but she took one of his hands in hers. She pulled him toward the bedroom. As she walked, she spoke over her shoulder softly. "For the first time in my life, I don't mind doing something reckless," she said. "Ever felt that way, Carlos?"

"Huh? Oh, no," Carlos said, "but I do now." He had barely heard her, his attention had been diverted by the way her buttocks moved under her tight jeans. He'd already begun visualizing….

An hour was lost, within which they gave in to reckless abandon. Time slipped by unnoticed. They were two souls, as one now, lost amid a maelstrom of passionate lovemaking. Like animals of a lower phylum, they grunted, groped, caressed and moaned. All that mattered was extinguishing the yearning, satisfying the innate desire raging inside.

Afterward they lay quietly for a while, amid a tangle of sweaty sheets. Each was enjoying the afterglow, occupied by their individual thoughts.

Elaine spoke first. "Did the thought of them coming back cross your mind yet?"

"No," Carlos said. "Anyway, right now, they're too far away and too damn scared." He could not help but flash a confident smile.

The thick curtains in the small bedroom were drawn almost closed, allowing very little light to penetrate. Dimness permeated the room, making Carlos' white teeth gleam against his dark skin.

Carlos stirred, placing both hands behind his head. "Hmm," he said, staring up at the ceiling.

Elaine was curious. "What? What are you thinking, Carlos?"

He smiled again before answering. "Do you happen to have any idea how well those jeans were fitting you?"

"No," she answered, playfully, "but you're welcome to tell me. That is, if it crosses your mind."

"Well, little lady," he grunted, rolling over and getting on top of her, "I think I'd rather show you."

It was fully dark when Elaine and Carlos exited the house. They walked quietly to Carlos' car. Again, the two were consumed by their thoughts. Neither spoke until after they'd gotten into the car. Elaine spoke first. "You're going where they are, aren't you?"

"Yes," he answered simply.

"But, then what?" she asked.

Carlos turned the ignition switch before he replied. When he did reply, he looked at her. The look he gave her made her feel uneasy. His eyes were piercing, unblinking. "What do you think they deserve?"

"I…I don't really know," she said. "But right now, I wish them something, anything no better than death. Scumbags!"

"Humph," Carlos said, "I don't know if that word fits those two." He did not bother trying to conceal the quake in his voice.

He put the car in drive and then he pointed to the glove compartment. "You asked me what would I do when I get to where they are. The answer's in there."

Elaine reached for the glove compartment. When she opened it, she could not stifle the gasp that escaped from her lips. "Oh! A, a gun…no, oh no, Carlos, not that. Are you going to…"

"Elaine," Carlos said sharply. His voice was almost a shout. "They betrayed us!" He banged one hand hard against the steering wheel.

Elaine was startled. She jumped, bringing both hands up, pressing them against her pounding breasts.

Before she had opened the glove compartment; before she had seen the metallic shine of the tool of death, Elaine had thought she wanted James and Sarah dead. But now… Her heart leaped. A lump lodged in her throat.

Elaine reached out slowly and closed the glove compartment. She lapsed into silence. Her mind played back pictures of the fun she and Sarah had shared earlier that day.

She had been temporarily distracted from the pain of betrayal by the sight of the gun. But now it was rising again, along with it though, anger. How could someone have done her that way, someone she thought was a friend?

Her fists tightened at her sides. Glistening streams of warm tears slid down her face. She did not bother wiping them away.

Carlos was speeding. To him, it mattered very little at the time. Both he and Elaine were consumed by poignant thoughts.

"How long do you think they..." Elaine's voice faltered, and then she managed to go on. "Do you think they've been seeing each other a long time?"

"No, I don't think that, I know it," Carlos said in bitterness.

Elaine made no reply. She did not bother asking Carlos how he knew. After a quiet moment, she asked Carlos another question. She spoke in a low tone. "Where are they?"

"Hill Road Park." Carlos' voice was not much louder than Elaine's was.

Through misty eyes, Elaine glanced at the street sign they were approaching. Hill Road Park was only a few minutes away now, too soon it seemed.

Elaine was scared. She had never thought she would ever even consider such an act...an accomplice to murder. She wanted James and Sarah to suffer, but murder?

Protest was the right thing to do, but somehow she could not seem to voice it. Her mind was at war, a tangle of confusion. The cold fingers of fear gripped her, crawled over her like a determined parasite.

Some of the words she and Carlos had spoken earlier came back to her as clearly as when they had first said them. "You're going where they are, aren't you?"

"Yes."

"But then what?"

"What do you think?"

"I don't really know. Right now I wish them..."

Carlos turned off the headlights and parked the car near the entrance to the park. He reached out, placing one hand on Elaine's shoulder. She jerked her head around, feeling her breath catch. She had not realized that they were parked. Her heart thudded ponderously, an ache within her heaving bosom.

Carlos studied her face. He could see the fear there. Her eyes were wide with it. He said, "You can stay here if you want to." It seemed that all she had the strength to do was nod her head in agreement.

Again, Elaine wanted to protest. But she saw the determination on Carlos' face as he reached for the glove compartment. She drew back. Carlos pretended not to have seen her recoil.

Carlos took the gun out; he avoided looking at Elaine's eyes. He could feel that she was staring at him. However, he was afraid that if he looked, he would see a plea in her eye.

Carlos stuck the gun in the waistband of his pants. He placed his hand on the door handle, hesitated and then pushed it open. He did not look back at Elaine.

Although Hill Road Park was outside of town, in a rustic area, Carlos scanned the immediate vicinity. No houses were close by. They lined the roadside further down from the park. Their dark silhouettes were pierced by squared and rectangular slashes of light. Carlos wondered, were any of the houses close enough to hear gunshots?

The light, evening breeze felt icy against Carlos' sweaty body. Nervous perspiration stuck his shirt to his skin. He scanned the park until he spotted the shine of metal far ahead. Was it James' car, or was someone else in the park too? He looked around again, more slowly. His eyes did not detect any more cars. Therefore, he started toward where James was obviously parked.

Elaine watched mutely. Her eyes scanned the park, and then she looked at Carlos again. The reason they were there seemed so unreal to

her, did not fit. The park seemed so good, so tranquil. A quiet pond stretched out in the middle of the park, a dark glassy sheet. The moon was reflected upon its ebon surface, a thin crescentic, silvery slice.

Elaine saw Carlos' dark shape move further and further out into the black of night. Her mind screamed, No! Come back, don't ... and the paralyzing hold of fear kept it there, only in her mind.

Her breathing was heavy. She could actually hear herself take in and expel laborious breaths. The rapid slamming of her pulse and the sound of her hard breathing created a weird rhythm.

Vivid images cast themselves upon the eye of her mind: James and Sarah lay on the ground, gaping holes in their heads and chests. Carlos stood over them, his dark face split by a white, demonic grin. The smoking gun hung loosely in his hand, gleaming like a jewel in the dark.

Suddenly Elaine knew what she had to do. She grabbed frantically for the door handle. The wet, hot perspiration on her palm made the metal feel chill, gelid.

As Carlos neared James' car, he tried to brace himself for what he was about to do. He knew there was no going back on such an act, no amendment for murder. Once carried out, the results were final.

He stopped about ten feet away. For a moment, a critical battle raged in his head.

The only light was from the moon, but he could make out their silhouettes. They were parked sideward, and Sarah's head was turned in his direction. It seemed that all she had to do was shift her eyes and she would see him.

Carlos could see violent gestures Sarah made with her hands. He supposed they were arguing. Fools! he thought, and reached for the gun. He felt the sting of tears, but ignored them. Just as he aimed, Sarah looked straight at him. First, surprise and then cold terror distorted her face. Her voice came out, a desperate cry, a useless shout. "Carlos! Oh, God! Plea..."

Carlos squeezed the trigger. The night was ripped asunder by two shots. A brief pause, and then two more shots followed.

Too late! Elaine's mind screamed, and then she screamed for real, a long, painful no. Her legs became like wet sponges. She stumbled for a few faltering steps and then fell to her knees. Hot tears gushed down unchecked.

The groaning sounded loud in her ears, but it did not seem to come from her mouth. "No...oh, no, Carlos...why-y-y?"

Her body bent at the waist until her face was only inches away from the ground. The arctic grips of fear and grief enclosed her, blotting out all else.

She managed to press her trembling hands hard against her sticky, hot cheeks and her eyelids.

Elaine's whole world seemed to be behind her crying eyes, a cold, painful and dark world. A voice spoke, cutting into her grief. "Elaine, let's go." Her head came up slowly, her glistening eyes wide in fear. Carlos was standing in front of her, one hand, he held extended toward her, the other gripped the gun loosely.

Elaine's gaze locked on the tool of death. She stood stiffly, and shaking her head no, she began to back away from Carlos. "Why, Carlos? Wh...?"

Carlos made a gesture with his hand, silencing her. "Elaine, I didn't do it. I couldn't," he said.

Her eyes blinked rapidly; she stared from Carlos to the gun. Her voice was hoarse when she spoke. "But...but I don't understand. I heard..."

"The shots," Carlos said, "were...well, let's just say, Jay won't have to worry about rolling his windows down."

For an instant, Elaine was rendered speechless. But then, she managed to find her voice. "Oh...Carlos, I'm so glad. I don't know what I would've done if..."

She stepped forward quickly, firmly pressing her moistened cheek against his chest. "So, what do we do now...about them, I mean?" she murmured.

"That's been taken care of," Carlos said. "Come on, let's..."

"Wait a minute," Elaine said, pulling away quickly. Uncertainty was in her eyes. Had Carlos lied? Had he killed James and Sarah? Was he now going to get rid of her, the only other witness?

The abrupt move caught Carlos off guard. He did not have time to say anything before Elaine was backing away. Her eyes were glued to the gun again.

Carlos, in that instant, realized what he was going to do, what he needed to do.

Elaine's eyes widened to the limits as she saw Carlos swing the gun up. "Oh, God! No, Carlos..."

In an instant, she spun on her heels and fled. For fear, the wind in her ears and her pounding heart, she did not hear Carlos shout at first.

"Elaine! Elaine! Stop!" he shouted. "I was just throwing the gun away. Look at me!"

Elaine didn't stop right away, but she threw a hurried glance behind her. She saw that Carlos had nothing in either hand. He held both hands high above his head. She stopped running then. She felt a bit of skepticism, but she stood watching as Carlos started toward her at a fast trot.

When he neared her, he slowed and then stopped. He spoke in choppy breaths. "My...God, girl...wh...what did you think...that I was going to kill you?"

She nodded. Carlos smiled, stepping forward, he embraced her. He could feel the tension in Elaine's return embrace.

"I understand," Carlos said. "What in the world was I thinking? I should've chosen my words a little more carefully. But I didn't mean I shot them. I'm sorry I scared you."

He backed up, holding Elaine's shoulders; he looked into her eyes. "Forgive me?" She nodded again.

Carlos smiled, and reaching for her hand, he said, "Come on. Looks like I've got some explaining to do."

They started toward the car. Elaine asked, "I believe you, but what did happen, and where are they?"

Carlos chuckled softly. "They're presently making their way to the road without clothes."

"What?" Elaine asked, "Are you serious?" Carlos smiled and nodded. "Indeed I am."

Despite all that Elaine had experienced, she could not help but laugh. It was a good feeling after having been through so much.

"This is what happened," Carlos said. "When I walked up, I had actually planned on shooting them. But, at the last minute, I changed my mind. I shot the side rear window out. And then, when they ducked, I shot the driver's side window out. I was so mad at myself for not being able to do what I really wanted to and then...the strangest thing happened. I said, Get out and crawl to me like the scum you are. But I did not say it loud. It was just a thought. Somehow though, they...they..."

"They really crawled to you!" Elaine said excitedly. She had spoken her words more like a statement of fact rather than a question. But Carlos paused and nodded. "Yeah," he said.

Elaine's eyes were wide with awe. "So," she said, "you can actually force a command into people's head? God, Carlos, I…I don't know what to say. I mean, should I be scared or, or…"

"Elaine, I would never force you to do anything against your will," Carlos interjected. His voice sounded as though he was somewhat hurt by her remark.

They arrived at Carlos' car on the driver's side. Carlos leaned against the door. Elaine stood a few feet away, staring at Carlos in wonderment.

Carlos folded his arms and smiled at her. "What's wrong?"

Elaine answered in a voice that clearly reflected the awe she felt. "I, I don't have the foggiest idea of how I'm supposed to feel now. I mean, do you realize what you can do? Carlos…you're like some kind of god or some…"

Carlos interrupted her. "I don't know if I'd take it quite that far." He flashed her one of his quick smiles.

"You know," Elaine said, "you never told me all that happened."

"Oh, that's right," Carlos replied. "What was I saying? Oh, yeah, after they crawled to me, they started begging me not to mess with their minds anymore. I could not believe it! But somehow, they could tell that I was controlling them. For a minute, I was so dumbfounded that I couldn't even move. After I got it together, I decided to try something else. So, I thought, Stand up and strip completely. They did! And then, I had them fill their clothes with rocks and throw them into the pond."

Elaine had temporarily forgotten about all the hurt and pain; she was laughing softly.

"Well," Carlos said, "you know the rest. Right now, they should be getting close to the road."

"And probably getting a little chilly too," Elaine said, rubbing her arms. She shook her head in mock sadness. "Too bad, isn't it?"

"Yeah," he said, feigning sadness himself. "But I think I'll let our little friends stay that way until we figure out what other kind of fun I can arrange for them."

"Why, Carlos, that's so mean!" she exclaimed. However, the giggle in her voice revealed how she really felt.

Smiling, she started for the passenger side of the car. "Are you ready to go?" she asked.

"Not yet," Carlos said, as he reached out and palmed one of her hands. He pulled her to him. Immediately their lips found each other's.

Carlos stepped away first and stared, pulling her toward the back door. She began to ask Carlos a question, but never completed it.

"Carlos, what..."

He interrupted her by turning quickly. He put one finger to his lips to silence her. While stepping toward her, he let her see his eyes roam lustfully over her body. Carlos planted eager kisses on various parts of her neck, moving toward her ear, invoking pleasurable moans from her. When Carlos got to her ear, he paused. Smiling, he whispered softly, "Oh, about your question, read my mind."

END

The day was hot, stuffy, the kind of day when even the breeze bore no cooling effect. The air even had a certain smell, a distinct odor that only heat can cause.

Two riders rode along a dusty, country stretch of highway. Little heat waves danced on the road ahead. Somehow seeing how the air reacted to the heat made the guys feel the stuffy discomfort more profoundly. The effect was like one feeling the pangs of hunger and viewing food. The visional effect would add intensity to the already present pangs.

The passenger swore loudly. "Damn!" was all he said for a moment. He shifted uncomfortably in the seat and unbuttoned his shirt down to his navel. His dark chest glistened with a thin layer of miniscule sweat droplets.

Roy Lee Rufra was a husky black man, black denoting race as well as actual color. The sweat on his skin gave it an oily sheen. He mumbled something under his breath then glanced over at the driver.

The driver cast him a quick, sideward look but made no comment. Kirk Bransic felt a touch of humor at his passenger's discomfort. But he didn't let it show. His pointy face didn't show anything but a silent hint of dangerousness. His skeletal, pimpled visage was one on which a smile would seem out of place. Kirk's eyes were blue, a cold blue. His over-all appearance was one that warned a person without him ever having to say a word.

Roy Lee had grown up in rural Alabama; when he spoke, his pronunciation of words always reflected his accent. "Seem to me that there heat don't bother you. What kinda blood you got?"

Kirk merely grunted. Roy Lee spoke a little louder. "Kirk, I sho' hate when you git like this here. Just ignore me, like I'm some kinda little girl or somethin'. You 'bout to git me mad."

Kirk looked over and met Roy Lee's gaze without saying anything for an instant. Tension hung in the air between the two. Then he said in a monotone, "Don't be mad at me. I didn't make you a big, black, ugly brute. Be mad at God." Seemingly he turned his attention back to the highway. But he scrutinized Roy Lee's movements out of the corner of his eye.

Roy Lee's big hand moved slowly toward the .38 caliber handgun stuck in the back of his waistband. "Roy, you should never touch a gun unless you are going to use it," Kirk said. His voice was low, yet it cut through the hot air like a razor. Roy's movements froze for the span of a few quick heartbeats. Then he forced a short, strained laugh. "What'd you think, Kirk, that I was gonna pull my gun on you?"

Tension moved through the air, a powerful almost touchable thing. Kirk spoke, but he didn't answer Roy Lee's question directly. His voice was emotionless. "If a man got shot while driving a car at this speed, I don't think anyone in the car would survive." He nodded toward the speedometer.

Roy Lee leaned over a little. His eyes narrowed. "Yeah. That there is a good point."

Kirk glanced at his big partner again. Just a trace of a smile touched his lips at each corner. It was not a warm smile though, nor genuine. "You know, Roy, you're the only guy in the world whose temper is as bad as mine."

In reply, Roy Lee only grunted. Kirk went on. "How many times did I save your life while we were in prison?" He still had a little smirk on his face.

"Two," Roy Lee said, flatly. "But ain't it funny how quick folks forget? Cause I done saved yours two times too."

Kirk's pointy brows raised quizzically. "Two times? What do you mean you saved my life two times?"

Roy Lee flashed a quick smile. His teeth shone like jewels against his black skin. "Well, I saved yours once when we was locked up." He smiled again at the look of realization on Kirk's face. "If you notice, your brains is still in your skull, not all over your pretty car seat."

Kirk chuckled shortly. "Roy, you're one crazy son of a..."

"Gun," Roy Lee interrupted. He noticed Kirk's brief hesitation. And an unrecognizable look flickered behind the gelid blue eyes. Then Kirk spoke. "Yeah, gun," he laughed. "Crazy son of a gun."

Both men's laughter resounded in the car. The laughs were not borne of mirth; they were reactionary, a release for tension.

Neither man was afraid of the other, but they both knew how to back off. Like in the animal kingdom, an inherent knowledge warned when to back off in certain situations.

Things grew almost quiet. Almost, except for the sounds of the muggy breeze rushing through the rolled-down windows and the rotation of the tires on the rough highway.

Roy Lee reached for the air conditioner control. He fumbled with it, swore and then let his hand fall away. "When you gonna fix this thing?"

"Humph, probably when hell freezes," Kirk said. "Maybe after we make a few more hits, I'll trash this…get something better to drive."

"Oomph," Roy Lee said, "that ain't gonna happen. You like paying for them whores and snorting that mess too much."

Kirk shot him a quick look but made no reply right away. "Well after we make this hit here, we ought to be able to do just about what we want. I heard that old man Drucker keeps his money in a safe. Says he doesn't trust banks." Kirk grunted a sound that passed for a laugh. "Too bad, he's going to wish he had."

"How much further is his store?" Roy Lee asked.

Kirk's hand went to the .45 handgun stuck down in the side of his waistband. He patted it. "Not far now, old boy. Not far."

Kirk glanced in the rear view mirror. "This is bound to be one of the sweetest hits yet. It's so deserted out here. I don't know why old man Drucker would want a business way out here in the middle of nowhere."

Again the stiff wind and the monotonous roll of the tires were all that could be heard. Kirk looked at Roy Lee, wondering why he had not commented.

Roy Lee was staring straight ahead, a look of deep thought on his face. Suddenly he spoke. "I don't know 'bout this one. You 'spose we can do another job, 'stead of this one?"

"What?!" Kirk asked, incredulously. "What the hell's gotten into you. You've never chickened out on a hit before."

"Well," Roy Lee started then paused, "I…it's just that… Well, when we first planned this here I had a bad feeling. Now it feels like the closer we git the…I just got a bad…." The sharp peal of a horn cut Roy Lee's statement short. Both men turned their heads sharply. "What the?!" Roy Lee said in alarm.

Kirk's eyes revealed the same alarm that was reflected in Roy Lee's voice. The two men watched as a jet-black '57 Chevy pulled up beside them. The car had tinted windows, as dark as the body of the car. Not even a silhouette of the driver could be seen through the ebon glass.

"I swear," Kirk said, "I'd been checking the rear view mirror. That car was not there a minute ago."

They stared wordlessly. The black car kept perfect pace with Kirk's car. Kirk eased his foot down on the accelerator in an attempt to pass. He managed to nose pass the black car only a little before it drove up even with Kirk's car again. Kirk depressed the accelerator harder. Again his car went a little beyond the other one. And yet, again, the black car pulled up even with Kirk's car.

Kirk frowned. He was beginning to become irritated. He pressed the accelerator even harder.

"Look!" Roy Lee shouted and pointed ahead. A large red car was swerving. It weaved over the centerline and back in a zigzag pattern. The car was still a few yards ahead, but Kirk slowed as a precautionary measure. He eased his car over nearly to the shoulder of the road. Remembering the black Chevy, Kirk glanced back. "Son of a freak! Where'd that car go?"

Roy Lee looked back too. His dark face had a frown of puzzlement on it. "Well, I'll be damn," Roy Lee said.

Temporarily they were distracted from their wonderment by looking again to see how close the red car had gotten. The big car was very near Kirk's car now. But somehow the driver had managed to get it almost under control. It still weaved somewhat though.

Kirk and Roy Lee watched circumspectly as the car passed them. The driver was a balding man with a deep tan. He had eyes seemingly too large for his elongated, narrow face. They were red, and the reason was obvious, as he passed. He turned up a bottle to his lips long enough for them to see that the label read: Jack Daniels.

He passed without weaving too close to Kirk's car. They watched briefly as the distance between the two cars grew. There was no other car in that direction. So they were reminded of the incident with the black Chevy. Neither man spoke of it; they didn't know what to say.

They rode along quietly for a while, each man enwound in his own pondering. Roy Lee broke the silence. "I didn't see anywhere that black Chevy could'a turned off. I say, that there was mighty strange. I got me a bad feeling 'bout this here, a right bad feeling...."

Kirk felt uneasy about the black car too, but he didn't want to discuss it. "Look," he said, "there's old Harry Drucker's store. Time to get down to business."

He slowed and turned the car onto the dusty driveway. A cloud of dust rolled up behind the car. It engulfed the car and then drifted past, slowly thinning and disappearing.

Kirk had parked a few feet away from the front of the store. He looked back at the road. There was no traffic to be seen. "Good," he mumbled. "I don't think there'll be any interference."

They had brought along ski masks tucked into a book bag in the back seat. Kirk took a quick look at the bag. He nodded his head in its direction. "We won't need the masks this time," he said. "Drucker wears glasses thicker than bottles. Sometimes his wife comes to help him out, but I didn't see her car around when we drove up."

Shifting his .45 from the side of his waistband to the back, Kirk reached for the door. "Come on, let's do it."

The two men walked toward the door. Out of habit, their gazes made examinations of the area they were approaching. The open sign hanging in the window, the restrooms off to one side, the peeling paint on the storefront, their eyes took in all these details. They could feel the familiar reactions associated with their planned crime. Adrenaline rush, pounding heart, racing pulse, these things had become part of a thrill for them. Though they'd robbed numerous times in the past, their bodies' reactions were always the same.

Old-fashioned chimes jingled and clinked when they opened the door. The interior temperature of the store was sharply different from the muggy air on the outside. It engulfed them, very lightly massaging the skin, a soothing coolness. Even the air smelled different, sharp and clean, mingled with the aroma of new merchandise.

The sharp, metallic clink of the chimes brought Harry Drucker shuffling from a room in the back. In contrast to the front of the store, the room in the back was dimly lighted. The light from a television could be partially seen flashing against one wall.

Harry Drucker was a small, stoop-shouldered man, gaunt to the point of appearing weak. His voice, though, was strong when he spoke, a baritonal boom. He shuffled up to the counter. His thick, gray and black brows raised quizzically. "Can I help you gentlemen?"

Kirk approached the counter. He placed one hand on the slick, cool surface. With the other hand he pointed to the cigarette selection behind the counter. "Yeah, let me get two packs of those Newport Regulars," he said conversationally.

"Alrighty," Harry said. Turning, he made a peculiar noise unique to old people when they do things as simple as rise from a chair. "Be anything else for you, young fellow?"

When he turned around, his mouth formed a silent O. Quickly he dropped the cigarettes on the counter and raised his hands as fast as he could manage. Kirk's .45 was pointed at his face.

"Take one of the biggest bags you've got back there and hand it to my friend here," Kirk said. He nodded quickly toward Roy Lee who was already moving around him. "You know the rest. If I see any cash left in that drawer, I'm putting a hole in your head, got it?"

Harry nodded, but he didn't move. It seemed the .45 held him in the grip of hypnotism. His bushy brows were raised high, and his eyes were stretched beyond their limits, it seemed.

When Roy Lee rushed behind the counter, Harry still couldn't take his eyes off the gun. He stared into the dark barrel, feeling sure that a hot piece of lead would come speeding down that dark tunnel at any moment.

"Move!" Roy Lee said. He pushed Harry aside roughly and grabbed up a bag. He snatched at the cash register drawer. It didn't open. "Open it!" Roy Lee shouted. Harry jumped, finally able to tear his eyes away from the gun. He hurriedly opened the cash register, and backed out of the way. His eyes looked up into the stone-cold eyes of Kirk.

Kirk had a contemptuous smirk on his face. "You didn't do what I asked you, old man. I don't like when people don't do what I ask."

"Sor...sorry, mister. Don't...please don't shoot me."

Kirk spoke, feigning contemplation. "Hmm. Let's see. I might not. But that depends on if you tell me where that safe is."

"Got it all!" Roy Lee shouted excitedly. His chest was heaving as if he'd just done something strenuous.

"Good," Kirk said. "Now hurry over there to the door. Peek out there and see if anybody's coming. Then turn that sign around to the side that says closed. Meantime, old Harry here is going to take me to his safe. Right Harry?"

Harry nodded mutely. Kirk motioned with his gun for Harry to come from behind the counter. "Come on, old man, don't let it take you all da…"

A girl's scream shattered the air. She was standing in the doorway to the back room. Her eyes were wide with horror. Her little body was rigid, and her small hands trembled at her side.

Harry and Kirk turned their heads sharply, at the same moment. Kirk's face was a mask of shock at realizing someone else was in the store. Harry's face took on a look of more fear, adding to that which was evident there already.

Roy Lee dropped the bag of money at the front door and ran back toward the counter. He stopped near Kirk. "What the devil?"

He looked in the direction Kirk and Harry were looking. "What the hell is that kid doing here?"

Instead of looking at Harry for an answer, he cast Kirk a pointed look. Kirk replied sharply, not bothering to hide the anger in his voice. "Don't ask me! What do I look like, a freaking psychic or something?"

The old man's wide eyes shifted rapidly from one face to the other. His voice came out in a near whisper. "That's my…my grandbaby." He paused briefly. Then he asked, "Can I put my hands down?"

It seemed that Kirk hadn't heard him; he was staring at the girl curiously. The old man looked at Roy Lee pleadingly. Roy Lee gestured with his gun and nodded. The old man lowered his arms slowly. He almost smiled with relief.

"How old is that girl, old man?" Kirk asked. Harry hesitated, seeming to know that the question was not an innocent on. "She…she's only thirteen…just a baby."

"Well now," Kirk said, "it's time for that baby to get a grown-up's lesson." He smiled. The smile didn't fit his menacing face.

Kirk took a step in the girl's direction. "Keep your eyes on that old fart. I'm going to have me a little fun with that baby," he said, chuckling.

The old man grabbed Kirk's elbow. "Please, don't…don't hurt my grand..."

Kirk turned quickly. He swung the .45 without warning, striking Harry near the temple. "Get your hand off me!" he shouted. His face was twisted in an animalistic snarl.

The old man grunted in pain. His eyes rolled back. One hand went toward the point where the gun had impacted. But it never reached its destination. Harry crumpled to the floor. Kirk strode on toward the girl without so much as another look at Harry.

Roy Lee's mouth opened suddenly, but he didn't say anything.

Though he was accustomed to violence, the act he'd just witnessed caught him off guard. He looked from the crumpled body to Kirk then back to the body again. He went to the old man and squatted beside him. When he saw the blood trickling from the gash beside the old man's temple, his eyes squinted. He looked up again to see Kirk dragging the girl into the back room. The girl was so terrified that she wasn't even resisting. But she was crying loudly and trembling all over. Roy Lee's jaw muscles heaved sporadically as he watched. Anger wasn't new to him, but this time, its cause was.

He was feeling for the old man's pulse when a piercing scream came from the back room. His head came up quickly. Roy Lee looked at the old man again then back toward the room. Suddenly he jumped to his feet and sprinted for the room. He could hear loud slaps, like shots, coming from the room.

And Kirk's voice was punctuating the slaps. "Get them off, I said! And shut up that godblame whimpering!"

Kirk had his pants and underwear down below his knees. His gun was lying slightly behind him on the floor. He had one of the girl's wrists gripped tightly in his hand. His other hand was raised, poised to strike the girl again. Roy Lee rushed in. His teeth were gritted together, a white gash against his black skin.

Kirk's back was toward the door. He looked back to see the big black man charging in his direction. In his mind he formed a question he intended to ask. But he never got the chance to verbalize it completely. "Roy, what the…"

Roy rushed upon him and released a stinging backhand across Kirk's face. Kirk fell clumsily to the floor, releasing the girl's hand. The little girl took advantage of her unexpected freedom. She ran to a corner of the room. Immediately, she slumped down with her back pressed hard against the wall. She pulled her knees up close to her chest. Closing her eyes tightly, she began to rock back and forth.

Kirk lay at Roy's feet. He stared up at the big man with a potent anger agleam in his icy eyes. He wiped his mouth with the back of his hand. It came away with a carmine smear on it. The red smear held his attention. He stared at it a moment. Then he spoke as if every word was something bitter. "Boy, you've really messed up. You shouldn't have hit me, you black son of a…"

Some intimation, a hint of danger caused him to stop what he was about to say. He looked up again to see Roy's .38 pointed unwavering at his face.

"Go on, say it!" Roy challenged. "But I sho' swear, if you do, I'm gonna put a bullet in that ugly face of yours. And if you ever call me a boy again, you'll die. Understand?"

The two men stared at each other in silence, a powerful silence.

At that moment, it seemed that nothing mattered to each man but the other.

Kirk's penetrating stare did not leave Roy's face as he made a slow nod. Roy stared an instant longer then put his gun in his waistband. Stepping around Kirk, he said, "Where I come from, nobody beats on old people or children."

Walking to where the little girl sat hunched in the corner, he could feel the weight of Kirk's stare. A mental picture formed in his mind, a picture of Kirk pointing the gun at his back.

His breath caught when Kirk called his name. "Roy."

Roy Lee turned slowly, thinking how stupid he'd been to turn his back. The urge to grab for his gun presented itself, but then he was facing Kirk. A pent up breath eased out when he saw that Kirk's gun was held loosely at his side.

It took only a matter of seconds for Roy Lee to turn so as to be facing Kirk, but to him it felt longer. When he'd turned completely, Kirk said, "If you ever hit me again, I'll kill you." He turned quickly and strode from the room.

The little girl still had her eyes shut tightly when Roy Lee approached. She'd stopped crying, but she was still trembling badly. He squatted in front of her. "That man won't hurt you again. I promise." Roy Lee got up. He had no idea of what else to say. As he walked away, his eyes blinked rapidly. He tried to ignore the layer of water he felt on them. Feeling sorry, he paused at the doorway and glanced back at the little girl. Her head was bobbing up and down in short, violent jerks. She'd begun to cry again. Roy Lee's big hands tightened into fists. He turned and walked away from the doorway.

As soon as he entered into the front part of the store again, his eyes fell upon a scene that needed no words to understand. Kirk was running his hand through his hair and pacing back and forth in front of the unmoving body of Harry Drucker.

Kirk looked up. He saw Roy Lee coming. "That son of a bastard!" he said. "He died on us!" He kicked the old man's stiffening body. Then drew his foot back for another kick. "That lousy son of a..."

"Don't," Roy Lee said. The single word wasn't spoken very loud. But the tone itself was enough. Kirk's intended kick froze. He looked into the bigger man's eyes. Something was in those eyes, something that would not tolerate a challenge. He lowered his foot slowly. His gaze remained on Roy Lee's face briefly. Then he opened his mouth, closed it, then spoke. "I'm not leaving without the rest of that money." He brushed pass Roy Lee, headed in the direction of the back room. "I'll bet that girl knows where that safe is."

Roy Lee turned quickly. Reaching out, he grabbed Kirk by the shoulder roughly. The smaller man turned sharply. "Don't mess with that child! I think you done put her through enough."

The two men stared at each other. Each could feel the heavy tension. Each man's chest heaved in anger. And each felt sure the other would reach for the gun in his waistband.

Inside of each man the intensity swelled. Their hot stares remained locked for what seemed an unending stretch. Roy Lee broke the stare and the silence. "Listen, man, we done already kilt somebody. Ain't that bad enough? Can't you just…" The wail of a siren could be heard approaching. The men's eyes widened in comprehension.

"Aw, man, let's get the hell out of here!" Kirk shouted. He turned quickly and ran for the door. Roy Lee was close at his heels.

Stopping at the door, Kirk grabbed up the bag of money. He peered cautiously outside. There was nothing in sight, but the piercing scream of the siren was growing nearer. "Let's go," he said. "I don't see any cops yet."

They ran to the car in gigantic strides, while frequently checking the road for any sign of the police. Kirk threw the money in the front seat between the two of them. He fumbled nervously with the keys. And the engine roared. The grinding tires kicked up clouds of dust as the car sped onto the road. The dust clouds hung in the air, shifting on the hot breeze, then dissipated.

Kirk was driving frantically. The things on the outside of the car flashed by in blurs of indistinct details. The road in front of the car rushed toward it, disappearing beneath it like a high-speed conveyor belt.

Within a matter of moments, the sound of the siren could no longer be heard. Only Roy Lee was aware of that fact. Kirk was still pressing hard on the accelerator. His face was set in grim determination; his gaze was straight ahead.

"Kirk," Roy Lee said. "Slow down. You 'bout to come up on that intersection up yonder." Kirk's speed remained the same. Roy Lee had to admonish him again before he finally slowed. "Kirk."

"Huh?" Kirk said. He glanced at Roy Lee. "Oh, the intersection."

When the men looked ahead at the intersection they were startled. The black Chevy was on the other side of the intersection facing them!

"Son of a bastard," Kirk said as he stopped at the stop sign. "Where in Hades does that car keep coming from?"

When Roy Lee spoke, his heavy Alabama accent was tinged with a hint of fear. "That there is an omen. My mama use to tell me that omens mean somethin' bad is 'bout to happen."

Kirk stared at the Chevy. It just sat there. "Why doesn't he come on across? He was here first."

He honked his horn. But the car remained unmoving. Impatient now, Kirk checked to see that no traffic was coming then he pressed hard on the gas pedal. The tires squalled as the car sped across the intersection. As they passed the black Chevy, Kirk stuck up his middle finger. "You stupid fart!" he shouted.

After they went a few yards, the Chevy pulled to the middle of the intersection and made a slow turn-around. Roy Lee was looking back when the car turned. "He's 'bout to follow us," he said.

"So what?" Kirk replied in an irritated voice. "What can he do, huh? Nothing, that's what. He can't do a thing." He took a brief look in the rear view mirror. On the inside, he did not feel as confident as he'd made himself sound.

The two men lapsed into silence; each consumed by his own thoughts. By their actions, it was obvious that they were thinking about the same thing…the car tailing them.

Black, gleaming like a gigantic jewel, the Chevy cruised along behind them. It never moved too close, nor did it let them get too far away. The car was persistent, like a predator on the prowl.

Roy Lee spoke suddenly, interrupting the silence as if they'd been talking all along. "Yeah, like I said, somethin' bad is bound to happen. Why you think he's been tailing us, Kirk?"

Kirk slammed his palm down against the steering wheel angrily. He pressed hard on the brakes and steered the car to the side of the road. He ignored Roy Lee's question when he spoke. "I don't know who he thinks he's toying with! But I'll show him! I'll show him…"

Kirk brought the car to a standstill on the shoulder of the road. He reached in his waistband and gripped the .45. He placed it in his lap.

"Look!" Roy Lee shouted. "He stopped." Kirk looked in the side view mirror. The black car was sitting in the middle of the road. He slammed his hand down on the steering wheel again. "What is he doing?" he yelled, asking no one in particular. He shook his fist out the window. "I'll kill you! You hear me? I'll kill you!"

His face was red with rage. He stomped down on the gas. Gravel and dust spewed out from the tires. "Kirk, we've got to take that money back. I got me a bad feeling 'bout this. Somethin' bad is gonna happen to us," Roy Lee said. His voice quavered, though he tried to speak calmly.

Kirk's chest swelled in anger. "No! Are you crazy?! You want to take the money back because some black car is following us? No way. I'll put a bullet in that sucker back there before…" Shock choked Kirk's words short. He'd glanced in the mirror, but the car was gone! The talon of fear gripped him. They had been driving along a straight stretch of road. There'd been nowhere for the car to turn off. Kirk was sure of it.

Roy Lee looked back. "I told you. See? Somethin' bad is…"

"Shut up!" Kirk shouted. "I don't want to hear anymore about your godblame omens. That was just an ordinary car." Kirk went on, but stammering, broke his words. "Th…the, guy foun…he found somewhere to turn off. We just didn't see it, that's all." He looked at Roy Lee quickly.

Roy Lee nodded slowly. "Yeah," he said without any conviction, "he found some road that we didn't see." His hand moved very slowly to his .38. His grip tightened on the handle of the gun. The solid feel in his hand gave him a little comfort...a little.

Kirk didn't notice exactly when it had grown dark. Nevertheless the night had descended, an immeasurable dark sheet. He looked over at Roy Lee. Roy Lee was sleeping; his chin rested on his chest. He was slumped slightly forward.

The headlights briefly illuminated a roadside sign. The sign read: Stantonsville 1 mile.

Kirk looked back. The sight of a pair of headlights made him swallow hard. He swerved purposely, while envisioning the black Chevy pulling up alongside him. In his mind, he saw himself point his .45 and pull repeatedly on the trigger.

The rhythm of his heart increased. His hand felt for the .45. He watched the headlights in the rear view mirror. The car was getting closer, fast.

The car came closer still. Kirk saw the signal light come on. He watched the steady wink, wink of the light.

Kirk began to raise the gun slowly as the car began to pass. He exhaled a low breath when he saw that the car was dark green, not black.

He was lowering the gun slowly when he looked over at his sleeping comrade. His hand stopped. His icy blue eyes flickered from the gun to Roy Lee's head. Then, they went back to the gun again. A slow chilling smile spread across his face. Still smiling, he extended his hand until the .45 was only inches from Roy Lee's head. "Hey, Roy," he said loudly, "got something for you."

Roy Lee's head came up slowly. He turned sleepily, his eyes barely open. Suddenly his eyes stretched. They looked like two large, white marbles with black centers. Throwing his hands up, he jerked his head to the side. "Come on, Kirk, don't play with that thing! You 'bout to scare me?" he said in a shaky voice.

Kirk moved the gun so that it was pointed directly at Roy Lee's head again. He laughed. "Who said I was playing? I didn't." He laughed again and lowered the gun.

Roy Lee exhaled loudly. He slumped back and ran his hand over his face. His hand trembled. It took a moment for him to gather his thoughts before he spoke. "That there was not such a good joke, Kirk."

Kirk stopped chuckling, but his face still had a comical look on it. "Man, you should have seen your eyes. Those suckers looked like golf balls. I bet you pissed your pants." He slapped his knee and started laughing again.

Kirk looked at the big man, looked into his eyes. He noted the squint, the hard set to his jaws, and knew that it was not a good idea to keep laughing. "Okay, man. No need to look at me like that. I had to wake you up. Guess I could've done it another way. I woke you up, though, because we are coming into Stantonsville.

"Stantonsville?" Roy Lee queried. "God, we must be at least 'bout seventy or eighty miles from Drucker's place."

"Nah," Kirk said, "more like a hundred, or more. See, I figure, if the cops are looking for us, they will hardly get to us way over here in Stantonsville. And anyway, all I figure is to get a room, stay till morning, then light out."

The car passed a sign that read: Welcome to Stantonsville. Kirk continued talking. "In the meantime, I say we plan something big. Say…a bank, maybe?"

He looked at Roy Lee. He was puzzled to see that Roy Lee was shaking his head slowly.

"Naw, Kirk, it ain't gonna be no more for me. If'n I was you, I do believe I would do the same thing."

Kirk pulled the car into the parking lot of a motel. He was shaking his head in disbelief and irritation. He parked the car, mumbling something indistinct. Pulling the .45 from his waistband, he tossed it on the seat. The gun landed beside the bag of money. He reached for the door handle. Kirk opened the door and got half way out of the car before he paused. His eyes flickered to Roy Lee's face briefly, and then he removed the keys from the ignition.

Kirk got out and took two steps in the direction of the motel's office. He turned back suddenly and walked to the car. Leaning in through the open window, he said. "You're going soft on me, Roy. We're going to have to fix that."

Roy Lee started to say something in his defense. "All I was trying to say, is…" Kirk turned swiftly and walked away. Roy Lee watched, as he did, a ponderous feeling of unease pulled at his subconscious. He was sure something was going to happen between him and Kirk. It would be something not easily avoided, something that presented no easy way out. Without realizing it, his hand moved to his gun. He left it there.

Kirk returned shortly. He was throwing a key into the air and catching it in the palm of his hand. When he got into the car, he tossed the key to Roy Lee. "Room eighteen," he said. "I asked the motel manager had he heard about that robbery and murder in Klinston. He said he hadn't but to play it safe, I think we should not be seen together too much. At least, not until we get further away. They may be looking for a black guy and a white guy together. So, I want you to go ahead to the room. I'm going to go get us something to eat."

Both men reached for Kirk's .45 at the same moment. There was a span of quiet while their hands remained on the gun. Their stares locked momentarily. "Kirk," Roy Lee said, "I think you should leave that. I'll put yours and mine in this bag with the money."

Kirk smiled a cold mirthless smile. He kept his stare locked with Roy Lee's. But he moved his hand slowly. "Yeah, I guess you've got a point."

Roy Lee picked up the .45 and placed it in the bag with the money. Then he reached in his waistband. Withdrawing his .38, he put that in the bag too. "We don't need to draw attention to ourselves," Roy Lee stated. He grasped the bag with one hand. With the other hand, he reached for the door handle.

Kirk watched through squinted eyes. The gelid smile returned to his lips. "Wait!" he said. He clamped a bony hand on Roy Lee's wrist. "How do I know that you won't take the money and run?" He chuckled, but the sound was flat, as mirthless as his smile. Roy Lee let go of the handle slowly. "Yeah, but, if I leave ever'thing with you, who says you ain't gonna do the same thing?"

Kirk chuckled again. "Si, amigo, what we have here is a Mexican stand-off." He laughed, reached in his pocket and retrieved the car keys, paused, then put the key into the ignition switch. He was still laughing softly when he cranked the car up and pulled out of the parking lot. "One of us'll just stay in the car while the other goes for the food." It was spoken like a statement, but he looked at Roy Lee as if for assent. Roy Lee nodded then looked away. He did not see when Kirk's eyes narrowed nor when Kirk shook his head slowly.

After returning to the motel, the men ate ravenously. Their eating was interrupted by desultory conversation. Neither man mentioned the black car. They ignored the mention of it purposely. Yet, it was there, engraved in their minds, a dark, persistent enigma.

At length, Roy Lee stood up and stretched. His gaze traveled to the bag of money on the table by the bed. But he made no mention of it. Instead, he said, "Throw me the keys. I gotta get some clothes to change into."

"Here," Kirk said, tossing him the keys. "Do me a favor? Bring me that brown suitcase. I've got a couple changes in there." He stood up and yawned. "Meantime, I'm going to hit the shower. After that, I'm going to bed. I'm beat."

Kirk started toward the shower. "We'll split up that loot in the morning," he said over his shoulder. He said it in a manner that left no room for option.

Roy Lee paused with his hand on the doorknob. The

authoritative tone Kirk had used sparked a vestige of anger in him. He looked back to reply, but Kirk had already gone.

Roy Lee stepped outside. Night breeze blew against his skin. The cool caress was a welcome change, contrastive to the hot air from earlier that day. He'd barely taken a step when shock slammed into him. The black Chevy was directly across from him on the other side of the parking lot! A man was leaning nonchalantly against the hood. His clothes were as black as the car. And, even in the dim light of the parking lot, Roy Lee could see that they shined.

The man wore a long trench coat and a fedora, as black and shiny as the rest of his attire. His white shoes stood out sharply against his otherwise all black ensemble. His face seemed abnormally long and narrow, especially in comparison to his wide shoulders. The whiteness of his skin made his face and hands stand out almost blindingly against the black clothing he wore.

The guy's head was slightly down. He was pulling slowly, thoughtfully on his long, dark goatee.

Time raced. Roy Lee's heart thumped violently. He prepared to take a step back. A strong compulsion to hide gripped him. But at the instant he picked up his foot, the man raised his head. At that distance, Roy Lee could not see the man's eyes, but he could feel the stare. The weight of the man's gaze held him briefly. With the tip of one finger the man pushed his hat up a little. Then he simply turned, walked a few steps, and got into the car. Roy Lee was stiff with fear, yet, somehow he managed to move incredibly fast. He turned, flung the door open, and stepped quickly inside. He slammed the door shut and pressed his back hard against it. His eyes darted from side to side. His breathing was heavy. "Kirk," he yelled, and then louder, "Kirk!"

"What?" Kirk asked. "What are you yelling about?"

Just as Kirk responded, Roy Lee pulled the door open enough to barely peek out. He'd begun to reply to Kirk when he received another shock. The parking space where the black Chevy had been was empty! But that was impossible! He'd only closed the door for a matter of seconds.

Kirk was calling to him, but Kirk's words were just indistinct sounds. Roy Lee's racing thoughts were loud, muffling Kirk's words. He stood there blinking rapidly. He flung the door open suddenly. Running wide-eyed into the parking lot, he turned in a short circle. His eyes searched as he turned. But there was no sign of the black Chevy. A feeling of unreality enveloped him. Frustration, anger, and confusion all crowded into his mind.

A fat man came out of a room on the other side of the parking lot. Right away, Roy Lee realized the man had come out near where the black car had been parked.

Roy Lee ran toward the fat man, waving his arms wildly. "Hey! Hey, can you tell me something?"

The fat man took one look at Roy Lee's wild eyes, his frantic behavior, his loping steps, and his eyes widened.

Fear needs no sound basis. It waits for no explanation or confirmation of sure danger. Fear merely attacks. Its dark depths swallowed the fat man suddenly. He started for his car quickly, with the peculiar wobble-shuffle seemingly inherent in obese people.

"Wait!" Roy Lee shouted, as he overtook the fat guy at his car. The man was fumbling, trying to get his door unlocked. When he realized that he wasn't going to be quick enough, he turned and threw his hands up protectively. "Don't. Pl…please, don't hurt me. Ta…take my wallet my…my car, whatever, just don't..."

Roy Lee grabbed the fat man by the shoulders. He had to shout over the man's babbling to calm him. "Hey, calm down. Nobody's gonna hurt you. Understand?" His grip tightened on the guy's shoulder, and he shook him roughly before the guy calmed down a little.

"Understand?" Roy Lee asked again. The man nodded. His ample jowls shook and his squinty eyes darted about nervously. "Where did that black car go?" Roy Lee asked. Letting go of the fat man, he half-turned and pointed to where the Chevy had been parked. "The one that was sitting right…" His mouth hung open. He stared incredulously. The parking space he pointed to was effectively blocked. A sawhorse stood on each side. And another one was placed at the front. His eyes bulged and then squinted in bewilderment. With a quick jerk of his head, he turned to look at the man.

"Bu…but, them sawhorses…where? How? They ain't 'spose to be there," Roy Lee sputtered.

He didn't wait for the man to make a reply. Turning, he stared at the parking space again. His next words came out very slowly. "Them saw horses … I seen that car there. I know I seen it…"

Roy Lee walked away. After every few steps, he glanced at the parking space. When he got to Kirk's car, he opened the trunk. His movements were stiff, the kind of stiffness invoked by only fear. He removed the suitcase that Kirk had asked for, then took out a smaller one of his own.

Kirk was sitting on the bed, wrapped in a large white towel. He looked up as Roy Lee entered. The bag of money was no longer on the table beside the bed. It was on the floor between Kirk's feet. He had one hand stuck into the bag. He started bringing his hand up, hesitated briefly, and then withdrew it. It held the forty-five.

At seeing Kirk pull the forty-five out, Roy felt a lump rise to his throat. Surely Kirk wasn't going to shoot him, was he…so near to other people? He stood just beyond the entrance. Without his being aware, his gaze kept going from Kirk's face to the gun in his bony hand.

Kirk brought the forty-five up to his eye level. He turned it slowly, admiring it like a precious stone. The dim light in the room hit the dark metal as it turned. Certain areas shined under the effects of the light.

Kirk's cold gaze found Roy Lee's eyes. He let a thin, tight smile creep to his lips. Roy Lee didn't like that smile. There was something innately evil about it. Certainly, it was not a smile of amorousness or humor.

Roy Lee broke what had seemed to be a spell by looking away. He didn't want Kirk to see the fear in his eyes. Kirk chuckled softly. Roy Lee pushed the door closed with his foot. He came further into the room and dropped the suitcases to the floor.

A short spell of quietness settled. Roy Lee could feel the tension of Kirk's eyes as he trudged to a lone chair. The quietness was broken when Kirk put the forty-five on the table. The contact of the hard wood and metal made a distinct clacking sound.

"So," Kirk asked, "what were you yelling about when I was in the shower?"

"I, uh…nothing," Roy Lee said. "It was nothing."

He got up, stretched, yawned and then walked to his suitcase on the floor. Kirk watched the big man as he squatted and rifled through his suitcase.

Roy Lee stood up with his change of clothes in his hand. He noticed Kirk watching him, but he ignored it. He started toward the shower. The feel of Kirk's intense stare was still there. It forced itself into Roy Lee's subconsciousness.

Just as he reached the bathroom, he said, "No more for me, Kirk. I'm through with this here." He paused in the doorway to the bathroom. His big body was just a dark silhouette against the pale interior of the bathroom behind him. "Mama used to say, there come a time in ever' man's life when somethin' on the inside tells him he got to make a change. She said nobody can tell that man, but his heart is gonna let him know. My heart done told me, Kirk. It's time for me to change."

Roy Lee waited in the doorway a moment, but Kirk said nothing. The big man turned and closed the door.

Kirk looked at the forty-five. His head made an almost imperceptible nod.

The wind made a constant rushing noise in Roy Lee's ears as he ran. He pumped his fists and legs desperately. His heavy breathing echoed loudly down the dark tunnel in which he ran. Old man Drucker ran behind Roy Lee. His hands were out-stretched, his fingers curled claw-like. He ran in stiff, jerky movements. But he managed to remain close to Roy Lee. Old man Drucker's face was twisted in a horrible smile. His teeth were stained with dripping blood. The blood was oozing down from a gaping hole on one side of his head.

It seemed that his neck had been broken. He ran with his head cocked to one side at an awkward angle. Roy Lee could clearly hear Drucker yelling and laughing maniacally behind him.

"Lordy, lordy, this is funny, I've found the man who stole my money," Drucker was shouting over and over. Each time after Drucker chanted he would burst into another fit of insane laughter.

Hot perspiration seeped from Roy Lee's pores. He glanced back repeatedly. His lungs ached. His sides hurt. He gave his attempt at escape all the energy he could muster. Despite his effort, though, Drucker was gaining.

"Lordy, lordy, this is funny, I've found the man who stole my money."

Drucker's fingertips snatched at the back of Roy Lee's damp shirt. He was narrowing the gap between the two of them.

Roy Lee felt his feet stumble over something. "No!" he shouted, to no avail. He slammed into the ground. In an instant, though, he was up again. Amid the rush of his pulse, the tremble of his body and his loud breathing, he realized that something was different. The tunnel had grown quiet. He jerked himself around. There was no one there!

His aching lungs continued to expel loud, harsh breaths. The sound of his loud breathing bounced off the tunnel walls, resounding eerily in his ears.

He stood trembling, straining his ears in the thick darkness. Fear caused his nerves to feel like things alive. His skin prickled all over like thousands of crawling insects.

A tap on his shoulder brought a scream to his throat. He turned. Drucker was there. The scream built up, but it didn't come out.

Old man Drucker's head was still at a weird angle. His thick brows were encrimsoned with blood. He smiled broadly, revealing bloodied teeth. Congealing blood oozed out at one corner of his mouth. The blood did not fall. It merely continued to stretch toward the ground, a long, glistening string.

Roy Lee wanted to run, but his legs refused to work. Fear held him to the spot.

Drucker spoke. His words came out distorted by the red, bubbling froth rolling out between his lips. "Your mama used to tell you that a time comes in every man's life when something on the inside tells him he's got to change. Too bad, you won't get that chance."

Drucker's age-gnawed hands shot out. His bony fingers clamped on Roy Lee's throat. A burst of Drucker's insane laughter echoed all around. Roy Lee pulled frantically at the old man's iron grip. He flailed at the old man's arms. Drucker's grip tightened. Roy Lee's eyes began to bulge from the pressure. He felt as if someone was forcing air inside his head, and that the air was trying to burst from his eye sockets. Darkness swam before him.

The sound of Drucker's voice broke through the fog gathering on Roy Lee's brain. Drucker's words repeated themselves, bouncing off the tunnel sides, echoes of doom. "See you on the other side, Rufra... See you on the other side...."

A sharp stab of pain in his side caused Roy Lee to snap his eyes open suddenly. He jerked himself upright in bed. Automatically his hand went to his neck. He grabbed at his throat frantically. Then he heard Kirk's chuckle.

Turning slowly he lowered his hands. Roy Lee rubbed his side. It throbbed. "Why you have to go and hit me that hard for, Kirk?"

"Because you were sleeping like a baby, kicking and screaming. Next time I get a room, I'll make sure it has two beds in it," Kirk said. "Now get some godblame sleep."

Roy Lee mumbled something in reply. And then he snuggled down, still holding his side.

A noisy car pulled up on the outside. The low murmur of the television next door came through the thin walls. Someone in another room shouted something unintelligible.

Kirk spoke suddenly. "Only the strong survive." He paused. "You know, that's not just a saying with no basis. You take, for instance, in the wild, an injured or weak wolf is not allowed to remain with the rest of the pack. The rest of the wolves turn on the defective link. They kill him."

Roy Lee mumbled something again. But he made no attempt at conversation.

"You're getting weak, Roy. You're getting weak," Kirk said.

The next morning the two men showered and ate in a hurry. Then Kirk went to return the motel key. He came back into the room and stuffed the .45 into his waistband. Pulling his shirt out he let it hang over the gun. He picked the bag of money up. Opening the bag he saw that Roy Lee's .38 was still there. "Come on, let's go," he said.

After they got into the car, Roy Lee asked, "When we was eatin', you promised me that we was gonna take that money back. You ain't done changed your mind, did you?"

Kirk turned the key in the ignition. He ignored Roy Lee's question.

Roy Lee began to question him again. "Kirk, you ain't done

changed your…"

"Damn it, Roy!" Kirk shouted, "I said we would take the money back. Now, leave me alone about it!" The tires squalled angrily as the car sped from the driveway. A white plume of smoke hung lazily on the clear, morning air.

The two men rode without speaking until they reached a country highway. Roy kept watching Kirk out of the side of his eye. He noticed that Kirk would, every so often, look in the rearview mirror and on each side of the highway. What was he looking for, Roy Lee wondered. The black Chevy, maybe?

"Kirk," Roy Lee said, a bit cautiously, "can we get to old man Drucker's store going this way?"

Kirk looked at Roy Lee. His gaze held no warmth. "I've got a stop to make. Got something to take care of." He cast a quick glance in the rearview mirror again. Then, he looked on each side of the road.

Kirk spotted a dirt path a few yards ahead. He slowed the car and pulled off the road onto the path.

Roy Lee watched quietly as Kirk put the car in park. He was puzzled. What was it Kirk had said? "Got something to take care of." Suddenly, realization hit him. Kirk was going to kill him! No! His eyes darted to the bag. He'd been a fool to leave his gun in there. He grabbed for the bag. But it was too late. Kirk snatched the bag away.

Roy Lee saw the flash of the big black forty-five. He saw when Kirk raised it. The butt of the gun slammed into the side of his head. White light flashed before Roy Lee's eyes. A loud grunt of pain whooshed from his lips. His senses reeled. Everything rushed at an impossible pace. Roy Lee felt the gloomy depths of unconsciousness pull at him like a vortex. He saw Kirk's lips pulled back hard against his teeth, saw the murderous look in his cold eyes, and felt sure he was doomed. Yet, his hand found the door handle. He snatched at it with trembling fingers.

Kirk raised the gun quickly to deliver another blow. But then, Roy Lee was half-falling, half-stepping out onto the dirt path. He staggered upright and began to run in desperate strides. He hadn't gone very far when he heard Kirk yell something. Then a sound like a clap of thunder ripped through the air. Roy Lee felt a powerful thump against the back of his head and to the side. His mind screamed, as loud as the shot, it seemed. "He shot me! Kirk done shot me!"

The path rushed toward him. He was falling. But he never felt when he hit the ground.

Kirk stood at the front of the car. He held the gun outstretched for a moment. Then he lowered it and started toward Roy Lee.

Kirk had left the car running, but after he had taken only a few steps, the car sputtered and then went silent.

"What the..." He turned. His gaunt face was a mask of puzzlement. He looked at Roy Lee again and then back at the car. Not being able to see movement, he figured that his first shot must have done what he'd intended it to do. So he rushed back to the car.

Kirk was breathing heavily. He jumped in the car, turned the key to the off position then tried to crank the car. Nothing happened. He slammed his hand down on the steering wheel. "Come on baby! Crank! Crank!" Kirk cursed. He hunched over the steering wheel and tried again. He didn't see the black car cruise slowly down the path. It was so quiet he did not hear it either. It rolled within a few feet of his back bumper. The piercing peal of the Chevy's horn startled Kirk. His heartbeat quickened. He jerked his head up, and turning, he saw the car sitting behind him.

The driver's side window came down. A pale white hand came out the window. Its long, thin fingers beckoned.

Kirk made his mind up quickly. Stuffing the forty-five back into his waistband, he pulled the shirt down over it. Next, he grabbed the bag of money.

The driver of the Chevy stuck his head out the window when Kirk got out. Kirk felt the man's eyes scrutinize him as he neared the car.

With one finger, the man pushed his black fedora up coolly. A strange smile spread across his long, pale face. He pulled thoughtfully on his dark, pointy goatee. "Looks like I'm right on time here."

Kirk stopped a few feet from the driver's side door. His mind prompted him to grab for his gun. In a flash of motion, he snatched the forty-five from his waistband and pointed it at the guy's face. "Yeah," Kirk said, "you're right on time to get out of the car and give me some answers, you meddlesome bastard."

The man smiled more broadly. He was so cool in his reaction that it puzzled Kirk to the point of anger. People were not supposed to smile in the face of danger.

Opening the door, the guy got out and stood up gracefully. The smile was still on his face. He stared straight into Kirk's eyes.

"Who the hell are you?" Kirk asked bluntly.

"Call me Reficul," the man answered. He stuck out his hand. Kirk took a quick step backward and raised the gun a little.

"What kind of a name is that?"

"It's just an alias that I use. But, at this point, I don't think that real names are...of importance," Reficul said, conversationally. His tone reflected not even a trace of fear.

Reficul's calmness was making Kirk feel strange. The guy was just too calm. "You are one crazy son of a bastard. You stand there smiling like this is some godblame social. Don't you realize I'm about to kill you, man?" Kirk asked.

Reficul cocked his head in amusement. “I don’t think so, Mr. Bransic.” Kirk’s mouth dropped open in disbelief. He hadn’t told the guy his name. Before he could recover from the shock, Reficul went on. “You see, that gun is not even working.” As he spoke, he pointed a long finger at Kirk’s forty-five. The cool smile returned to his face. His arm remained outstretched briefly, his finger pointed, as if adding emphasis to what he’d said.

Kirk chuckled shortly. “Not working? I just shot this gun a few minutes ago. I’ll tell you what. I’m going to ask you some questions. If I don’t like your answers, we’ll see if you’re right about the gun.” He raised the gun to the height of Reficul’s head. “How did you know my name? And why have you been following me around?”

Reficul smiled again. And then he actually started to chuckle. He waved his hand nonchalantly as if shooing a fly. He turned his back and reached for the car door. “Go ahead, Mr. Bransic, pull the trigger.”

“I want some answers!” Kirk shouted. The man’s attitude was making him angry. “Don’t you turn your back on me, you son of a…” Click. Click. Click. Kirk pulled the trigger repeatedly. But true to Reficul’s words, the gun would not work. Kirk’s mouth shaped a silent, “What the…”

“Told you, didn’t I?” Reficul asked. He had gotten in the car and closed the door. His forearm propped on the edge of the door, he leaned out and smiled.

With trembling fingers, Kirk checked to see if there were any bullets left in the gun. There were. A commixture of fear, confusion, and anger rushed over him. In reaction, his breathing grew fast, his face reddened, and he stepped back. He let the forty-five clunk to the dirt.

“What … what did you … how did you do that?”

Reficul ignored Kirk’s question. “I think, Mr. Bransic, that you’d be more concerned about getting out of here. You know, somebody could’ve already called the police. And, I have no idea that you’d want to revisit prison.”

Kirk looked at his own car quickly then back at Reficul. His thoughts were rushing. He didn’t like nor trust the strange man in the black Chevy, but he knew the guy had made a good point.

Kirk hurried toward the black Chevy. As he walked, he stuck his hand into the bag of money. “Okay,” he said, “but if you try anything, I’m going to…”

Reficul interrupted him. “No need to toy with that thirty-eight, Mr. Bransic. No need at all.”

Kirk’s face froze in shock. He let the gun fall from his fingers. Then he was at the passenger’s side door. Just as he opened it, Reficul motioned with his thumb toward the back. Kirk hesitated then closed the door quickly and reached for the back door.

He threw the bag on the empty seat. Then he slid in. He looked up to see that Reficul was watching him in the mirror.

Reficul laughed a soft, throaty chuckle. He put the car in reverse. The tires kicked up dust clouds. The tires had barely touched the highway, when Reficul braked sharply, rammed the car in drive, and sped off.

Kirk kept looking over at the bag on the back seat. He wanted to get the gun. But he kept remembering the incident with the forty-five. Somehow, his strange rescuer had caused the gun to malfunction. What had he done? How had he done it?

"What are you," Kirk asked suddenly, "some kind of master magician or something?"

"Yes, Mr. Bransic, or something. You have a lot of questions about me. So I'm going to answer all your questions." Reficul paused. "Well, actually, I have a better idea. I'll let you come up with the answer. You'll be surprised to see that one word will answer all your questions."

"One word?" Kirk asked. "How can one…"

"Patience, Mr. Bransic, just a little patience," Reficul interrupted. "Pick up that tablet beside your bag back there. And…"

"There's no tablet back…" Kirk felt his body stiffen. "Wait a minute. That wasn't there when I got in here. How did you…."

"Shh, Mr. Bransic," Reficul said. "Remember, patience. Now, to continue…oops, I almost forgot, I suppose you need something to write with." He raised his hand up a little higher than the seat. Kirk watched. Reficul snapped his fingers. A long, shiny ink pen appeared between his fingers.

Kirk stared, unblinking until Reficul spoke, prompting him to take the pen. "Uh, Mr. Bransic, I do believe this is for you."

Kirk reached out slowly. His fingers pressed the pen firmly, as if assuring himself that it was actually real.

Reficul continued. "This is going to be really simple, I assure you. Open the tablet. Write my name at the top of the page. By the way, it's spelled R-e-f-i-c-u-l. Got it?" he asked.

"Yeah," Kirk said, "I got it."

"Very good," Reficul said. "Now, I want you to spell Reficul the other way around. Start with the el and work your way back through all the letters."

Kirk mumbled something. Then he scribbled L-u-c-i-f-e-r. He dropped the pen and writing tablet as if they'd burned his hand. His head came up fast. He opened his mouth to scream. But at that very moment a powerful force slammed into his chest, forcing the wind from his lungs. And a blinding jolt of pain caused him to close his eyes briefly. When he opened them, he was standing in the middle of the highway. The bag of money sat at his feet. Just as he began to reach for the bag, something urged him to turn around.

Unspeakable horror assaulted his vision. Kirk's eyes bulged. Something from a nightmare stood there, something that escaped definition. It was big and dark, as black and shiny as the Chevy had been. It dwarfed Kirk's frail frame by at least four feet. The head was wide at the top, narrowed down to a pointy chin. Horns, like a bull, glistened whitely where ears should have been. A long tail waved behind it, above its head. The thick appendage moved as if it floated on alternating air currents. The entity stared down at Kirk through eyes white like fresh snow. The eyes were eerie; they had no pupils.

Kirk was completely frozen in horror. Sweat shined on his face.

Lucifer smiled. He stuck his hand out, clamping down on Kirk's shoulder like a steel vice. Kirk winced. His lips trembled violently.

One instant, the two lone figures stood on the highway. The next, the highway directly beneath them disappeared with a frighteningly loud suction. The two falling figures rushed toward impenetrable dark. A long horrible scream burst from Kirk's lungs. "Nooooo!"

Whump! The highway closed. It looked as if nothing had ever disturbed it. The large paper bag reappeared suddenly in the same spot it had been in earlier.

The journey from the depths of unconsciousness was a slow, dark one. Roy Lee opened his eyes very slowly. His vision was blurry. A constant throb pounded the back of his head and caused the back of his entire neck to feel sore and stiff. Nausea swept over him as he lay there attempting to remember what had happened. Suddenly it all came back to him in shocking clarity. Kirk had tried to kill him!

Where was Kirk now? Why didn't he hear any footsteps? Was he actually already dead and this just a prelude before he plunged off into abysmal darkness?

He waited, not daring to move a muscle. Roy Lee didn't know how long he forced himself to lie there waiting, listening. But it seemed like forever. Finally, he got shakily to his hands and knees. He remained in that position until the nausea lessened, and then he stood up. Turning slowly, his insides knotted, he expected to hear the boom of the forty-five at any instant. Nothing happened.

His brows raised in bewilderment when he saw the car parked where Kirk had left it. Lifting one hand to his aching head, he started toward the car. His fingers detected a deep cut slightly in the back of his head but mostly along the side. His hand came away sticky.

Roy Lee approached the car slowly. He was even more

bewildered to see that the keys were still in the ignition switch. After checking to be sure that Kirk was nowhere around, he got in the car and started it up. He took the same direction that the black Chevy had taken. He'd been driving only a short time when he spotted the bag in the road. Curious, he parked the car on the shoulder of the road. Walking to where the bag was, he stopped and picked it up. Old man Drucker's money! Roy Lee's thirty-eight was still in the bag too. Reaching into the bag, he took out the gun. He stared at it a moment, and then suddenly hurled it as far as he could.

Walking slowly, he started toward the car. Got to find a way to get this money back to Drucker's store without being seen, he thought.

Rudy Vargella sat in his car at the intersection, waiting for the light to change. He scratched his shaved head thoughtfully, as he looked in the rearview mirror. The black '57 Chevy was still behind him. For some distance now it had made every turn he'd made. Numerous times he had slowed to let the car pass, but the car had slowed too.

Must be some kind of weirdo, wanting to play car games, he thought.

Rudy glanced up. The light changed. He pressed down on the accelerator hard and fast. Tires squalled. Rudy's car sped across the intersection. "Well, eat my dust, pal. I don't have time to play."

As his car sped away, Rudy glanced in the mirror again. To his amazement, the Chevy remained at the intersection. He shrugged and slowed his car down.

Dominick Sabastan had known Rudy for years. Together they had committed numerous criminal acts, all for money. Now, according to Dominick, he and Rudy were about to get into the big time.

He pushed his lanky frame back from the table. Dominick looked at the map he'd placed on the table. There were two handguns and a marker lying near the map. He smiled. Everything was ready. Now, all he had to do was wait on Rudy and go over the plans with him.

Dominick looked at his watch then he started toward the door. It was time for Rudy to show up. Just as he entered the living room, he heard Rudy's distinctive knock. His steps quickened in anticipation.

Dominick opened the door to see Rudy standing there smiling. Rudy had a brown shopping bag in his hand.

"Hey, Nick, good to see you, man," Rudy said. Rudy proffered his hand. Dominick shook the other man's hand in a firm grip.

"Come on in the kitchen, man. I've got everything laid out. You won't believe how easy this hit'll be."

"But, Nick, over the phone, you said we were going to hit a bank, right?" Rudy asked.

"Yeah, Rudy. But believe me, man, this bank here will be a piece of cake."

The two men stopped at the table. Dominick leaned over and pointed to a spot on the map. "This is Vanceburg, here. Like I said over the phone, it's just a small country town. And get this…they have only two policemen on duty, on every shift. The way I figure it is…"

A loud knock startled the two men. They looked at each other, puzzled. "You expecting someone, Nick?" Rudy asked.

"No," Dominick replied, "but go ahead and answer it." He picked up one of the guns. "Me and my partner here, we'll be right behind the door, just in case it's somebody like a nosy cop."

Dominick walked over next to the living room door. He put his back against the wall. Gripping the gun in both hands, he nodded for Rudy to open the door.

Just as Rudy peeked out through the peephole, another knock sounded. Rudy stepped back and opened the door.

A man stood there in all black. His pointy, glossy black goatee looked out of place against his narrow, pale face. His pallid face had a smile on it. He took off his black fedora and held the hat between his thin fingers.

"Yeah," Rudy asked, "what do you want?"

The man's eyes seemed to twinkle as he spoke. "Well, just, I guess I should introduce myself. You can call me Reficul."

END

Frank Mawby eased his black, mid-size Pontiac into the driveway. A gleeful, yet cruel smile spread across his face.

A frequent visitor sat curled, and asleep on the top step. The grayish-brown cat had no idea that he was about to experience excruciating pain. And Frank Mawby was all too willing to be responsible for the administering of such.

Frank could induce pain upon any creature and not feel the slightest twinge of guilt. He'd always been a bully for as far back as he could recall.

Sometimes a person's character can be accurately determined by a careful look at their facial features. Frank was such a person. He had hard, wide jaws, tiny, cold blue eyes and a nose that spread too far. His pale skin seemed to be out of congruency with his rust-colored hair. Shaggy brows and moustache were the only things discernibly consistent about his appearance.

The bony cat was about to become Frank's victim for the third time within the same week. Frank got out of his car slowly, quietly.

He was still smiling as he tiptoed toward his unsuspecting victim. Big and blocky, Frank almost seemed comical, tiptoeing, but the grim objective took all the humor out of the scene.

"Two times not enough for you, huh?" he whispered to the slumbering cat as he approached.

"Now git!" He drew one big foot back, preparing to deliver what would have probably been a killing strike. But the door opened at that instant. "Frank!" his wife said.

The split-second pause was enough to throw his timing off. It also allowed the intended victim time to escape, but with some cost.

"Damn woman!" he shouted as he saw his startled prey scramble for the edge of the steps. The cat leaped but not quite quickly enough for Frank's big boot caught it in mid-leap.

A pained meow sliced through the evening air. It caused Frank to smile somewhat satisfactorily. But his wife cringed. She knew how the cat felt. Her small, thin body had been subjected to Frank's cruelty at times also.

"Your dinner is ready," she said, not being able to completely keep disgust from her tiny voice.

Frank grabbed her wrist as she turned away. He held her tightly, shaking one thick finger in her face. "Woman…if I know you'd done that on purpose, I'd…"

He pushed her aside roughly, leaving her standing in the doorway rubbing her wrist. She closed the door, feeling a little satisfied. It felt good to have almost stopped Frank from hurting the poor defenseless cat.

"Lizella, get your scrawny butt in this kitchen!" Frank bellowed.

Lizella stiffened at hearing the angry voice. The all too familiar lump arose in her throat. Her heart pounded ponderously as she choked back the fear and headed toward the kitchen.

Frank was standing in the middle of the kitchen; his big fists were clinched and propped on his hips.

Lizella took only a few small steps toward her husband once she entered the kitchen. She seemed to be trying to shrink, vanish inside herself, much like a small child, reluctant to face chastisement.

She fumbled with her hands and kept her eyes averted, just staring nervously at the floor.

Frank spoke again, causing her to look up at him, slowly though, hesitantly. "Lizella, come here. Right here in front of me," he said.

Although fearful, Lizella hung back, hoping desperately that Frank wouldn't get abusive this time.

Dropping her eyes away from Frank's hard gaze, she took a small step and then paused.

"F-Frank, I…"

"Lizella," he interrupted, "I said get over here in front of me. Now!"

Frank's voice was beginning to rise again. Suddenly he moved; Lizella shrank back again. He took two, long, angry steps toward her. "I said get over here!" he shouted as he snatched her by the wrist, pulling her face to face with him.

She could feel his violent anger in his grip and his torpid breath as his nostrils flared.

Frank stared down at his wife, neither of them saying anything. He turned, yanking her hand.

When they got close to the table, Frank let go of his wife's wrist. Grabbing her by the back of the neck, he ignored her whimpering and pushed her closer to the table.

"Look, look at that garbage!" he said, pointing to the meal she'd prepared for him. "You really expect me to eat that mess? Now get over…"

"Frank, Fra-Frank please! You…you're hurting me," Lizella interrupted. Her voice was a whisper of pain.

Frank laughed short and hoarsely. "Oh!" he said. "Hurting you? Well, you hurt me when I come home to this…this slop that's suppose to be supper. Get over there and fix me something, something I can eat, woman!"

He pushed her toward the stove. She flung her small hands out to stop herself from slamming into it. Despite her effort, her hip smashed into the hard edge of the stove.

"Oh!" she exhaled painfully. Tears welled up in her eyes, not just tears of pain; anger was fueling them also.

She heard her pulse race in her ears; her eyes squinted tight and then she spun.

Frank didn't see her reaction, because he was now headed out of the kitchen, head down and grumbling.

When Lizella spoke, it cracked loud and sharp, like an angry whip cutting the air.

"Frank! Franklin G. Mawby, that's it! That's the last time, the very last time you'll put your hands on me that way..."

Her last words were low, guttural, and almost masculine.

Frank stopped short, stiffening like he'd slammed into an invisible wall. For a moment, he paused, then he turned on her like a wild beast. His eyes were turgid, wide with disbelief.

"What? What did you just say to me, woman?" He was staring savagely at her as he spoke, and several slow, thundering steps followed his questions.

Frank felt a little doubt when he noticed the squint and gleam of Lizella's eyes. His steps were reflective; they faltered. Then he brushed aside the uneasiness, and came on more confidently.

Lizella did not move but for the trembling that gripped her small frame. She was not trembling out of fear; it was anger.

There was a knife holder sitting on the counter beside the stove. It held five knives in various sizes. A huge wooden-handled butcher knife protruded higher than the rest.

In a flash of motion, Lizella swung her head wildly; her look rested on the knives.

Frank's eyes bulged at seeing where his wife's gaze rested. Quickly he increased his steps. Lizella was much faster, however; she darted for the knife holder. Snatching the butcher knife from its place, she swung around again, facing her husband. Her small shoulders were slightly rigid and heaving up and down with every hard breath.

Frank came to an abrupt halt about three feet from her. Some of his anger vanished, being replaced by fear, fear that irritated him.

"Look woman, I know..."

"Shut up!" Lizella shouted, interrupting what Frank had intended to say.

Frank started to take a half step backward, but his pride restrained him, forcing him to put on a brave façade. His eyes, however, reflected no bravery at all. They were shifting restlessly from the knife to Lizella's face.

Lizella only stared; her eyes alight with the potency of fury. She held the handle of the knife gripped tightly with both hands, blade pointed toward Frank.

Frank took one step forward; uncertainty made him hesitate. He knew he'd never seen Lizella so adamant, act so strongly about anything.

It definitely unnerved him, but Frank was obstinate, unwilling to show fear.

When he started to take another step, Lizella's voice stopped him cold.

"You take one more step toward me...and I swear, by God, Franklin G. Mawby, it'll be your very last. I'll drop you where you stand!"

For emphasis she raised the big knife high over her head. The steel blade was struck by the kitchen's light in its ascension. A steely glint sliced through the air.

Despite the distance still remaining between them, Frank's body went stiff. And feeling that his wife had seen his reaction, he could no longer look at her. Embarrassment colored his face; he felt his face grow hot. To cover his embarrassment, he fumbled to make a coherent sentence, but failed.

Frank's face wore the look of one thoroughly confused. Turning quickly, he walked stiffly from the kitchen. "I...I'm going out," he said. Frank said other things, but they were mumbled.

She could hear him mumbling still as he strode through their den.

Momentarily, all that she heard was the sound of Frank's ponderous steps, her rapid breathing and the rushing pulse in her ears. Then the door to the den slammed shut. Frank had gone.

Lizella felt a kind of elation; she'd finally stood up to Frank. That...was wonderful! she thought.

Turning, she placed the knife on the counter top. Her palm rested on it briefly, and a hint of a smile showed at the corners of her mouth.

Paula Johansen drove her white Toyota Corolla into her driveway. The setting sun's light played on the shining white metal. It shined brightly off one certain spot on the hood, too bright to look at for long.

Paula parked the car, and getting out, she brought along a worn black briefcase. Her shoulders were slightly stooped from the fatigue of a long day's work.

Paula was the complete opposite of her sister Lizella, and she was six years older. Her face was rounded and pale, whereas, Lizella's was a bit hard looking and darker. And Paula, while pleasant to look at, was not pretty. However, Lizella was pretty, but the stress of her abusive marriage was taking its toll on her looks. Dark circles had begun showing under her eyes since the last time Paula had visited.

Paula trudged up the steps to the front door; her face took on a frown. She was envisioning her younger sister's visage.

The keys jingled like a door chime as she stuck one into the lock.

Despite the heat of summer, the round, smooth doorknob was just a little cool to her touch.

Once inside the house, Paula hurried to the phone. Her sister's haunted countenance was still poignant in her mind's eye.

Lizella roused herself from a tired sleep.

"Hello," she said.

"Hey girl!" Paula replied. "I've been thinking…well, actually, I've been worried about you. When's the last time, I mean, has he put, has he hit you lately?"

There was a moment of silence. And then Lizella started to laugh. It was low at first, but gradually it grew in loudness, becoming more intense.

Paula, assuming that Lizella was tickled by her blunt questioning, spoke hurriedly into the receiver. "Zella, remember what Mom used to say, don't you? If you've got something to say, just say it! So now I've…"

"Oh, I'm not laughing at how blunt you were. It's not that at all. Girl, you know by now, I know you're just like Mom, straight to the point. I was just laughing because…" Lizella giggled and then continuing said, "I can still see his face. He practically ran from me, girl. His eyes were…"

"No way!" Paula shouted, excitement rising in her voice. "He actually ran from you? What…what on earth did you do, girl?"

Bringing her giggling under restraint, Lizella answered. "Well, the cat…"

"Cat?" Paula questioned. "When'd you buy a cat?"

"Not my cat. It's a stray that's been hanging around," Lizella replied. "And if you'd stop interrupting like an old woman, I'd explain." Lizella giggled again; she knew her older sister was sensitive about her age.

"Now you wait just a minute, sister," Paula said. She raised her voice, pretending to be angry. "I know you didn't just call me old. After all, I'm only six years older than you are. Now, what's the difference between thirty and thirty-six?"

Paula was smiling when she asked the question. Her round cheeks rose, making the skin tighten and producing a squint to her blue eyes.

"Hmm," Lizella responded, "let me see. You take 365 days, multiply that by six and, whew! Too much for my brain! Got a calculator?"

Both women laughed this time.

"No, I don't have a calculator, smarty pants. And even if I did…"

Paula stopped what she'd started to say. "Zella, how in the world did we get on this conversation? You were telling me something about a cat."

"Oh yeah," Lizella replied. "The cat was sitting on the top step when Frank got home from work. Well, he didn't see me peeking out the window. I watched until he got ready to kick it, and then I opened the door. He didn't know that I'd done it on purpose, but I could tell he suspected that I had. Anyway, he was steaming, looking for something to argue about. So he called me into the kitchen, told me, 'I'm not eating this slop,' and before I realized what'd happened, he grabbed me. He pushed me into the..."

"Stop!" Paula shouted. Her breathing was getting quicker, and her grip tightened on the phone. "I don't really want to hear anymore, just stop. I'm sick of hearing about how...how that bastard keeps hurting you! How long, Zella? How much more of his...his trash are you going to put up with, huh?"

Lizella could tell that her sister was getting angry; she was silent for a moment before replying. Then reticently, she answered. "Paula...I...I don't know. I mean, what..."

"Yes, you do know!" Paula retorted. "You know exactly what to do. Zella, I've told you over and over, you can come to stay with Brian and me. Away from that monster! I just can't understand why you..."

"Enough, Paula!" Lizella interjected sharply; her own voice was getting an edge. "You're right, we've been through this over and over. And every time, I tell you the same thing. I can't. I'm a grown woman, and then too, what can I do? Here I am, thirty years old and can't do a thing. No degrees. No special talents. So tell me Paula, what is..."

Paula bit down on her teeth; she spit her words out furiously.

"Look girl, how foolish can you be, huh? And just how damn dumb do you think I am? I know what it is. You...you love that beast, don't you? I guess things won't be good enough until I wind up having a stupid corpse for a sister, huh? Well?"

Click. Lizella slammed the phone down! She reached up slowly, wiping at a lone tear trailing down her hot cheek.

She heard her sister's words echo in her mind. They stung with the force of a slap; she knew that Paula's words rang true and meaningful.

I'm a fool, she thought, loving someone that treats me like an animal.

Lizella wiped at the warm clear liquid again; it was slowly rolling down both cheeks now.

"No more," she whispered through clenched teeth. "No more, Frank."

Lizella bit down on her bottom lip, holding it between her teeth.

Languidly she walked into the kitchen, her head down until she got to the refrigerator. Opening the refrigerator door, she paused, frowning.

The big butcher knife lay where she'd placed it earlier. She turned her head ever so slowly until her gaze found the shining steel.

For a moment, she seemed held, transfixed, even fascinated by the gleaming instrument, the metallic friend.

Hypnotically, she walked the little distance to the counter. Reaching out for the knife, she suddenly halted her thin hand, staring intently. After a long pause, she reached a determination.

Closing her hand around the large handle, she was hesitant at first. But picking the big knife up, Lizella headed for the bedroom.

The tears had ceased to run down her face, leaving only faint, dry traces of their ever having been. Her skin was tight in the areas where the tears had dried; she felt it pull every time she sniffled.

Words of solemn determination resonated through her mind. Never again, Frank, she thought. Never again.

Paula sat on the couch in her den. Her gaze traveled back and forth from the television to the remote.

Sighing heavily, she ignored the urge to phone Lizella back. Fighting back the guilt, she leaned forward, picking up the remote from the coffee table. Her rust colored hair moved with her. The long shiny curls cascaded down around her round face.

Casting a last look at the telephone, Paula mentally shook her head and clicked the television on.

Disinterested, she watched as channels flicked past; she let go of the channel button when she heard the jangle of keys at the door.

Smiling inwardly, Paula stood up quickly. She'd been so distracted by her thoughts that she'd temporarily forgotten that it was around the time that Brian usually got home.

Brian stepped through the doorway; his face lit up in a smile. Paula approached to greet him before he was very far into the room. It was a routine that had never vacillated much during the years of their marriage.

Brian's smile broadened when they embraced. His deep dimples accentuated his smile, something Paula still found attractive.

They embraced. "Tired?" Paula asked.

"No, not really. You?" Brian responded.

"Yeah, sort of. But not so tired that we can't take a ride to Nehold Garden," she said winking at him.

"Chinese food, huh? Sounds good to me. Ready?" Brian queried.

In the car, Brian made several attempts at conversation, but

Paula made only brief replies. After riding for a while, her short replies began to irritate him. He called to her, his voice conveying a questioning tone.

"Paula?" He frowned, noting that she was staring distractedly out the window. Raising his voice, he called to her again. "Paula, what's wrong? Did I do..."

"Huh? Oh, sorry, honey. I...my mind is somewhere else." She couldn't stop her face from coloring in slight embarrassment.

"Well," Brian said, "wherever it is, I want you to go get it. I'll be darn if I'm going to remain married to a mindless woman." He smiled.

She could not help but laugh a little. Paula hit his shoulder with a playful punch. "Clown," she said.

Brian smiled at the retort, flashing straight, white teeth. But the smile was fleeting. Taking on a more serious tone, he questioned, "Your sister again?"

Sighing, Paula flashed him a quick, worried look before answering. "Yeah...that...that beast has been bullying her again. God! I wish she'd just leave that piece of trash."

Brian reached over, placing a hand on his wife's shoulder, then said, "Baby, try not to get worked up about it. It's her choice. But I'll tell you; I'd like to put my hands around that sick bastard's throat. Anyone that beats on a woman deserves a taste of their own medicine. Damn! It angers me. I'd just ...."

"Brian! The turn...don't miss the turn," Paula said, pointing to the Nehold Garden Restaurant's driveway.

"I think I'll go by to see how she's doing early tomorrow," she said.

"Correction," Brian added, smiling, "we'll go by there first thing in the morning."

Paula smiled back, and then her attention was drawn to a payphone near where Brian was parking.

"Go ahead," she said, "I'll be right there. I just need to find out how she's doing."

"Okay," Brian responded, "and tell her I said hello."

When Frank Mawby exited the bar, he staggered; the reek of alcoholic drink swam heavily around him.

The darkness was thick, hanging a vast sheet of ebony all around the surrounding buildings.

Stepping further into the parking area, Frank frowned, wrinkling his nose. The scent of fresh, light, summer rain drying on asphalt, wafted through the night air.

Lighting in the parking area was vague, adding to the creeping sense of uneasiness Frank had suddenly begun to feel.

Even though on the verge of being drunk, he could detect the strange sense of heightened awareness one feels when being watched.

Shrugging mentally, he fought down the urge and ambled on toward his car.

Acting like a little girl, old boy, nobody's watching you, he thought. It was only an attempt to ease the creepiness that refused to relinquish its hold on him.

He was almost at his car when he gave in to his instincts. Quickly, he glanced around at the few remaining cars in the parking lot.

There was no one in any of the cars. It made him feel somewhat embarrassed. Despite the embarrassment, he was also a bit relieved.

I knew it, he mumbled through the haze of near inebriation.

Turning his head toward his own car, Frank managed a half-smile. The smile froze on his face.

He'd just glimpsed a face, someone ducking in the back seat of the car. It appeared that the trespasser had on a skull mask and a charcoal black hood.

For a moment Frank stood stock-still, as rigid as the smile on his face.

Fear gnawed at Frank's courage, but his nature replaced it with a rising anger.

Death. The face he'd seen resembled the common depictions of death. But the eyes he'd seen were glowing, glowing like an intensely burning fire.

For some reason, the burning glow of those eyes remained etched into Frank's mind. He took a half step, paused, and then in long, angry strides went to his car.

"Alright," he said, reaching out, preparing to yank the back door open, "game's over. Get your…"

Frank's mouth sagged weakly; the same weakness suddenly attacked his knees also.

The back seat was empty. Empty! The door was still locked. Distrusting his own senses, he yanked on the handle again. "Damn it! What in the hell…"

"Frank," a voice called out, interrupting his thoughts.

Frank jerked himself around with a speed belying his size. Eyes wildly searching the parking lot, he struggled not to let fear overtake him.

His mind and his heart raced as wildly as his roving eyes. He searched his mind desperately for a rational explanation to what he'd seen and heard. None came immediately.

When the mind is jolted by the inexplicable, delusion follows. The mind proceeds to trick itself into accepting something explainable.

Frank Mawby's mind was no exception to the rule. He forced himself to conclude something that seemed logical. Too much to drink. You've had too much to drink.

His thought, though accepted, gave him little comfort. Frank pressed his back hard against the car as he moved to open the driver side door.

Digging into his pocket for his keys, he struggled for effort to still his trembling hand. He couldn't keep his eyes from searching the parking lot.

Fear enhanced Frank's senses. Things seemed sharper, clearer. Even the jangle of his keys sounded incredibly loud.

Turning quickly, he inserted the key into the lock. His hand trembled again.

Frank cast frequent glances over his shoulder. His breathing became heavy. He swallowed, hard and dry, several times, but the lump kept forming in his throat.

Swinging the door open, he got in quickly. His eyes went to the rearview mirror; they didn't look elsewhere until after a long moment.

Frank ran a nervous hand across his forehead. It came away sweaty. Frank had not showered when he'd gone home earlier.

The smell of sweat was pungent in the air, air made hard to inhale by fear.

Involuntarily, his eyes kept swinging to the rearview mirror as he sped from the parking lot.

In spite of the summer heat, Frank felt a definite chill, like a breath of arctic breeze.

Frank made it to the outskirts of town without passing much traffic and without further strange happenings.

His breathing had returned to normal when he turned onto the rural road that lead to his home.

Silhouettes of trees and shrubbery flashed by as Frank sped along. The silhouettes were darkened even more by the density of eventide along the country road.

At the bottom of the foliage, darkness was more intense, blending the foliage with the color of night.

Something up ahead caught at Frank's attention, making him more alert.

Questions went through his mind. A woman? This time of night, in the middle of the road? Must be hitchhiking.

The figure appeared to be dressed completely in black, something resembling a cloak.

Something was weird though; the cloak was flapping about wildly. Frank recalled that the night was not windy. At that distance, no face could be clearly seen, and whoever stood in the road, had a hood over their head.

For a better view, Frank flicked on the bright lights.

Shock grabbed him, stiffening him; he inhaled loudly.

The bright lights illumined the face. It was a pale face, inhumanly pale, the same face he'd seen in his car!

"What the… How?"

For an instant, Frank's mind repeated the words he'd asked himself. Then he spit out more words, words tinged with both anger and fear. "Prankster, huh? I'll show you a prank, you sick son of a…"

Slamming his foot down on the accelerator, he sent the car hurtling forward.

Swerving toward the centerline, Frank noticed that the figure held the same position. It not so much as even budged.

The speedometer reading was climbing rapidly. Before Frank even realized it, he was passing through the spot where the figure stood.

No impact! Frank did not feel the expected impact. Instead, the car's interior plunged suddenly into pitch darkness.

A loud whooshing assaulted his ears. An intense cold enwrapped him. His teeth clicked together, hard.

The car shook like a toy amidst a windstorm.

The entire occurrence lasted only a matter of seconds, but the effects were profound.

Frank shivered with cold; it was a deep aching cold, penetrating deeper than his flesh.

He was afraid to venture even so much as a glance behind him, fearing what he would see.

Seconds before the expected impact, Frank had seen eyes, horrible eyes! They were unlike any human eyes. What was going on?

His mind whirled, and his heart was a thudding ache in his chest.

He's seen those eyes only once before, those deep sunken holes, vacant of life. They were like small glowing caverns, alight with the red-yellow color of fire.

The face…God, the face! It was a white, hideous construction of bone, not a mask. Somehow Frank knew it was not mere synthetic fabrication.

God, it was real! But what was it? Frank's mind wrestled with his thoughts, turning the words over and over.

Gripping the steering wheel mightily did nothing to weaken the frigid talons of fear.

His senses were reeling, sharpened by fear and the rush of adrenaline. Streams of tepid sweat trickled down his back. Upon his sticky skin, the rivulets of warm sweat felt like things alive.

The speedometer's needle breezed past eighty-five. Frank was unaware of the acceleration. His foot was still pressing hard on the accelerator.

Lizella blinked, coming awake. The darkness in the bedroom was ponderous. She had not bothered to turn the bedside lamp on, or the overhead light.

Something moved. The noise was so slight that it was perceived more as a feeling than something actually heard.

Lizella's eyes shifted nervously.

Several seconds vanished off into the realm of no return.

Straining her ears, she detected nothing further.

Tensing her muscles, she prepared to get up. But wait! There it was again.

Something had definitely moved. Something had stirred, causing her to awaken. What?

There…there is was again, a rustling by the closet in the corner.

Frou-frou. It was like cloth swishing, the sound of skirts rustling.

Lizella laid on her stomach, resting her head on a pillow, the pillow under which she'd placed the butcher knife.

Minutely, she raised her head. She hoped the tiny movement went undetected by the eyes of the watcher.

Easing her hand under the pillow, she gripped the knife's handle tightly.

The heavy thumping of her heart pounded rhythmically against the softness of the mattress.

The corner she'd heard the noise come from was behind the direction her head was turned.

Hoping she could catch the intruder by surprise, she leaped up suddenly, gripping the pillow in one hand, the knife in the other.

Lizella flung the pillow toward the corner, shouting, "Alright, whoever you are, I've got a weapon. Don't move! Don't try anything."

Two fire-colored spots shined through the darkness, perforating the veil of gloom.

The glowing spots were about eye-level; she kept her eyes on them while backing hurriedly to the light switch.

Her eyes didn't even waver as she backed up to the wall. Fumbling to the side, her fingers brushed past the light switch. She tried again, this time flipping the light on though.

Her face formed a tight frown; there was nothing in the corner but the closet. What were the fiery things she'd seen?

Had she actually seen anything at all?

Her lips formed the word, stress. But they only moved silently.

Too much…too much stress, she thought.

Wrapping her arms tightly around herself, Lizella shivered. The room had grown cold.

Tires rushing over gravel snatched Lizella out of her deep state of pondering. Frank was speeding the car into the driveway. The tires ground loudly on the gravel, abruptly coming to a halt.

Quickly striding over to the corner where she'd flung the pillow, she stooped, retrieving it. Standing upright again, Lizella folded her arms, crossing them in front of her.

She kept the pillow, concealing the hand that held the knife.

Sitting down on the edge of the bed, Lizella bit down on her back teeth. She waited, her eyes agleam with something akin to anger.

Her earlier words of determination came back to her. They rang out loud in her mind, as clear as if she were speaking them.

"No more. No more, Frank."

Some of her sister's words came back too, fomenting tears in her eyes. But she blinked, trying to stop what was about to happen.

"Look girl, how foolish can you be, huh? I guess things won't be good enough until I wind up having a stupid corpse for a sis…."

Frank called out from the den, interrupting Lizella's thoughts of what Paula had said earlier.

"Lizella! Lizella, I want you to get in here and fix me a sandwich."

Lizella didn't respond. There was a pause in which relative quietness settled. Suddenly, the quiet was broken by a succession of heavy, rapid steps.

Rushing into the bedroom, Frank was stopped in mid-stride and mid-sentence.

"Woman, didn't you hear me? I told you to…"

Frank couldn't see the knife she held; it was concealed by the pillow. But Lizella's eyes! Her eyes were boring into him. Her head was slightly bent in the direction of the floor, but she was staring from under her brows.

Lizella spoke slowly, as if each word was being spit out like something bitter.

"You get it yourself!"

Frank gaped. And when he tried to speak, it was done haltingly. "I don't know what's gotten into you…I…I'll tell you…"

Lizella's eyes never wavered from his face, and it made Frank extremely uncomfortable. He threw up his big, beefy hands in a gesture of hopelessness. Turning sharply, he hurried from the bedroom.

"I'll just get it myself," he said over his shoulder.

Though anger was the prevailing emotion, Lizella felt a tinge of humor. Her tight, thin lips curled slightly, a hint of a smile.

After a few minutes, she could hear Frank's heavy steps return.

Despite her anger, her body stiffened in response.

When he got as far as the doorway, he paused, chewing on the last bit of sandwich he'd made. Eyeing Lizella warily, he came slowly on into the room. But he left plenty of room between them.

Turning her head, Lizella let her steely gaze follow his every step.

Frank watched her from the corner of his eyes, but when he got to the far side of the bed, he turned his back. Sitting on the edge of the bed, he removed his shoes.

"Whew, boy am I beat," he said. Silence.

Then there was a light squeak as Lizella got up. Keeping the pillow and the knife, she walked to the doorway that Frank had just entered. Leaning against the doorjamb, she watched Frank's large back. She could feel her hand tightening behind the pillow. The hard handle of the knife caused a dull ache, yet still, she squeezed.

Frank sighed heavily, and stood to remove his shirt. Clearing his throat, he said, "I guess I'll go take a shower."

Lizella said nothing, made no response, adding to the uneasy silence.

Frank took off his undershirt, and turning to face Lizella, made yet another attempt at conversation. "I've been thinking, what would you…"

Lizella turned, and without hesitance, she went through the doorway.

Momentarily, he stared at the now vacant space where his wife had stood. Finally though, he shrugged his shoulders and headed for the shower.

The indifference, which is indicated by a shrug, was not present on his face. He had stiff lines across his forehead, and he shifted his view from side to side as he walked.

Lizella had walked to the couch in the den; she sat staring in the direction of the phone.

Words came to her; words that made her feel frustrated, weary and confused, all at once. Do I still love him? What am I going to do…leave, live with Paula and Brian? Humph, then what? I think I'll call Paula and…no. Tomorrow?

Groaning inwardly, she looked around the room; she looked with the gaze of a stranger, as if her surroundings were new.

Sighing heavily, Lizella placed the knife in the corner of the couch. She stared at the thick, wooden handle, the gleaming metal blade.

Shaking her head, she put the pillow on top of the knife, and then she laid her head onto the pillow.

Lizella was so fatigued mentally that she was fast asleep within a matter of minutes.

When Frank came out of the shower, he headed for the bedroom. But with a sudden change of thought, he veered his direction. And peering into the den, he saw that his wife was sleeping soundly.

Frank's face took on a malicious grin; he headed toward the couch, walking stealthily, barely making any noise.

Approaching the couch, Frank reached his big hand toward Lizella's hair. Inches from grabbing a handful, he paused suddenly. Wait! Something was wrong. A horrible chill made him tremble suddenly. The light fluttered. There was a subdued pop. The light flickered and went out.

Frank felt his chest begin to rise and fall rapidly, but the rest of his body remained virtually motionless.

"Frank," a voice said. And though it was dark, Frank's eyes shifted wildly, straining in the darkness.

His eyes caught light coming from the hallway, and in a sudden rush, he headed for the light. When he reached the hallway, he turned to look at the den again. Not a power failure, he thought. Then what the devil ...

The light in the den flashed, coming back to full luminosity just as if it had never been out.

Flicking rapidly, Frank's eyes stretched; and immediately he turned. At a fast stumbling pace, he went into the bedroom.

In the bedroom, he sat on the edge of the bed; he mopped at his sticky forehead.

His big hand came away trembling and sweaty.

Looking strangely at his trembling hand, Frank scolded himself. You big baby, what are you afraid of, huh?

Nothing happened. Nothing unusual happened. That voice. That...you didn't hear a thing. Your imagination is getting the best of you, old boy. Take it easy. Get some sleep.

After lying down, an unnatural chill crept over him. And Frank's eyes couldn't stop their surveying of the room.

Finally though, his wariness was subdued by tiredness, and he succumbed to the overpowering pull of sleep and alcoholic drink.

Frank Mawby was in a dark place, a cold, dark place. He shivered, and sticking his hands out, he tried to feel for something. All that he could feel was a weight, a very light weight. It weighed upon his hands, his arms; his entire body could feel the weight. It was the gloom. The darkness was so thick that he could actually feel its presence! It breathed.

Frank turned frantically; arms flailing like those of a blind man.

He was turning in a full circle; his mind was screaming for help.

Stubbornly though, he refused to cry out verbally.

"Frank," a voice said. It seemed to ride the darkness, coming from every direction.

"Frankie boy, I've come…"

"No!" Frank screamed. He snatched himself upright in the bed. Sweat rolled down his face. Frank shivered; he was cold, very cold.

Through the rest of the night, Frank tossed and turned fitfully, and morning seemed to have arrived too quickly. He got up stiffly.

Rubbing at his eyes, he noted that Lizella was not on her side of the bed.

Fine. He trudged sleepily through the hallway, arriving at the bathroom door.

At the bathroom door, he reached out for the doorknob, but it turned before he could grip it.

Lizella opened the door and froze, a quick flicker of fear shined in her eyes. Frank, too, was caught off guard.

Their eyes held each other's for a matter of seconds. Suddenly Frank moved, and brushed past Lizella's body, almost knocking her down. But Frank didn't even halt in his stride.

Regaining her balance, Lizella stepped out into the hallway. In her mind, she was hurrying away, but in actuality she took only slow, stiff steps. She could feel Frank's stare and hear his grumbling.

But then the bathroom door thudded shut.

Lizella let go of a long exhalation. Until then, she hadn't even realized that she had been holding her breath.

Paula Johansen sat up quickly. She was breathing heavily.

Reaching out quickly, Paula gave Brian a rough shake. "Brian…Brian! Get up," she said.

"Huh? What?" Brian asked. He cast her a sleepy look and then closed his eyes, nestling down against the mattress.

"Brian! Come with me to see Zella this morning."

Lifting his head slowly, he murmured, "Oh, oh yeah, that's right."

"Hurry!" Paula insisted. "I feel, I…something is wrong."

"Okay…I'm moving. What about breakfast? I'm hungr…."

"No, no Brian," Paula interjected. "Let's go! I told you, something is wrong. I know it." With that, she was springing up from the bed.

Brian was getting up, grumbling, but not without irritation. "Umph, 4:45 in the morning. Boy, I'll tell you…"

In a few minutes, Paula was tugging at Brian's sleeve, pulling him hastily down the steps.

"Okay, okay! Ease up speedy, I'm coming. And since you're in such a hurry, I don't know why you want to drive that foreign toy of yours. My car is much faster," he said jokingly.

She glanced behind her, catching his smile. "Yeah, it's fast alright. Fast heading for the salvage yard," she said, giggling childishly. She then began to sprint toward her car.

"Ha! Very funny," he said catching up to her. "My trash heap is a perfectly fine piece of … garbage," he chuckled.

When they reached her car, they both were laughing.

Shortly after pulling out of their driveway, the car's speedometer needle was steadily climbing.

Lizella came from the hallway and went into the den. She halted when she got near the couch. Looking at the pillow lying on the couch, she thought of what lay under it, the knife, her weapon and inanimate friend.

Starting toward the couch, Lizella took a few steps, but then, her thoughts stopped her.

No, she thought. I refuse to walk around in my own house having to carry a weapon, having to be scared. I refuse.

Changing her direction, she went into the kitchen. Taking down a small bowl, she poured cereal into it. The cereal was Life cereal, and the brand name caused her to start having thoughts of her existence.

Life, humph, not much of that going on around here. Scared all the time. Have to carry weapons…ridiculous.

Going to the refrigerator, Lizella removed a small jug of milk. "I'm so tired of th…this life. I have to get away, do something, something different. Paula was right. If he hits me one more time, I'll…"

Frank was entering the kitchen, sour-faced as usual. He paused at the doorway, scrutinizing her face, and then his eyes went to the jug in her hands. Within that brief moment, Lizella paused also; then she came back slowly to the table.

Frank watched her pour the milk as he came over to the table, close to where she was standing. He was wearing a smile, but it was not jovial; it was a cruel one.

Putting his big hands on the table, he leaned over, coming close to her face. For an instant he only stared at her. She pretended to ignore him. But the quick thudding of her heart let her know that she couldn't ignore him; she was too afraid.

Turning away from Frank's malicious glare, she placed the rest of the milk back into the refrigerator. Taking her time in turning around, she told herself, "Just keep ignoring him, maybe he won't get…"

"So, where's breakfast?" Frank asked sneeringly.

"I…I didn't cook anything," Lizella replied.

"Oh, I can see that, but I want you to get…"

"No," Lizella said, interrupting Frank. "I'm tired of the way you…you…"

Frank's face reddened; he took two loping steps and raised his hand to slap her. He stopped, hand still poised, when he saw that Lizella only stared him in the eyes. She didn't even flinch.

The doorbell rang, but neither of them moved, their positions remained the same momentarily. When it rang again, Frank tore his gaze away from her and headed for the door.

Opening the front door, Frank's eyes clouded over with displeasure. But he did not bother to attempt hiding it.

Brian and Paula's stares were no different from Frank's own.

A moment of tense silence prevailed as the three traded stares.

Frank kept his hand on the doorknob, and he purposely had himself in a position blocking entrance.

Brian spoke first, but it was clear that there was no friendliness in his tone.

"Frank, so, how's it going?"

"Alright," Frank replied, still keeping his position.

"Well," Brian went on, "mind if we..."

"Who is it?" Lizella asked, coming into the den.

Frank only grunted, and turning away from the door, he moved aside. But he didn't go far away. Moving back only a few feet, he crossed his massive arms, watching with evident disgust.

Lizella rushed forward and flung her arms out toward her sister. "Paula! Paula," she said, "I'm so glad to see you!"

Brian and Paula came on into the house. Brian took a position a little distance away from the women. He was smiling as he watched the two giggle and hug like children.

The two were trying to talk at the same time. Their words kept jumbling into each other's. This made them giggle all the more so.

Brian cleared his throat, causing the two women to part and look in his direction.

"Uh, excuse me, please, but it seems someone forgot to speak," he said.

Both Paula and Lizella feigned looks of innocence. "Who?" they asked simultaneously, then they giggled again.

"Very funny," Brian said, his face lighting up with a broad smile.

"How are you, Brian?" Lizella asked.

"Fine, just fine," Brian replied. "Now, that's better."

He smiled again, but it turned into a hard look when he saw Frank move toward the women.

Taking several long steps, Frank came to Lizella's side and grabbed her by the shoulder roughly. He turned her away from her sister to face him.

Brian reacted; he took a half step forward. But then, he stopped. His fists closing and opening at his sides.

Frank said, "Why don't you get into the kitchen and fix me something to eat!"

"No, Frank," Lizella said calmly.

Without warning, Frank backhanded her; she fell against Paula, and then crumpled at her big sister's feet.

"Zella!" Paula shouted, kneeling to examine her younger sister. Paula could see blood trickling down the corner of her sister's mouth.

Instinctually, Brian took two leaping steps.

Something must have warned the larger man, because he was turning to meet his attacker. A mixture of shock and anger was etched into Frank's face.

Brian's first punch landed, glancing off the edge of the big man's jaw.

Frank rocked back, but did not fall; a feral rage lighted his beady eyes.

Brian had reacted without really thinking, but when he saw the big man shake his punch off, his mind cleared somewhat.

Frank was a towering menace; he was three inches over six feet. And though he was not muscular, his body was fairly solid, a formidable opponent.

Brian was muscular, but he stood only six feet, and he was outweighed by at least thirty pounds.

He worked out regularly, so he felt that he was in far better condition. But he was certain, if he were to win this fight, he needed luck, a lot!

Moving quicker than what Brian had expected, Frank threw a wide swing, but it landed. Brian was caught off guard and knocked backward. He crashed into the coffee table, splintering it.

Lizella was up now; she and Paula gasped when Brian went down. Frank's punch had landed so solidly that the two were certain Brian had already lost the fight.

The impact was tremendous when Brian landed. It jarred him, causing his teeth to click together loudly. And his eyes snapped shut.

Frank stepped forward quickly, sure that he would be the victor. He'd seen Brian's eyes snap shut and assumed that he'd knocked him unconscious.

Brian's head felt thick, and indeed, he was on the verge of unconsciousness, but he kept his eyes closed purposely. He wanted to gain a little time, to catch Frank off guard. It worked.

He heard Frank's footsteps stop near him.

"Ha!" Frank boomed. "Look at your pretty boy, hero. Look at him!"

Turning his back to Brian, he sneered at the two women while pointing at Brian.

"I'm going to mess that face up. I'm going to teach him a lesson he'll never forget."

Both women wanted to help, wanted to move, but everything was happening too fast. They stood unmoving, locked in the grips of intense fear.

Brian could feel his head clearing, his strength returning.

Opening his eyes minutely, he peeked through, seeing that Frank's back was turned.

Frank went on bragging, taking note of nothing except the fear on the women's faces.

"And I don't think there's nothing anyone can do about…"

Lunging up from the floor, Brian drove his shoulders into the back of Frank's knees.

"Wrong!" Brian hissed through gritted teeth. Frank's eyes widened upon impact, and he crashed ponderously to the floor.

Before Frank could orient himself, Brian reacted quickly. Straddling Frank's back, he grabbed two tight handfuls of Frank's hair and began slamming Frank's head into the floor.

Frank's arms flailed wildly, and he emitted pained grunts every time his head banged into the floor. Suddenly though, Frank's flailing and grunting stopped. Brian, however, did not notice. Anger had dulled his senses.

His face was twisted in rage, and he was still slamming Frank's face into the floor while spitting out harsh, emotional words.

"Where's that badness now? Huh? You lousy excuse for … for a man! I ought to … to kill you, right now, right …."

Paula had to call to Brian. "Brian, please stop! Don't kill him. Look, he's not even moving."

Brian looked up to see his wife rushing toward him. For a moment he seemed dazed; his eyes were empty of all but the light of fury; slowly though, realization began to seep in.

He uncurled his fingers slowly from the big man's hair. Frank's head thudded to the floor; it then rolled to one side, but otherwise he moved little, except for the movements of his shoulders. They moved jerkily in unison with his raspy breathing.

Brian stood shakily, reaching for Paula's hand. Within that brief instant, his eyes and Lizella's made contact. His face took on a questioning look, but Lizella nodded, giving him an unspoken, "I'm okay, you didn't do anything wrong."

Paula was hugging her hero. With one hand she was tenderly touching his face.

He could hardly issue a reply between her barrage of questions. "Did he hurt you? Are you okay? He's not going to die, is he? What happens if...when...?"

"Whoa, whoa," Brian said. "Take it easy. I've only got one mouth. I can't make but one reply at a time."

Lizella was standing by the door; her eyes shifted constantly between her downed husband and the two huggers.

Paula was about to resume her flow of questions when Lizella approached.

"Brian," she said, "is there..." she stopped, feeling the soft touch of her sister's hand alight upon her shoulder.

Turning, Paula faced her sister, her eyes conveying a silent message of solicitude. She opened her mouth to speak, but at that moment, Frank groaned and rolled over.

Brian walked over, and touching the two women by their shoulders, he lightly steered them toward the door.

"Come on," he said, "let's go."

Frank rolled over, and when he saw the three leaving, he tried to make a sudden lunge. Instead, he plopped down again weakly, moaning and tenderly cupping his face in his big hands.

When Brian, Paula and Lizella left, they didn't bother closing the door. And from where Frank was lying, he had a clear view when he lifted his head again.

Cursing, he made another effort at getting up. This time he was successful. However, when he got to the door, the three were riding off in Paula's car.

Frank's face grew hard; he stood in the doorway a long time gazing, even after the car was out of sight.

Finally, he turned slowly, ambling toward the bathroom while gingerly touching his nose and lips. They both felt sore, numb and exceedingly heavy.

When he looked in the bathroom mirror, his eyes widened. His face looked worse than he'd thought. "Damn!" he said, "I can't go to work like this."

Biting down hard upon his back teeth, Frank opened the medicine cabinet and thought, That's not the end, pretty boy, not by a long shot.

Evening found Frank drowsy, sitting in the den brooding. He held a bottle of whiskey in one hand, and the television remote hung loosely from the other. Frank stared at the television, but he was unaware of what the screen was displaying. His eyes were not receiving any outside reception; all that he could see was inside, a vision of revenge.

Turning the bottle up, he drained the remaining liquid greedily. Then placing the bottle and the remote on the table, he stood up a bit unsteadily.

"Humph," he uttered; realizing that he was quite drunk.

He managed to make a bumbling trek to the bedroom. Seeming to forget what he'd come into the bedroom for, he paused at the foot of his bed. Soon though, he plopped down on the bed and sat staring at the wall.

The thought of revenge crossed his mind again. Frank smiled inwardly, and reaching up, he touched his swollen face again. And then he lay back. "No, it's not over yet, not yet, pretty boy."

Before long, the pull of drowsiness became too strong for him. Relenting, he drifted into a drunken snooze, thoughts of vengeance whirled in his mind.

Frank was in a dark place again. Dense darkness surrounded him from every direction.

I've been here before, he thought. He then stuck his hands out before him, flailing at the thick darkness. It was maddening.

He started stumbling with his hands still outstretched. Fear was his companion. It caused his mind to whirl, searching for some answers, any answer.

Why…why am I in this place? What is this? Is anyone here who can help?

A sinister laughter interrupted Frank, as if supplying an answer to the questions in his mind. The laughter was like the overpowering darkness, everywhere.

The darkness was cold, but Frank's face was beading tiny balls of sweat.

He began to turn in a small circle while still feeling the darkness.

"Hey…hey, please…help. Help me," he moaned. "Please? Where are you? Who are…"

The laughter increased in intensity; it became unbearably loud. Responsively, Frank slammed both hands over his ears. But the laughter penetrated easily, getting even louder.

Hands pressed tightly against his ears, Frank fell to his knees weakly. Groaning horribly, he shut his eyes tightly.

The laughter stopped. A calm deep voice called to him. "Hey, Frank. Frankie boy."

"Huh! What?" Frank's voice quaked badly.

The laughter started over again. It seemed to rush upon him from every direction. And suddenly it was right before him.

His pounding heart hammered his chest thunderously. It seemed that the rhythm shook his whole body with every thump.

Opening his eyes cautiously, Frank beheld a sight that would have forced a tearing scream from his lungs, had he been able to scream.

A face. That face! The skeletal face he'd glimpsed in his car and on the road.

He could not see a body. The darkness was hung too densely. The face was eye-level. It leered at him, bone-white, jutting out from the dark, sinister grin, and piercing eyes aflame.

A scream swelled within Frank's chest, but stuck, rendered impotent by the clammy hand of cold terror. He clawed at his gaping mouth with hands of a man terrified to the brink of insanity.

Without taking the time to stand, Frank scrambled backward on his hands and knees. Suddenly there was no support under him. Frank fell. He did scream then, a long terrifying rush of pent-up breath.

Such momentum propelled Frank that the rush of wind in his ears was nearly unbearable. Every second his body tensed tighter and tighter, readying itself for an awful impact. It didn't come.

Frank landed on his bed. But he felt very little impact. The feeling, instead, was like the sudden jerk and descent of an elevator. The bed springs creaked with a tremendous sound. Frank sank deeply into the mattress.

The mattress sprang back up violently, and all was still. All was still, that is, except the spasmodic hammering of Frank's heart.

In a trembling jerk, he sat up abruptly. His sweaty shirt stuck to his skin. The sweat permeated him with a biting chill.

Hell of a dream! he thought. I've really got to cut down on so much drink...

Death stood at the foot of the bed. This time the face was minus the evil leer. It only stood there staring, as immobile as a statue. Frank could actually feel the eyes piercing into his own.

I'm still dreaming, he forced himself to think. The desire to get away from the weighty stare was overwhelming. He tried to spring from the bed. Though he'd issued the mental command, Frank couldn't move! The force of the fiery glare hypnotized him.

He tried shutting his eyes, but even they refused to be governed by his will.

Sharply the voice of death cut through the air. "You know, Frankie boy, people who die in their sleep, they...well they have good reason."

Frank's face contorted; it writhed with the effort to speak. No sound came. His speaking faculty, too, was absent.

Death went on. "There are three categories."

Frank knew he was in his own house, in his own bed, but it had to be a dream.

His mind screamed that determination repeatedly, so loudly that the voice of death was temporarily a murmur.

"Some die of old age," Death continued. "Others die of certain sicknesses..."

Placing a long, fleshless hand under his chin, Death grew silent and tilted his white, white, boned-face. Frank waited, wanting to speak so badly that his throat ached with strain. At least his mind was capable of functioning. And it did function, screaming, screaming a soundless question. What about the third category? Death's elongated face came up slowly, returning to its former position. He fixed Frank with a look of mock surprise.

"Ah, yes," he said, "the third category. Well, Mr. Mawby, the people in the third category die rather...hmm, let us say, mysteriously."

His voice died down, trailing off into the air like a whisp of vanishing smoke.

Death dropped his head again. And placing his boned hands behind him, they clacked loudly. He began pacing back and forth, the width of the foot of the bed.

Frank's temper had always been easily piqued, and it didn't fail now.

His face contorted again when he tried to shout, but the shouting was only in his head. What is all this about anyway? And what does any of it have to do with me?

Death stopped his pacing and, again, fixed Frank with a stare. This time, though, he chuckled before he replied.

"Dear, poor child. You don't know do you? You really don't know what this is all about? Maybe it's just a dream, huh, Frank?"

Death sounded concerned, but immediately after speaking, he chuckled again.

As suddenly as the chuckling started, it ended with Death's teeth clicking together loudly. The sharp sound shot a sliver of tension through Frank's body.

"Let me explain," Death said. He pointed one long, skeletal finger upward. "Sometimes he allows me to come a little early."

Death smiled. It was obviously gratifying toying with his victim, watching the agony on his face, in his eyes.

"No need to get so excited, Mr. Mawby," Death said. He emitted a short laugh.

"You see, you've not even heard the best part yet. The people in the third category are usually very cruel people. And, thus, their demise is something especial. They have to experience the pain of death as many times as the number of their age. You, Mr. Mawby, are thirty-seven."

Death stopped talking to watch Frank's eyes stretch to their limits. He rubbed his skeletal hands together in anticipation. The sound was like dry wood scraping against another hard surface.

Slow, painful seconds ticked away. Death pointed one elongated finger directly at Frank. He spoke in a low conversational manner. "I've come for you, Frankie."

Frank's breath hitched, hanging painfully in his chest. White, hot pain exploded within. He wanted to grip at the pain in his chest. Furious effort did not avail him. Franklin G. Mawby still could not move.

His mind whispered what he knew, deep down, was not true. I'm dreaming. I'm dreaming. This is just a dream.

The pain was so powerful, worse than anything he'd ever felt. Paralyzing.

Sweat poured out of his skin profusely. He struggled for every breath.

The sound created a weird unmelodious rhythm.

Death's laughter echoed all around, adding yet another strange note to Frank's death repetend.

Without doubt, Frank knew he was dying. He tried vainly to believe that it was a mere nightmare. But pain could never be so real in a nightmare.

Suddenly he was able to move again, and his voice came back. He used it too, not to talk, but to scream. He screamed in agony, loud and long. Then he fell back on his bed, his body wracked by spasms. His eyes rolled back and closed very slowly. His body twitched, and then he lay still. Franklin G. Mawby was dead. He'd come to his end once, but there were many more times to suffer...thirty-six more.

END

The sky was subfusc, an expanse of seemingly abysmal darkness. Omnipresent, the dark stretched out, thick and unbroken. It was unbroken, that is, until sudden, jagged talons of lightning ripped it. Plangent peals of thunder accompanied the tearing bursts of lightning.

Nature's unleashing her brand of tumult was not without effect. In his bedroom, fourteen-year-old David Holis' sleep was rudely interrupted by the storm. He mumbled and stirred. His eyes moved rapidly under closed eyelids.

The thunder boomed, resounding like amplified gunfire. Lightning flashed—white ragged fingers cutting the blackness.

Thunder clapped. The sound rumbled powerfully, and then weakened somewhat, seeming to travel off into some distant void. An exact replication followed. Jolted from his sleep, David's eyes snapped open. "Ma!" he expulsed.

In one stiff, jerky motion, he sat up. His eyes wide, his breath raspy and rapid, he scanned the room.

Although the bedside lamp was on, the room was not very well lit. But it took David only a short time before his eyes started to adjust to the dimness.

Rigidly he sat with the fog of drowsiness slowly dissipating. Then he looked toward the stairs, flung the bed covers back, and jumped to the floor.

No question arose as to what was wrong. Yet he was driven by an unrelenting impetus, a sense that something was indeed awry.

David slowed little as he reached the landing to the stairs. Rounding the banister, he leaned into a rapid descent.

His breath was coming hard. His bare feet made light slapping sounds against the steps as he ran. And then he reached the bottom landing suddenly. The landing was in semi-darkness, only partially affected by the light at the top of the stairs.

Not certain why, David stopped on the landing. The feeling that something was amiss was so intense that it sapped his motivity.

His heart thumping madly, David stared toward the living room. It was dark except when a lightning flash cast its ephemeral light.

He knew that his mother often sat in front of the big window near the front door, sometimes even late into the night. David had never asked why, but he supposed that she entertained the same hope as he...the hope that his father would come. But the hope was futile; it always remained merely a hope.

From where he stood, David could see into the living room through an arched opening that led into it. But he couldn't see the big window. Nor was he sure that his mother was sitting in front of it now. Despite the incertitude, some inner feeling unglued his feet from the floor. And he started toward the living room.

Except for his pajama pants, David was not garmented. The frequent flashes of lightning hit against his face and bare torso.

With every flash, his chocolate skin was rendered coppery briefly.

His steps slow and nearly stealth, David walked into the living room. He paused when he saw the silhouette of his mother sitting in the chair in front of the window.

A lull in the storm allowed an eerie silence to settle. In the quiet, David's pulse throbbed in his ears loudly.

"Ma?" he said. His voice was low. There was no answer. Raising his voice, he called again. "Ma, you awake?"

Staring at the back of her head, he started forward again. "Ma…" Straining his eyes into the dark, David detected no movement.

His mother's head was canted. The angle at which it reposed didn't seem right to David.

When he came within a few feet of her, thunder crashed again. Several bursts of lightning lit up the room.

David sucked in a hard breath and froze. His eyes bulged at what he saw. A dark hole gaped at him from the back of his mother's head.

Sheer horror, shock, anger and disbelief clashed inside him. As if sensing the peripety, the thunder rolled in rapid succession and the lightning came in continuous blinding flashes.

During the lightning flashes, David's widened eyes caught glimpses of gruesome details that would forever be grafted onto his memory: the red puddle on the floor, the dark hole in his mother's head, and the gun that lay not far from his mother's chair…these things would always be a nightmare somehow wrested into a reality.

David screamed in anguish. The strain of it seemed to grate the soft flesh of his throat. His next utterances were mumbles, jumbled words expelled from trembling lips. Tears welled up, spilling down his cheeks in hot, fast streams.

Lightning flashed. Thunder hammered its echoey cadence.

David swung his eyes to the gun on the floor. All the pain, the horror, the anger…he had found a culprit.

His hands tightened into fists at his sides; his body trembled, and his eyes narrowed. "Get away!" he shouted as he jerked his head toward the door sharply. The gun leaped from the floor, cutting the air in a dark, metallic blur. Thunk! It slammed into the door near the top. The barrel held it there, imbedded in thick wood all of two inches deep.

Breathing as if he'd run a goodly distance, David stood staring at the gun, as much in wonderment as in hate. He would never remember how long he remained zombified before he called the police.

That was fifteen years ago now. In spite of the expiry of years, at times, David could still feel the hurt as if that night had been recent.

He had changed. The once skinny fourteen-year-old had grown into a well-built, two hundred and ten pound man.

Though much had changed, at twenty-nine, one thing virtually remained the same. David still hated and blamed his father as much as he did at fourteen.

He stood in the back room of his combination curio, portrait painting shop. His mind slowly found its way back from the past.

The shop was composed of two rooms and a bathroom. The front room contained numerous shelves lined with various curios and objects d'art.

Several glass-topped counters were spaced so as to form aisles. The counters, too, held curios.

Different size paintings hung, sparsely spaced, upon the walls. Some of the paintings were ones David had painted himself.

The back room had a few small tables in it. And there were other things there…things relative to painting.

David stood in front of a tall easel. Upon the easel a portrait of a gerontic couple reposed. David angled his head slightly, giving the portrait scrutiny. He then picked up a long-handled brush from a table near the easel. Dabbing the brush into a blob of paint, he stepped back and eyed the portrait again.

After a moment, he stepped close to the canvas and applied a few brief strokes with the brush. Satisfied, he dipped the brush into a tall container of water on the table. Several other paintbrush handles protruded above the top of the container.

Picking up the container, David carried it into the bathroom. He set the container onto a wide, porcelain sink which was positioned directly in front of a square mirror.

Pausing, David looked in the mirror. At twenty-nine his appearance was still rather youthful. His thinly cut goatee and dark brows stood out well in contrast against his brown skin. His jawlines were modelesque. And below each cheekbone there were clear indentations that were not so deep as to appear unattractive and skeletal.

His eyes were brown, noticeably much lighter than his skin. But they were not incongruous enough to clash totally. Rather, they were accentuations.

Vestigial indications of a smile touched his lips as he looked at his eyes in the mirror. His wife had said that he was the only man she'd ever seen with eyes like a doll. He was glad that such a statement had not been made to him during his four-year incarceration for manslaughter.

The thought of prison caused him to bite his bottom lip momentarily. Then he sighed and put all the paintbrushes into the sink. If it hadn't been for that damn Leeza...

Well, that was all behind him now. It was over, another life.

He was busy washing the paintbrushes when he happened to glance into the front room through a large window that had been cut into the wall.

His brows went up in surprise. Someone was inside his shop. Her back was toward him; it seemed the woman was admiring one of his dioramas, one of which was placed in front of each of the large front windows.

David hadn't heard the door chimes when the woman had come in. But that was not the entire reason why he'd been surprised. But the main reason was that the woman had obviously ignored the closed sign hanging in the window of the shop.

Quitting his brush-washing task, David headed for the front of the shop. Since it was Saturday, he'd not come to sell any merchandise, but only to complete the portrait. Evidently, though, the woman really wanted to buy something.

Stepping into the room, David said, "Excuse me, can I help…" The woman turned.

"Leeza!" David froze. His lips parted; they remained that way as she started toward him.

Her dress was short and tight. The hem was well above her knees, revealing smooth, caramel tinctured thighs. The dark blue material was cut low at the top, letting her ample breasts show, ripe and enticing.

"Yes, it's me," she said, stopping too close to him. She was smiling.

David's gaze lingered on her breasts for longer than he was aware. Leeza was not incognizant of that fact. Her smile widened.

David averted his gaze. "Leeza…I…"

She chuckled and stepped closer. Putting her palm against his chest, she made a sly movement that poked her breasts out a little further.

As if magnetized, David's eyes were drawn to the evocative swells of her brown bosom again.

This brought another chuckle from her. "You still like what you see, don't you? Why don't you touch…"

He stepped back. "I saw you looking at that diorama." Stepping around her, he continued. "You interested in buying it?"

David walked toward the front of the shop while he talked. He stopped in front of the diorama, his heart pounding fast. She still had an effect on him. But he didn't want her to know it.

Leeza didn't answer his question. For a moment the only sound was the lightly resonant tapping of her high-heeled shoes as she approached.

The diorama was about four feet long; it was completely glass-encased except for the top. It contained a frontier scene: A bearded replication of a man was nearest. The eyes, the rugose face, and even the overalls had been apparently done meticulously. The details were strikingly realistic. The log cabin was as if someone had shrunken an actual log cabin to augment the diorama.

A little boy and a shaggy dog were crafted in an energetic sprint. Not far from the dog and the boy, a woman was stooped in a garden which ran alongside the cabin. Even the vegetables in the garden had been done so well that they, too, looked real.

Leeza stopped so near to David that her perfume seemed to be on him instead of her. It was a sweet smell, faintly reminiscent of candy and flowers.

He didn't look directly at her when he spoke. But he could see her at the side of his vision.

"So, is this what you want to..."

"No," she said, "I don't want that stupid thing. I want you back."

She stepped in front of him quickly. Throwing both arms around his neck, she mashed her lips against his hungrily.

Caught off guard, David stood wide-eyed and motionless. But a sudden burst of anger vanquished his immotility. Snatching her arms down, he stepped back quickly. "What the hell?"

She took a short step with one hand half extended. "Baby..."

David's look made her stop. She dropped her hand listlessly. She tried to smile. "I...I just want..."

David interrupted her. "I don't care what you want! You should have thought about what you want before you... Aw, forget it. Just go."

Leeza's eyes were wide and watery. "No. You go ahead and say what's on your mind."

He turned his back, attempting to calm himself. "You hurt me more than any woman—no, all women I've ever loved, Leeza. I kept trying to live with all your jealousy, all your cheating. I really tried... You wouldn't be satisfied, though, no matter what."

"But David, we were young. That's the kind of stuff young people do," she said.

David turned to face her. "We were young?" He managed a humorless smile. "We were young? Incredible. I just can't believe you!" He shook his head. "Pitiful. You'll never change. Still got an excuse for everything."

There was a moment of quiet. The two of them stared at each other. And then David said, "Let me tell you something. I spent four years in hell...in prison because of you and your ways..."

He sucked in a deep breath, bit down on his teeth and then blew the breath out. "A man died...at my hands...because of you. And you have the freakin' audacity to stand there and say, we were young. Well, missy, those are not some magic words that can erase..."

"Wait! Wait a minute," Leeza said. "You're blaming me? I

didn't make you hit Contrell."

His breath was coming hard and fast. David stared at her. He was wordless temporarily. He shook his head hopelessly. "I use to have my suspicions that you were crazy, but now I'm sure of it."

Leeza's eyes showed how deeply the words had cut. "You don't have to say such mean things to me. I…"

Anger emanating from his eyes, David stepped up close to her. "Let's get the facts straight: You were cheating with this guy. I caught you. He had a knife and a false sense of what's right or wrong. He came at me. I defended myself. The guy died, and I went to prison. But I can't blame you?" He paused to catch his breath. "Well, who the hell am I suppose to blame, huh?"

His eyes were hard and unblinking. Leeza looked away from the hot stare.

Hesitantly, she moved her hand until her palm was against his chest once more. Her voice was tremulous. "David, I…I'm sorry. Believe me, I am." Her eyes pleading, she stared into his eyes.

He shook his head, forcing a short laugh. "No you're not. If you were, you would've thought of those weak apologies way before now. But nooo, you never thought to put any of that in your letters when I was in prison. You never said you were sorry, not even once."

He looked down at her hand distastefully. "Now take your filthy hand off me."

For a moment she left her hand on his chest. But then, letting it fall slowly, she looked down, away from him.

A thin-strapped purse hung from one shoulder. Sniffling, she reached into the purse and brought out a long, blue kerchief. Her lips trembled as she dabbed at her eyes and looked at him.

It was quiet except for Leeza's intermittent sniffling. David stared at her, waiting.

At five-foot eleven inches, Leeza was barely less tall than he. Her hair framed a face that was oval, smooth and a buttery tan. The ebon pupils of her eyes shone wetly, as black and shiny as her hair. Her lips were bright with a rubious shade of lipstick.

Looking at the face before him, David felt a twinge of compassion, just a twinge.

Her voice cracked. "That…was a very hurtful thing to say."

He smiled without mirth. "Leeza, after all you put me through, I really don't give a damn. Furthermore…"

He failed to see the slap coming. But he jerked with the impact. Reflexively he drew his hand back intending to reciprocate. His eyes squinted, he kept his hand poised.

"Go ahead," she challenged.

David was tempted. But he lowered his hand slowly. "Nah.

Generally I don't put my hand on trash."

Without warning, Leeza's hand flashed. The slap brought water to his eyes. David swung back-handedly. The blow landed on the side of her face and against the corner of her lips.

"Oh!" she exclaimed as she was knocked partly around. She crumpled to the floor clumsily.

David cursed to himself. And instinctively he moved to help her up. But when he stooped to reach for her, she sat up and slapped at his hand. "Don't touch me!"

He stepped back and watched as she blinked rapidly and shook her head as if trying to clear it.

When she got to her feet her lips were pressed together in a tight line. Her eyes were cold as her gaze steadied upon him.

The momentary quiet was a leaden thing, thick upon the air.

David moved his hands as if he was about to embrace her. He started to take a step. "I'm sorry. I..."

She threw one hand up, palm outward. David halted. "No you're not," she said. "I don't believe you."

She stared at him. He let his hands fall to his sides.

Leeza winced when she wiped her mouth with the back of her hand. Her hand came away with a rubrical smear of lipstick and blood.

Pointlessly, she whispered, "I'm bleeding." Sticking her hand into her purse, she pointed a blazing stare at him. "You...you split my lip."

Leeza was slowly bringing her hand up out of the purse when David repeated himself. "I'm sorry, Leeza..."

Her hand stopped. A twisted smile touched her lips. "Sorry or scared?"

Within a couple of heartbeats David looked from her eyes to her hand, then back to her eyes. Something was not too sane about those eyes just now.

There was yet a brief reticence before he said, "Sorry." He couldn't help shifting his eyes back to her hand which was still mostly concealed by the purse.

A short throaty chuckle came from her lips. David frowned. Two more chuckles followed, in the same manner, before she threw her head back and laughed deeply.

David's frown deepened. She's gone, he thought. Crazy witch! She's gone.

She stopped laughing abruptly. A curious light seemed to be in her eyes when she looked at him. "David Gregory Holis, no, I don't believe you are sorry... But you should be."

She stared at him for a moment, turned sharply, and walked away, a shrill laughter trailing behind her.

Even after she opened the door and stepped out, David stood unmoving for a while.

He was still looking at the door when the phone rang. It was sitting atop one of the counters near the cash register.

David started for the phone, glancing over his shoulder once. The thought to lock the door crossed his mind. He was a little more than uncomfortable with the thought that Leeza might return. That look that had been in her eyes was hard to forget.

"Hello, David Holis speaking," he said into the phone.

"Oh really!" the voice on the other end of the line said. "Thanks, I really can't recognize my own husband's voice."

David smiled. "Very funny, baby." He gave his watch a glance. "Oh, I guess you're wondering what's taking me so long."

"Yeah, I am. Anything wrong? You sound kind of funny," Aretia Holis said.

Again, he thought of Leeza and the maniacal look that had been in her eyes. "I, uh… no, I only guessed about the time it'd take me to finish that portrait. Took longer than I thought."

His wife started to say something, but David went on. "Well anyway, I finished with it, and I'm on my way, okay?"

"Okay," Aretia said. "I love you."

"Love you too," David replied. "See you in a little bit."

He thought of going to the back of the shop again to finish washing his brushes, but opted to leave them until Monday. For the most part, the brushes were fairly clean from their initial washing anyway. So he cut the lights off and then walked slowly from the shop.

Driving home, David thought about his encounter with Leeza. He tried to deny that there were any feelings left for her, but… His forehead wrinkled in thought. What did she do to me? How can I still feel anything after so long…after all she did?

Until the incident in the shop, the last time he'd heard anything from her he'd had a year left on his prison term. The contact had come in the form of a letter. Some of the wording was still recollectable.

"Dear David,

How are you? I know it must be a shock to hear from me, but I just had to write. What can I say? I dream about you all the time, and I think about you a lot. I just don't understand. What did you do to me, David?

It's not that I can't find anyone, because I do have a boyfriend. He's very nice to me. And he gave me an engagement ring. But I don't even feel like wearing that thing most of the time. You're the reason. I keep trying to put you behind me and move on. But it's so hard."

David wasn't sure if his memory was at one hundred percent regarding the exact wording. And much of what the letter had said was forgotten. However, there was one line that he felt he'd never forget. That line had been declaratively phrased. It had read: "I can't get over you, David." If anything in her letter reflected truth, he felt that it was that line.

Despite the infidelity, jealousy and arguments crammed into the few years with Leeza, there had been something that he'd thought was love. And even while he was in prison he'd often felt that he could never get over her. Even now, there was something.... But why? His mind had been made up some time ago; there could never be another try with Leeza.

The sound of a horn snapped David out of his reverie. He had been sitting at the stoplight, allowing his mind to drift. He drove away from the stoplight feeling a little irritated. Why'd she have to show up? He'd hoped that Leeza and the chapter of his life that had involved her was forever closed.

They could've had something really special. There'd been something unique about the way they'd been able to make each other laugh. And there'd been something about her being able to understand him at times when he'd really needed someone to unburden on.

Then, there had been their lovemaking.... David forced himself to think in a different direction. That had been another era. It was over. It was gone.

When David drove into his driveway, he was thinking about Aretia. She was a good wife and companion, but there were some things that had caused repeated arguments. Their neighbor had been at the center of more than one of their quarrels. David had noticed that the guy's car was present in the next driveway. That meant the guy was at home.

Turning the ignition off, David glanced toward his neighbor's house. Disgraceful! he thought. Sucker ought to drop dead...he and anybody like him.

Seven-year-old Niculaous Molden sat on the plush carpet intrigued by something displayed on the television screen. He had scant, straight eyebrows above roundish, infantile eyes. A small, perky nose sat above lips that seemed on the verge of a smile.

Niculaous looked up when David opened the door and stepped in. "Daddy!" he shouted as he jumped up and ran with outstretched arms. Although Niculaous wasn't David's actual son, the boy had utilized the parental appellation without doubting its propriety. The boy's real father hadn't been seen since Niculaous was three, and Niculaous didn't remember him. So to him, David was his father. Neither Aretia nor David had bothered telling the boy anything to the contrary. They had discussed the subject on various occasions, but had decided not to divulge something that would likely hurt Niculaous' feelings.

David dropped to one knee, preparatory to Niculaous' embrace. Niculaous crashed into him while flashing a gapped-tooth smile.

"Umph!" David feigned a sudden loss of breath. "Dang boy, you hit like a freight train."

Niculaous stepped back while David ruffled his hair. "What's a freight train, Daddy?"

While answering, David stood up. "Well, it's about the same as a regular train, but it doesn't have seats for people. And it carries things that are sold. The things that are carried are called freight. Got it, Nick?"

Niculaous nodded. "Uh-huh."

"Okay," David said. "Where's your mother?"

"I think she went in the kitchen," Niculaous answered.

With Niculaous trailing beside him, David headed for the kitchen. David supposed that Aretia was rewarming lunch. He glanced at his watch; it was two full hours beyond lunch time. It was no wonder she had called him at his shop.

David imaged some of the events that had occurred between him and Leeza while in his shop. He thought about what he'd told her at one point: "You never said you were sorry, not even once." What if she had? he wondered. What if…

Niculaous tugged at his hand. David looked down. "Look, Daddy. I forgot to tell you, Chris gave me this when I was playing in the yard." Niculaous extended a ten dollar bill up toward David.

"Chris…!" David said just as he and Niculaous stepped into the kitchen. He felt the pressure of his teeth pushing hard against each other.

To be continued…

Eric Benedict reached for his glass of ruby wine. He raised the glass to his lips. Sipping the sparkling liquid, he eyed his date over the wineglass.

She sat at the opposite end of the well-polished, oval table. The soft light in the restaurant made the polished wood gleam like dark glass.

Eric felt complacent as he watched the woman across the table. He'd never seen skin so white, so smooth. And the eyes, they were large but not overly so. The shiny, dark pupils seemed to be as dark as her silky hair. Her hair was long, uncommonly long, considering that most contemporary hairstyles were worn short. It disappeared down below the height of the table.

The woman toyed with her fork. She put it down and reached for her glass of wine. Before her hand touched the glass, she said, "Eric, why are you watching me again?"

He smiled. "Simple. You're the most beautiful and intriguing woman I've ever seen."

She lifted her glass. A slight smile came to the corner of her lips. Her eyes flickered. Over the glass, her gaze found his and lingered briefly.

"Why, thank you, Eric. That's so sweet of you. But I'll bet that you say the same thing to your wife."

Eric's eyes widened. His face reddened. "My…my wife? I don't have… I, I'm not going to lie to you. But I'm amazed. How did you know?"

She sipped her wine, put her glass down and then proceeded to answer. "Well, I…guess the best way to answer your question is, I noticed the impression around your ring finger."

Eric looked at his hand. He laughed. "That ring was always a little big. I don't see how you can see any impression."

He turned his hand, examining it in the mellow light. "Simply amazing. I don't see a thing, and my vision is twenty-twenty."

His brows were slightly raised when he looked up at his date. The question he hadn't directly verbalized was clearly readable on his face.

The woman smiled; she'd detected his wonderment. "I guess it wouldn't hurt to tell you, I'm from a…let's say, unusually perceptive species of people. Our abilities were far above the average person. Of course, that includes sight. Our abilities were tools necessary for our survival."

Her voice quaked. She lowered her head briefly. "Unfortunately, our keen abilities were not enough to ensure our continual existence."

When she raised her head again, Eric could see that her eyes shined with water. Intrigued, he asked, "Species? What a strange word choice. Why'd you pick that particular word?"

"Because," she replied, "that is the most accurate diction. My people were a species."

Eric leaned forward. Curiosity compelled him to continue questioning her. "Why do you say were?"

She looked straight into his eyes. She answered him in a sad monotone. "I'm the only one left."

Eric cocked his head slightly to one side. He squinted at her. "Help me to understand? Are you saying you're from a race that no longer exists?"

"Something like that." She nodded. Melancholy made her voice seem drained, weak.

She went on. "My father was a scientist. He sought ways to preserve our kind. You see, we were hunted. We…"

"Hunted?" Eric's voice was incredulous. "What in the world…"

"Yes," she interrupted. "They hounded us almost into extinction. Finally, my father and I were the only ones left. My father had been wounded at the time, though. But he and I escaped. He'd only managed to bring along some of his chemicals and notes. He worked night and day. It was frenetic, because he knew it was just a matter of time before we were tracked down. And he knew that he was dying from the wound."

Eric stared across the table at his date. Though he was intrigued, he was a bit confused. Surely she had to be making some sort of joke. Yet, as he studied her face, she seemed so grim. If she wasn't joking, then what? Was she some sort of psychopath masquerading as a normal person?

"Eric? Eric, do you hear me?" she asked.

"Uh, oh, yeah. Sure, I hear you."

"Good," she said. "For a moment, it seemed that you weren't really listening. It is so important that you do, because I've kept this story inside so long. I've never told anyone before."

She hesitated briefly before going on. "My father worked to develop a drug that would alter a deadly condition intrinsic among my kind. He sought to invent something that would enable us to survive the sun's rays. He was successful in his endeavor. And…"

Eric chuckled. "Wait a minute. This stuff about the sun's rays. It sounds like something from a vampire movie or…"

She interrupted him. "I know how it probably sounds, but I'm being truthful with you, Eric. I know what you're thinking, that I've drank too much wine and have been reading about the strange murders around here."

"Yeah, I'll admit that you have drank quite a bit this evening. And add that to the way the *Bartenfield Daily* has written about the murders, I think maybe your imagination is doing a little overtime."

Eric smiled. "Humph, missing blood, marks on their necks. Shoot, the way those reporters write things up, they'll have a person believe anything. I mean, come on, blood sucking creatures? Ha," he laughed and reached for his fork.

Savoring a mouthful of food, he studied his date's face. She wasn't eating, only toying with her fork again. Darn weird, he thought. She sure looks serious.

"Not hungry, huh?" he inquired.

"Well, not for food, anyway," she said. She lifted her head. Looking at him straight on, she let her tongue snake out and slowly trace the contour of her top lip. Moistened now, the perfectly shaped lip glistened in the light. The lipstick she wore was ruby, like the wine.

Eric felt the stir of sexual arousal. He'd understood the hint.

"So," he said, "tell me a little about your family."

"Family?" she responded. "I don't have a family anymore." She sounded irritated.

He frowned slightly and thought, She's acting like that story she told me is actually true.

Not so complacent as he'd been earlier, he refilled his glass and took a large swallow. He'd dated weird women before, but he was beginning to think, this woman takes the cake. What does it really matter though, he thought. It's not like I'm looking for a wife of something. I think, tonight, she's ready to give in. Humph, after that, she'll be just a sweet memory like the rest of them. He sipped his wine and then put his glass back down. Her eyes met his over her own glass.

Eric glanced at her food; it still remained barely touched. He was amazed that the woman continued to maintain her composure, considering the amount of wine she drank on top of very little nourishment. That surely must have something to do with that crazy story she'd concocted.

"Everyone has some family," Eric said. "So, I don't understand what you mean...that you moved, that you disown them?"

She looked at him strangely. He was sure that he detected irritation alight in the dark eyes.

"Yes," she responded tensely. "I've moved, quite often. But no, I would never have disowned them."

As if that was the end of the matter, she reached for her wineglass again.

Eric watched her a moment longer. He thought about her last sentence. She'd even looked as if the story she'd told him was a reality.

The uneasiness that slowly invaded his subconscious was relentless, powerful. It felt more like a monition, a warning of impending danger. Something was definitely wrong about the woman. Something. What, he could not fathom. With effort, he suppressed the feeling. He waved to a passing waiter. "Waiter, check please?"

Later, at the hotel, they spent their passion in a tangle of sweaty sheets. Afterward, the woman got up quietly. She moved to the window like a wraith.

The hotel room was dimly lit. The overhead light had been turned off. But a light played over her shapely body. Her pale, white, naked flesh was striking against the soft, dull light in the room.

She stood at the curtain. One thin, white hand held a small section of the curtain back. She seemed pensive. Her head was tilted upward slightly, her gaze on the full moon hanging against the dark sky.

A light rustle of the bed sheets caused her to turn her head a little toward the bed. She didn't turn her head enough to see that Eric had awakened. But she felt his eyes on her body.

"You know, I used to worry that I would be tracked down and killed like the others. But I've since learned to fit in, just like one of your kind. I rent a house here in Bartenfield. I have a job. And I even go out in the sun. I've adapted. Had to, in order to survi…"

"What? Don't tell me you're still on the vampire story," Eric said.

The last vestige of sleep was melting from his mind. At first, he'd not been paying much attention to what she'd been saying. Now, fully awake, he heard her clearly. And it angered him that she was carrying on like the story was real.

Eric shook his head. He smiled, but not because he was in the least bit humored. To him, it was incredible that such a beautiful woman could be so screwed up, mixing fantasy and reality.

"You're a strange woman, you know that?"

She turned from the window and smiled. "That's not what you really think, is it, Eric?" She walked slowly toward the bed.

Eric sat up a little. "What do you mean?"

Before answering, she placed one knee upon the bed. A devilish smirk showed on her lips; it even reached her eyes. She straddled him. Then gently, she placed one hand on his chest. He eased back under the gentle pressure she exerted.

"I think, sweetie, that you believe I'm off my rocker," she said. A throaty chuckle followed.

Attempting to sit up, Eric's chest pushed against her hand. She easily kept him pinned against the mattress. The woman was strong. She was amazingly strong. It frightened Eric. He'd never felt that kind of strength exerted by a woman before. He relaxed, letting go of the fear. What was he fearful about? After all, he was a man, and she, a woman. What could a woman actually do to a man via harm?

She slowly leaned forward. Her eyes were fixed on his neck. As her face descended, Eric thought he saw a flicker of bright red light her eyes. But that was impossible. Surely, it must have been a trick of the light in the room. In any case, the thought was soon forgotten.

Her soft moans filled his ears as she licked and sucked his neck gently. Eric could not help but emit a low moan of pleasure.

"Ow," he said suddenly. "Not so hard, alright?"

She'd begun to let her mouth open and close, rubbing the skin on his neck. Her teeth clicked together repeatedly. She writhed slowly on top of him. Her breathing became hot, heavy against the warm skin of his neck.

It seemed that she had not heard his plea. She bit down harder. He jerked his head to the side. "Hey…what the he…"

She clamped her hand down, covering his mouth. His mind screamed when he felt the teeth puncture his neck.

Eric clawed frantically at the hand over his mouth. It was far too strong. He kicked while his muffled screams were louder in his head than they were in the room.

Hot blood gushed out. He could feel it slide down his neck. His kicking became more desperate, but futile. His eyes strained painfully against their sockets. The pressure was so intense that he felt as if his eyes were being forced from his head.

Frantic, desperately, he made a fist. He pounded the woman on the side of the head. The blows rocked her. The thumps were solid. But like a giant leech, the woman remained attached.

Eric felt the life oozing out of him. His heart pounded madly. Strength borne by fear surged through him. He heaved his body upward in a sudden burst of desperation. Caught off guard, the vampire became partly dislodged. Taking advantage of the new situation, Eric twisted quickly and rolled on top of the creature. Then, toppling off the edge of the bed, he scrambled for the door. Hot sweat coated his skin. The steady roar of his pulse reverberated inside his head.

On the slick floor, Eric made a few frantic moves, something between crawling and slipping. Finally he made it to his feet, but by then, the vampire had recovered. In his mind, he screamed as he raced for the door. Too late! The vampire sprang from a crouched position. The leap was smooth, defying gravity like one propelled by a trampoline. A deep, feral growl sliced through the air. No longer was the woman's face a visage of beauty. It was contorted, beyond anything even remotely resemblant to human. Her lips were rolled back, revealing one pointy and glistening cuspid at each corner of her top lip. Momentum held her hair strung out behind her in fluttering, black threads.

Eric's sweaty fingertips had barely touched the doorknob when he felt the weight of the creature slam into his back. His forehead hit against the door with a resounding crack! Eric's vision blurred as his knees buckled. He was numb, on the verge of unconsciousness. That fact was an advantage, for he barely felt when the pointed fangs broke through the skin over his throbbing jugular.

Bartenfield College was composed of numerous large, red brick buildings and several smaller ones. The buildings were scattered; their roofs and corners jutted out sharply against a pale-blue morning sky.

A lively, verdant lawn stretched out away from the buildings. The lawn was intercepted here and there by concrete walkways. Glossy shrubbery lined some of the walkways.

Eugene George Garrison pulled up into the college's parking lot. After he parked, he sat in his car a moment, scanning the assemblages of milling students. He was hesitant about getting out. Some of the students often ridiculed him. They nicknamed him Egg, misusing the initials of his first, middle and last name.

Eugene sighed. He looked in the rearview mirror and brushed dark strands of unruly hair away from his face. He stared at the eyes in the mirror, eyes like his mother's. The comparison made him sigh again. It was always painful when something reminded him of his mother. Where she was, he did not know. Nor, did he know why she'd left. He remembered walking into the house one day and seeing his father staring at a short letter his mother had left. It didn't explain, just made clear that she'd not be returning.

The slightly brown color of Eugene's skin and his dark hair was due to his father's lineage. Sometimes it resulted in ridicule just as his name did. He knew that he was not to blame for his father's or his mother's choice of whom they had chosen to love. So, why did he often feel guilty and ashamed when someone called him half-breed? The fact that his father was black and his mother white was something he felt he shouldn't be ridiculed for. But that was just the way things were.

He leaned over, gathering his books and his book bag. When he looked up, he groaned inwardly. Oh, no. Three guys were headed across the parking lot. He could not hear what they were saying, but they were headed directly for his car. One walked a little ahead of the others. A wide, mischievous grin was on his face. Eugene recognized the guy instantly. He was the captain of the football team. And he had been bullying Eugene off and on ever since the beginning of the school year.

Eugene felt anger rising; he fought it down. Getting out, he closed the door and avoided looking in the troublemakers' direction. He was hoping to avert a confrontation.

His steps were tense as he started across the parking lot, heading away from the approaching trio. He could hear the guys' giggles as they came closer. He felt tension grip him tightly. He knew he should walk faster, get to the buildings before they caught up, because under his quiet persona lay a violent temper that needed to be controlled.

Brad Richardson was the lead instigator. He shouted across the parking lot, although he was not far from Eugene. "Hey!" Eugene kept walking. "Hey, half-breed, do you hear me talking to you?"

At the commotion, other students stopped to look. A few started towards what they hoped would be a confrontation.

Brad and the other two guys increased the pace of their steps. Brad spoke again, making sure that his voice was unnecessarily loud. "Hey, weirdo, I'm talking to…"

Eugene turned so swiftly that it caught Brad off guard. The show of bravery stopped everyone in their tracks, including the troublemakers. Eugene faced the three who'd been following him. He looked directly at Brad; his gaze was cold and unwavering. His jaw muscles pulsated, responding to the pressure he was putting on his back teeth. When he spoke, his voice was as cold as his stare. "What do you want?"

Brad had to close his mouth before he answered. He was still shocked. He had not expected Eugene to respond in the way that he had. "I heard that you are in Sandy's class."

"Yeah, that's right," Eugene answered. "And?"

"And," Brad responded, "someone said they saw you talking to her. You know that Sandy's my girl, right?"

"Humph," Eugene grunted. A tiny trace of a smile touched one corner of his mouth. The smile wasn't reflected in his eyes; they were still cold.

He turned without another word and started walking off. He ignored the crowd that had gathered. Some in the crowd whispered among themselves. Then someone shouted, "Brad, are you going to let him get away with that?"

Brad's face colored with embarrassment. He scanned the crowd of students. Then he started after Eugene. "Come on, guys. We're going to teach that punk a lesson."

What happened next shocked everyone. Without even looking to see if the troublemakers were following, Eugene stopped. Stooping, he placed his books and book bag gently on the ground. He turned. His eyes were gleaming with water, and the fire of anger showed in them. Fists clenched at his sides, he waited.

Curious students tagged along behind Brad and his two buddies. The whole crowd stopped when they came within a few feet of Eugene.

The air was tense. The onlookers were quiet, watching with eyes of intrigue.

Just for an instant, Brad and Eugene stared across the distance remaining between them. Then unexpectedly, Eugene started toward

Brad. Out of the corners of his eyes, he saw Brad's two buddies move around to each side of him.

Eugene's lean, muscular frame exceeded Brad's by three inches. But, it seemed to be more, with the two standing so close.

Eugene leaned over. His hair almost brushed Brad's face. His words came out through clenched teeth. "If you and those two punks don't back off, I promise you, you'll be sorry. Now, I'm going…"

One of the guys rushed from the side. Without seeming to take his eyes off Brad, Eugene jerked up one leg. It shot out so quickly that some in the crowd sucked in audible breaths. The would-be attacker forced himself to an abrupt halt. Eugene's heel was only inches from his chin. His eyes were wide. His gaze was riveted on Eugene's heel.

Not even the slightest of sounds could be heard for a moment. And then Eugene slowly put his leg down. He turned, picked up his books and, once again, headed for one of the buildings.

No one moved or said anything at first. Brad was as awed as everyone else. For the second time that morning his mouth hung open. He turned, saying to no one in particular, "Did you see that? I can't believe it…." He walked away. His two friends tagged along. They heard the crowd whispering words of wonderment. Some were laughing. Brad knew that they were laughing at him. He promised himself he would get even. Nobody embarrasses Brad Richardson and gets away with it, nobody.

Eugene walked into one of the buildings. He headed for his first period class. Sandy Fields met him at the door when he stepped in. Her eyes showed the admiration she felt. "God, that was really cool! I saw you from the window. Where'd you learn to do…"

Eugene cut her off. "Brad is your boyfriend, right?" Sandy nodded, looking puzzled.

"Well, if you love him, you might ask him to leave me alone. Somebody could get hurt…bad."

Before Sandy could say anything, he walked to his seat. Sandy stared after him.

Their seats were on different rows, but they were side by side. All during first period, Sandy kept turning her head slightly enough to see Eugene's face. Eugene pretended not to see her watching him.

A few minutes before first period ended, he looked over to see her scribbling something in a hurry. When the bell rang, ending the period, she stood up and placed what she'd been writing on his desk.

Eugene noticed that she was smiling when she turned to leave. He stared at the paper a moment. The words read: In reference to what you said at the door, I have two statements. No, I don't love him. But, yes, I'll ask him to leave you alone. You'll still help me with my lessons, right?"

The note was signed, San. It had an awkwardly drawn smiling face beside her name.

Man, what a straightforward girl! he thought. Wouldn't Brad be surprised to find out that she's really not his girl, as he likes to put it.

Folding the note carefully, Eugene put it in his book bag. He felt warm and cheerful inside. A picture of Sandy's long, black hair, big dark eyes, and white, smooth skin was vivid in his mind. When he gathered his books and left the room, he was still seeing the image.

The night was dark, a vast, ebony expanse. It provided a contrastive backdrop for the white glow of the globose moon.

Under the dark sky, a car swerved dangerously close to the road's centerline. The car weaved repeatedly, creating a weird pattern. For anyone watching, it would have been easy to deduce the cause of the erratic driving.

Someone was watching. However, the watcher happened to be a passenger in the swerving car. But she seemed unperturbed by the manner in which the car traveled. As a matter of fact, the woman's giggles proved that she wasn't the least bit concerned at all.

The drunken driver rattled off a string of tasteless riddles, his voice as unsteady as the car. "Why did the ghost go to the dance contest?" he asked.

"Hmmm," his passenger answered. "I don't know, Henry. You got me again. But what say, you be a good boy and tell me, hmm?"

"Well," Henry replied, "he went so he could boo people. Get it, boo people?"

Henry let out a drunken chuckle, and the woman joined in. "Oh, Henry, you've got to be the funniest guy I've ever met."

Henry raised his brows before he spoke. "Speaking of that, I think it's kind of strange that I met you at all. I mean, I go to Jimmy's all the time, and I've never seen you there. Well, I mean, except for tonight, that is. Boy, but I'm sure glad I did."

Henry cast his passenger a quick, lustful look. Though he was quite drunk, his eyes could appreciate what he saw.

The woman wore a tight, short dress. Sitting as she was, Henry could see a hint of her white panties. She sat facing him slightly, her legs parted just enough to tease.

The dress was jet black, low cut in the front and snug enough to reveal that she'd not bothered to put on a bra.

Her hair was dark, as dark as her dress. It hung in silken strands, down to her waist. Some wisps of it played around her face, affected by the wind coming through her partially rolled down window.

She saw Henry glance at her. It made her emit a girlish giggle.

"If you want to experience what's coming to you, you'd better keep your eyes on the road, Henry," she said. "But then, compared to what I've got for you, you may rather run off the road, directly into a tree."

Henry laughed. "That's a heck of a way to let a man know that you're too hot to handle. Makes me all the more eager to..." Henry glanced over at the woman; she wasn't smiling. Her cool black eyes stared back at him for a moment. But then she smiled. Henry could tell it was forced. It made him feel uneasy. He managed a half-hearted smile and then turned his head. He didn't see when his passenger's smile broadened.

"What's the matter, Henry?" she asked. The trace of a smirk was at the corners of her mouth. "Did I bother you with my comment?"

"No...no, of course not," he lied. "I was just thinking, you never told me your name. And what would a pretty girl like you be doing hanging at a bar like Jimmy's?"

"Well," she said, "you'll find out shortly why I was at Jimmy's."

Henry glanced over at her again. She smiled and shifted on the seat, allowing Henry to see more of her panties. "And," she continued, "as for my name...well, when I finish with you, you won't know it anyway." She giggled again.

Henry tried to laugh, but he was feeling too uneasy. Something was wrong; his passenger's comments were really strange. Was she some kind of mental case? Or maybe, she had a terrible sense of humor. Henry's thoughts wandered. Boy, I sure hope I didn't pick up some sort of weirdo, for all those drinks I bought her though, I'd screw her anyway. Man, seems like we've been driving for hours. What kind of chick lives way out in the country like this? I should've talked her into going back to my... Henry felt her hand slide over his thigh and lightly massage his crouch. She seemed to know exactly how to arouse him. Her touch wasn't too rough.

While still massaging him she spoke in a low, seductive voice. "Henry, I don't know if I want to wait until we get to my house," she said. "I'm getting so-o-o hot."

She leaned over, nibbled at his ear and then whispered into it. "There's a dead end road just up ahead. Why don't you make it there as fast as you can so I can give you what I've got for you? I promise, I won't hurt you," she paused, "not for too long anyway."

Henry looked at her; he frowned. But he didn't say anything.

The car swerved toward the dead end road. Its headlights briefly illuminated the road sign. The sign read: Deadmen Road. Henry turned onto the sandy road. The headlights made the sand appear to dissect the surrounding darkness.

Henry parked the car and leaned over. He slurred his words when he spoke. "You know, you are so pretty but kind of strange. Why'd you pick a place like this? I've got plenty of money, we..."

The woman giggled and interrupted. "This is the perfect place, Henry. Probably, you'll be doing a lot of screaming."

Henry laughed. "Oh yeah, little lady, we'll just see about that."

He reached for her small, perky breasts. One hand missed, but with the other, he fondled her breast.

She slapped at his hand. "Now Henry, aren't we a bad boy," she purred. "Before I have you, let me show you something first."

Henry started to protest. "Aw, come on. I was really getting..."

"Now, Henry, be a sport," she murmured. She flicked her tongue out and slid it slowly across her top lip. "Pleease?"

"Aw, alright," Henry replied, "but you're really going to get it, I mean good."

"Oh, Henry, I like that. I can hardly wait. Now turn your head, and don't look until I say so, alright?"

"Okay," Henry answered. He turned his head, expecting that at any moment he would hear the sounds of her undressing. Instead, he heard her soft laughter. And then he felt a light tap on his shoulder.

Henry turned; his face was a mask of confusion. His once beautiful passenger was still there, but ghastly different. Her eyes glowed a fiery red; her lips were curled back in a hideous snarl, revealing two glistening fangs.

To Henry, time seemed to race on at an impossible pace. His heart too, thumped at a rate far exceeding normal.

"What kind of...of a joke is...?" The woman lunged. Henry tried to dodge, but she was far too fast.

When the needlepoint fangs pierced the skin of his neck, Henry screamed. She had been right; Henry would do a lot of screaming.

Minutes later, a car slowed before reaching the intended destination. Its lights glanced off the road sign ahead long enough for the sign to be read: Deadmen Road.

When the car turned onto the sandy road, the beam from its headlights bounced off the shiny metal of a car ahead.

"Damn!" the driver exclaimed. "Vicky, looks like somebody had the same idea we did."

He prepared to put the car in reverse, glanced up at the car again, and said, "I don't think I can squeeze by. We'll just have to...whoa, what the devil?"

"What is it, Earl?" Vicky asked.

Earl squinted. "I think somebody's in trouble." He eased his foot down on the accelerator. The car rolled along slowly until it came close to Henry's rear bumper.

Earl put the car in park. He reached over and patted Vicky's thigh. "Stay here. I'll go check it out."

Vicky did not have the same view of Henry's car that Earl did. When Earl got out, she leaned over in order to improve her view. Still, she couldn't see what had alarmed him.

Henry's driver side door was open. He was hanging out, his head nearly touching the ground. A dark pool was forming on the sand beneath Henry's head. Earl's headlights made the pool shine.

Earl's steps were slow as he started toward Henry's car. His every step sounded loud to him. He felt an urge to tiptoe. Stopping within a few feet, he starred at where the blood was seeping from. It oozed from two small punctures in the side of Henry's neck.

Earl's heart felt heavy, hammering hard against the inside of his chest.

Vicky's voice split the night air. "Oh, God! That guy...I think he's...he's dead."

Earl had not realized that Vicky was standing a few feet behind him. He had been unaware too, that he'd been staring at the dead man.

At the sound of Vicky's voice, he jerked his head around. He turned quickly. Not needing any further prompting, he started toward her.

Vicky held both hands against her breasts; her breath was coming hard. It seemed she couldn't take her gaze off the thing that had once been a living being.

Earl grabbed her by both arms and shook her firmly. "Vicky. Vicky, let's go."

Vicky didn't respond. Earl turned her head away. He then took hold of her by the back of both her arms and guided her to his car.

For a moment, the sound of tires grinding against sand was all that disrupted the night's quiet. Then, after the sound of the car faded, nature's sounds arose amid the silence. An occasional scuttle of little feet, the rustle of leaves and foliage whispered through the quiet.

Another sound added its rhythm to the admixture of nature sounds. This one, though, not a product of nature at all. It was a low plop, plop, plop. The dark, crimson pool beneath Henry's head was slowly spreading.

The magnificent moon, sounds of little night creatures and the whispering breeze went unnoticed. Such things no longer made a difference to Henry. His pallid face was turned toward the sky, eyes wide but seeing nothing.

Brad Richardson was lying back in a large recliner. It was positioned in front of a 56" television.

The television remote dangled from his hand, hanging over the edge of the recliner. His eyes were closed; he was somewhere deep within the realm of sleep.

His fingers relaxed slowly, relinquishing their hold on the remote; it fell to the floor, clattering over the stained, polished surface.

Brad's eyes sprang open. He jerked his head up, scanning the room around him. Then as the threads of drowsiness vanished, he realized what had caused the noise. He spotted the remote a little way from the recliner.

Standing, he stretched, yawned and ran one hand through his short, dark hair. His hair was left sticking out in all directions after he ruffled it.

Brad walked over to the remote, stooped and picked it up. The phone rang just as he straightened. "Hello, this is Brad speaking."

"Hey, man, this is Travis," a voice said from the opposite end of the line. "So, what's up, Brad?"

"Nothing much, Trav," Brad replied, "just waking up."

"Just waking up? Brad, you sleep more than an old lady does. Hey, did you catch the six o'clock news?"

"No," Brad replied. He glanced at his wristwatch. "I didn't even realize I had dozed off for so long."

"Well, I guess it's understandable," Travis said, "considering that you were all over that football field yesterday. But listen, that's not what I called about. Remember how we'd been speculating about who could be killing those guys that have been turning up? Well, the question is not who, but what. What do you think about vampires?"

"Vampires?" Brad queried. "Trav, have you lost your damn mind? You know as well as I do that such things don't exist. Fantasy, that's what I think. Where'd you get such a crazy…"

Travis interrupted. "Well, remember the media has been kind of hush-hush about letting the public know the details."

Although Travis' wordage sounded more like a question than a statement, he went on without letting Brad reply. "Not any more. They found another body on Deadmen Road. But, I don't see what all the fuss is about. Shoot, that shouldn't even have made the news." He paused, his lean face taking on a mischievous grin.

"Trav," Brad said, "sometimes you puzzle me. What are you saying, that a man's death isn't important enough to make the news?"

Travis laughed. "No, but finding a dead man on 'Deadmen' Road is common sense, not news." He laughed again.

"Trav, your sense of humor really stinks," Brad said, without reciprocating the laugh.

"Yeah, Brad, I've got to agree. Stinks like dead men, huh?" Travis grinned. And this time Brad laughed.

"You are one sick dude," Brad said. He was thinking how Travis seemed to be able to make a joke out of almost every situation.

"You are precisely right, old buddy, but as a famous sailor used to say, I yam what I yam." Travis emulated Popeye the sailorman so well that it brought another laugh from Brad.

When Travis spoke again, his voice carried a hint of reflection. "What was I saying? Oh, yeah, that last guy they found was minus quite a lot of blood. And, get this, he had puncture wounds in the side of his neck! Finally, they revealed that those other dead guys had the same kind of marks. Now, I rest my case, Mister Skepticism. Any…"

"Trav," Brad interrupted. "You've really been watching too many horror movies. Or, have you been hanging around Egg? Hey, what is that weirdo's real name?"

Travis answered with a frown as if he'd just bitten something bitter. "Eugene George Garrison. Ugh, imagine being stuck with a name like that. No wonder he doesn't protest his nickname. But, personally, I thing Egg sounds as ridiculous as Eugene George Garrison does. Hey, imagine him making love to a girl. Oh, Egg! Ooh, Egg…."

Travis chuckled into the phone. From the other end of the line, Brad couldn't help but laugh too. "You are indeed a real clown, you know that?"

"Of course I do," Travis replied. They both laughed. Travis stopped laughing suddenly; his narrow face took on a frown. "Brad, I'd almost forgotten…I could have sworn that I saw Egg pass San a note at the game yesterday."

Brad made a noise with his lips, an exhalation of disbelief. "No way, Trav. My Sandy? San and Egg? That couldn't happen in a zillion years. She did admit that they have talked though. She said it was dealing with schoolwork. But, a letter? Nah-h, no way."

There was a moment of quiet. Brad held his lip between his teeth. The gesture and the look on his face made it clear that he'd started thinking something serious.

"Trav, where do you think she's been the last few times she broke our dates?"

"Hmmm…that's a good question. Listen, Brad, I know what you're getting at, but Sandy's not like that. Does she have any idea how often you mess around on her?"

"What? Trav, where in the world did you dig that question up from?"

"Well," Travis said, "not taking sides or anything, but if she did...you know...mess around...."

"Whoa. Sounds like you know something about where she goes when she's missing some nights," Brad said.

"Brad! My God, man, I'm your best friend. I wouldn't hide anything like that from you. I was just saying..." Travis paused, then, after a moment, went on. "Let's get off this subject, huh?"

A moment of quiet tension hung about both Brad and Travis before he answered Travis' question. "Yeah, let's change the subject ...but, you don't think that she'd...you know...."

"Nah, man," Travis said. "Hey, you want me to come over, bring some beer maybe?"

"Yeah, come on over, but skip the beer. I've got something in a little plastic bag. All it needs is rolling and lighting."

"Cool," Travis said.

A dark blue sedan crawled to a stop in the driveway of a modest two-story brick house. It was the style of sedan driven by detectives.

The man in the driver's seat wore spectacles, seemingly too narrow for his broad face. He adjusted his glasses and glanced back at the mailbox. The mailbox was at the beginning of the driveway.

He opened his car door, looked at the mailbox again, and sighed tiredly. "Might as well," he mumbled.

When he walked to the mailbox, his stride didn't reflect the same tiredness that his sigh had. His legs carried his six-foot frame smoothly across the concrete driveway.

The mailbox was tall—a shiny, black rectangle of metal positioned atop a weathered 4x4. The man stopped in front of the mailbox. He didn't open it right away. Instead, he gently touched some of the glossy white lettering riveted to its side. The letters on the mailbox read: The Garrison Family.

"Humph," he grunted softly. "Family." He was thinking of how his wife had left him. He felt that two, just him and his son, Eugene, didn't quite make up a family.

After he looked in the mailbox and turned from it, his walk did seem tired now. His face wore a look of melancholy as he reached for the doorknob. But what he saw when he stepped through the door made him smile a little. Eugene Garrison was stretched out on a narrow, black couch, his mouth agape in comic repose. He was snoring very quietly.

His father eased the door shut. Then he tiptoed toward the couch. He was grinning. But suddenly, his grin froze. Eugene had stopped snoring. And his father was close enough to see that Eugene had tensed up. He waited until Eugene seemed to be relaxed again, then continued to tiptoe.

"Okay, Dad, I know that's you," Eugene said without opening his eyes.

His father smiled broadly. "Boy, you're amazing. Would've made a heck of a man for the Special Forces."

Eugene sat up, smiling. He moved his long legs, giving his father room to sit down. "Well, Dad, look who taught me. I mean, while other kids were learning sports, you taught me how to survive, Special Forces stuff."

"Son," Eugene's father said, "old John Garrison has made a lot of mistakes in life, maybe that was one of them." He paused reflectively. His eyes briefly revealed a trace of sadness. Then he spoke again. "Your mother," his voice came out hoarse, so he stopped, cleared his throat and started again. "Your mother, she never did approve."

Eugene looked away from his father a moment. He didn't feel right seeing the poignancy of his father's thoughts in his eyes. To him, his dad had always been impervious. But his father's eyes said differently. Even an ex-special forces man, a tough homicide detective, could be affected by something.

"Dad," Eugene said, "are you going to start looking for another…I mean, have you thought about dating?"

John nodded. "Yeah, thought about it." He didn't need to say any more; Eugene understood the succinct reply.

John suddenly reached out, ruffling his son's long hair roughly. "Look whose asking about dates. Boy, it's time you brought some pretty little thing over to meet your dad. I know good and well I didn't raise one of these." He held one hand out and flipped it over and back a few times.

"Aw, Dad, come on, you know I'm not gay," Eugene whined. His face turned a little livid. He threw a playful punch at his father. His father caught his fist inches from his shoulder.

"Dad, you've still got it," Eugene said. "Oh, Dad, I'd almost forgot, no pizza tonight. I won't be back 'til pretty late."

John's face showed his disappointment. "It's still a little early son, not even dark yet," he said. "Sure you won't have time for a few bites with your old man?"

Eugene had started getting up. He paused. "Aw, Dad, you're trying to make me feel guilty. But I'd planned on getting a little practice with my crossbow before it gets dark. Then I've got to go see this girl, Sandy. I've got to help her on a chemistry lesson."

"Ah," his father said, "keeping secrets from your old man, huh?"

"No, Dad, it's not like what you're thinking. We…we've just got this lesson that she wants me to…"

"Does this lesson deal with the birds and the bees?" his father asked. He was smiling broadly.

"No, that's biology, Dad. I'm talking about chemistry." They both laughed. "Sandy's just a friend. She's about the only one at school who doesn't think I'm a weirdo."

John Garrison smiled again. Arching his thin, black brows, he said, "Oh, is that right? A friend, huh? So, why don't you tell me a little

about..."

The sharp jangle of the phone interrupted. John reached for the phone. He laughed. "Probably just a friend. Hello. Hello?" He frowned.

He shrugged and prepared to put the phone down when someone spoke. It was a woman. Her words were slurred at first, then they became broken by sobs.

"Is this John?"

"Yeah, this is John Garrison," Eugene's father replied. "Who is..."

"I'm so...so sorry," the woman interrupted. "I...I had to...I, I...." Click. She hung up.

John Garrison was dumbfounded. He stared at the phone, then slowly he placed it back in its cradle. "What a weird world." His voice was just a whisper. "You know son, for a minute there, I thought that woman sounded a little like your mother."

"Really! Dad, what'd she say?" Eugene asked.

"Not much at all. Just sounded like whoever it was wanted to make some kind of confession. She said that she had to do it. What it is, I don't have the slightest idea. She probably didn't either, at least not now. She sounded really drunk. Sounded like she was crying too."

"You think possibly it could have been Mom?" Eugene queried.

"No, son, I'm afraid your mother is excluded. Like I said, that woman was drunk; your mother never drank a day in her life."

John Garrison grew quiet for a moment. Contemplatively, he cupped his hand under his chin. Leaning forward, he rested his elbows on his knees.

"One thing really bothers me about that call. Drunk or not, she knew my number and my name. That, I can't figure."

Eugene patted his father's shoulder. "Try not to worry, Dad. Maybe that was just a one time thing, huh?"

"Yeah, maybe you're right son."

"Listen, Dad, I guess I'd better be going," Eugene said. He headed for the door.

When he reached for the doorknob, his father spoke. "Before that call, I was just about to ask you to tell me a little about your friend. But, no...I guess you'd better get..."

"Oh, that's right, Dad," Eugene said. He glanced at his wristwatch. "I've got enough time to tell you."

He walked back to the couch and sat down again. "Well, let's see... Sandy has this long, black hair. It hangs down to her waist. And, Dad, you should see her eyes, they're big and dark like marbles. Her skin is so smooth and really white like..."

Eugene stopped talking, noticing for the first time that his father was frowning. The look on his father's face befuddled him. "What? What is it, Dad?"

"Eugene, that...that sounds like the description of the woman last seen with Henry Johnson!"

Eugene raised his brows quizzically. "Henry who?"

His father answered in a monotone. "Henry Johnson, he's the last guy that's been found dead. They found him over on Deadmen Road. Guy had puncture wounds in his neck. Looks like I'm stuck trying to nab a killer with a really weird sense of foul play."

"Dad, I didn't know you'd been assigned to that case. Tell me more about it. What else have you..."

"Whoa, whoa, son, slow down. First of all, I'm not supposed to have told you that much. Second, what in the world would you do with police information?"

Eugene smiled. "You must not be my Dad. Because my Dad taught me not to answer questions with questions."

John returned his son's smile. "Touché," he said. "Honestly, though, there's not much to tell right now. What I do know is that one of the last people who saw Henry alive was the bartender at Jimmy's. From what he said, the woman who left with Henry looks about like your friend..."

He paused; noting that Eugene was looking somewhat troubled. "No need to start thinking the worse though, son, alright?" Eugene nodded his response.

"I hope you do realize that I will...I will need to question your..."

"But, Dad," Eugene started to protest but changed his mind.

"I'm sorry, son. It's just a part of my job, just procedural. Mind telling me her address?"

Eugene hesitated before answering. "It's uh, 2032 West Meadowbrook Drive."

He stood to leave, walked a few steps and then paused. "See you later, Dad."

"Okay," his father said. "And, son, thanks."

John watched as his son walked toward the door. A frown of puzzlement crept over his visage. "Hey, son, forgetting your crossbow?"

"Nah, Dad, it's already in the car," Eugene replied. "See you later, alright?" He didn't hear his father's response. The echo of John's earlier words held his attention. "That sounds like the description of the woman last seen with Henry Johnson."

Eugene walked to his car, distracted by his thoughts. Sandy. Sandy's the only girl I know with hair, skin and eyes like that. But, nah, couldn't be.

Brad and Travis sat in Brad's living room. They sat at opposite ends of a large burgundy couch with big, fluffy pillows. Both guys stared bleary-eyed at cartoon images on the television screen. Foolish grins were on their faces. They didn't seem to notice that the television was blaring.

Pinched tightly between Brad's fingers was the remnant of a smoking marijuana cigarette. The smoke writhed slowly upward, white threads of fog-like consistency. It danced lazily, blending with smoke that already hung upon the air.

Travis looked over at Brad. He could see that the burning end was very close to Brad's fingers. His grin broadened. Brad looked over at him. He started to ask a question but never completed it. "What are you…ouch!" he exclaimed, dropping the cigarette to the floor.

Travis fell over toward his corner of the couch. He was holding his side and laughing raucously.

Brad dived over on him. He started hitting Travis with playful punches. "You knew! You knew, didn't you, clown?"

Travis was attempting a poor defense while emulating the way Brad had sounded. "Ow! Ow! Ow! Okay, okay," Travis said, "you owe me one."

"Darn right, I do," Brad said. He stood up, grinning. "Tell you what, go make a couple of sandwiches, and we'll call it even."

Travis frowned and stood also. "Aw, man, that's some way to treat your guest, Brad. Next time you come to my house I'm…"

Brad made a fist in Travis' direction. "You want some more, champ?" he asked.

Travis cringed, feigning fear. "Oh, no, not the fists of legend." He smiled and headed for the kitchen.

Brad watched him an instant, and then he picked up the remote and turned the volume down on the television.

Travis shouted needlessly. "Hey, aren't you going to do something about that smoke before your parents get here?"

"Don't have to worry about that," Brad responded, "they'll be away for at least two weeks. Vacation."

"Oh," Travis said from the kitchen. He spoke loudly, still not realizing that the volume had been turned down on the television.

When Travis came back he had four sandwiches on a platter. Brad looked up at him when he came into the living room. He was pressing the remote's channel button, watching disinterestedly as the channels flashed past.

Travis sat down beside him and extended the platter in his direction. Taking one of the sandwiches, Brad said, "You must want us to choke on these."

"Oh, dag," Travis responded. He gave the platter to Brad. "What do you want, water or juice?"

"Juice'll be cool," Brad responded.

Sighing, Travis heaved himself up and headed for the kitchen again.

Brad set the platter on an end table near the couch. He took a voracious bite out of his sandwich and pressed the channel button on the remote again.

Travis plodded back into the living room. He gave Brad one of the two glasses he carried.

Bored, Brad put down the remote. His voice was languid with boredom. "We've got to find something to do. Just sitting around is a waste of a good high. Hey, I've got an idea. Why don't we make some prank phone calls?"

He noticed a look of disinterest on Travis' face. "Aw, come on, Trav. It'll be fun…something to do. I'll tell you what, I'll go first." He didn't wait for Travis' response. He picked the phone up with a broad smile on his face. His eyes shined with anticipation as he punched a random phone number.

A phone on the other end of the line rang once, twice, then someone picked it up. "Hello," a man said.

Brad fought hard to keep himself from giggling. He answered in a voice that sounded like a drunken person. "Yeah, you, you know what time Jessey'll be getting back?"

"Sorry," the man replied, "you have the wrong number. I don't know anyone by that…"

"Jessey Lee Baker," Brad interrupted. "Yeah, oh, yes, you do know her. This is the number she gave me, so don't you tell me that crap!"

The man spoke again, his voice hoarse with anger. "Listen here, you son of a…"

Brad slammed the phone down, giving in to laughter. By that time, Travis was laughing too. But when Brad picked the phone up again and held it in his direction, his laughter stopped abruptly. "Your turn, Trav," Brad said.

Travis put his hands up defensively. “Nah, man, no thanks.”

“Aw, Trav,” Brad began, then shrugged. He replaced the phone in its cradle. But after only an instant, he picked it up again. A mischievous smile worked its way to the edges of his mouth.

Brad punched another number. The phone on the opposite end of the line rang several times. No one answered. He replaced the phone for the second time. But a thrill had kindled within him now. So again, he picked up the phone and punched in a number at random. This time the other phone rang only once before someone answered. “Hello, can I help you?” a woman asked.

Brad held back a laugh and answered in a voice like a drunken person again. “Can I…I…speak to…to Jessey…Jessey Lee Baker, please?”

A big smile was on Brad’s face, but it froze upon the woman’s reply.

“I am Jessey Lee Baker,” she said.

“What?” Brad said, “I…uh…I…”

The woman giggled. “You sound shocked. You did want to speak to me, right?” Her voice was soft, sexy, almost musical.

Brad found himself envisioning a face and body matching the intriguing voice. The intrigant spoke again before he could gather his thoughts. “What’s wrong, sweetie, hmm?”

A funny feeling went through Brad. The mere sound of the woman’s voice was invoking sensuous thoughts.

Travis could read the confusion on Brad’s face. Brad quickly positioned the phone between his jaw and shoulder. He pointed to the phone and then pointed toward Travis. He then jerked his thumb toward the kitchen.

Travis stared at Brad, a lack of comprehension evident in his manner. This caused Brad to roll his eyes upward, as if to say, you numbskull. He pointed to the phone again and then started to point at Travis. The woman’s voice stopped him.

“Hey, are you still there?”

“Oh, sorry,” Brad said. He looked at Travis again. Travis formed a silent oh with his lips. He now understood that Brad wanted him to eavesdrop from the phone in the kitchen. Travis grinned, nodded and stood up quickly.

The woman continued; the sweet, melody stirred something inside of Brad again. “Tell me, what do you think of vampires?”

Before he could reply, he heard Travis lift the other phone from its cradle. He coughed loudly, intending it to be a distraction. His ploy failed, and he felt a nervous tension, realizing that Jessey must’ve heard when Travis picked the phone up. Her next question confirmed his intuition. “Is someone there with you?”

Brad cursed silently, naming Travis something that would've made him blush. "No," he lied hastily. "I think there's something wrong with this line. It's been acting up for a while now."

He waited momentarily for the woman to speak: she said nothing. It was obvious by Jessey's lapse in conversing that she was in doubt of Brad's explanation. After a brief quiet though, she went on. "You never answered my question."

"Oh," Brad said. "Personally, I think that they are fabulous creatures."

"You do!" Jessey exclaimed. "I think that's great. You know, you're the first person that I ever heard say that. I think they're wonderful too, though, you and I must be two in a zillion."

Brad was frowning; Jessey'd assumed the wrong definition for the word fabulous. But still, he was puzzled by her excitement. He felt an urge to hang up. Something was weird about Jessey.

Instead of submitting to his urge, he decided to explain. "Jessey, I meant fabulous in the sense of relating to fables. I didn't mean..."

"Oh," she said, interrupting. She actually sounded a little hurt. Brad's brows went up in a deep frown. Weird, he thought.

The hurt had vanished from Jessey's voice when she spoke again. "Well, you already know my name, so why don't you tell me yours?"

Brad laughed. "Sorry. I can be such a dunce sometimes. My name is Brad, Brad Richardson."

"Hmmm," she said, making it sound as if she was savoring something sweet. "Sounds like the name of a real handsome fellow. Are you?"

"Most girls think so," Brad answered. "What about you? Do you look as good as you sound?"

Jessey emitted a soft giggle. Her answer was not much different from Brad's. "Most guys think so."

Brad smiled. Although he still felt that Jessey was weird, he was feeling curiously drawn to her. "You know, you're the second person to ask me about vampires today. What made you ask a question like that?"

Brad didn't understand the hesitation. "Well, I uh...I'm curious, that's all. I'd wondered what someone else's thoughts were about the murders that have been occurring. Evidence seems to suggest the impossible. What I mean is something that most people think is impossible...vampires. Consider that last guy, Henry. He had teeth marks on his neck just like the others. And a lot of his blood had been sucked out."

Brad felt his skin prickle on the back of his neck. He heard when Travis put the phone down. He coughed as he'd done previously, attempting a distraction. This time, however, Jessey didn't question him about the sound.

Looking toward the kitchen, he saw Travis motioning frantically. He was motioning for Brad to hang up. Brad shook his head and continued talking. He didn't know what Travis wanted, but he figured whatever it was, it could wait. Still, he wondered about the wild look he'd seen in Travis' eyes.

"Listen," Brad said, "I know you don't know me, but would you object...what I mean is, could I possibly see you sometime?"

He was a little surprised by her answer. "Of course. Actually, I was hoping I might have you for dinner sometime soon. What's your number? I could call you to see when the best time would be for us to get together."

Hardly able to contain his excitement, Brad quickly told Jessey his number. For some reason, he felt the need to be honest. He wanted to tell her that he'd just dialed her number at random, but he decided not to; she didn't seem concerned about it anyway.

"I'll call you again soon," Jessey said. "Take care."

"You too," Brad said. He hung up the phone. Turning, he saw Travis hurrying toward him.

Travis' voice was high-pitched when he spoke. "Brad, do you know what you just did? God man, you just put yourself in danger. You've got to do some..."

"Whoa. Whoa, Trav," Brad said. He brought up both hands, palms facing Travis. "What are you talking about?"

"Brad, she's the vampire!" Travis said. His voice was still shrill, and his eyes were wild.

"What? Trav, old boy, you've lost your mind," Brad said. "First, there's no such thing as vampires. And second, what is the chance of me just calling the killer's number at random?" He gave a short laugh. Then he studied Travis' face for a moment. "Damn, man, you're actually serious, huh?"

"Uh-huh," Travis replied. He paused. "Brad, listen, just hear me out. She said some things that were really spooky. That's why I hung up. There's no way that she could have known some of those things, unless she is the killer, or maybe a detective. And I'm willing to bet you anything, she's definitely not a detective."

Brad smiled. But he noticed that Travis' eyes said that he wasn't joking. He started to say something but waited, sure that he'd be able to explain away any incriminatory supposition Travis could point out.

Travis continued, "I saw the news about that last guy they found. They said nothing about teeth marks, but she did. And..."

"Trav," Brad interrupted, "couldn't she have read about that in the newspapers?"

Travis was shaking his head even before he answered. "No. That story just came out in today's paper."

Contrastive emotions compelled Travis' voice to become rapid, his words nearly running together. "The paper, today, didn't mention teeth marks. So why'd she choose that particular word, huh?"

He kept going, not allowing Brad time enough to respond. "All the paper said was that the guy had marks on his neck like the other victims. And she told you that the blood had been sucked out. The news only said that a large amount of blood was missing, not sucked out. But the biggest thing is, she said the last dead guy's name. The release of the guy's name isn't even public yet!"

Something like shock flickered in Brad's eyes. He suddenly sat up straighter. Cupping his chin in his hand, he stared at Travis. Then he shook his head and laughed. But it was not a very convincing laugh. "Trav, there's probably some other explanations. Like, okay, suppose she knows someone who is working on that case. They could've told her those things…right?"

Travis looked down; he ran on hand through his hair. His gaunt face took on a look of concentration. "Well," he said hesitantly, "maybe you've got something there. But still, something's not right. I can feel it, Brad."

Travis put his head down again. He felt that there was another point that he wanted to bring out, something else he could not put his finger on.

Brad slapped him on the back lightly. "Come on, Sherlock, Jessey's not a killer. Why don't you…"

Travis looked up sharply, eyes agleam with excitement afresh. "That's it," he said. "That's the other thing that bothers me. You made that name up as a joke, right?"

Brad nodded. He already understood the point Travis was going to make, but let him go on.

"Now," Travis said, "why did she go along with you then, knowing that her name was not Jessey Lee Baker?"

"Hmmm," Brad said, frowning. "Now, that is something to think about. Kind of strange, but even that wouldn't mean she's a killer, Trav."

He smiled and stood up. "Come on, you can leave your car here, ride with me to San's house. I'll buy the beer."

Travis got up too. He smiled, but it was a smile hindered by what he was feeling. Something was wrong about the woman Brad had talked to. But what could he do about it? Certainly, he could not go to the police with nothing more than his personal theorem and a gut feeling. Yet, as he followed Brad out the door, he knew he would think of something. He had to.

Eugene had driven out away from the city to practice shooting his crossbow. He had set up his targets in a wooded area away from the road. By the time he was getting bored with practicing, it was growing too dark to see the bull's eye well, so he gathered his things.

He trudged back toward his car, his senses alert as they always were. His mind played back vivid scenes of the things his father taught him, survival things. He remembered how proud he was when his father came home wearing a miscellany of medals. John Garrison had been one of the best men that the Special Forces had ever seen. And he taught Eugene as if he expected that his son would follow in his footsteps.

Occasionally, they still practiced. But Eugene had lost some of his quondam enthusiasms since ninth grade. Two bigger boys had jumped him and...Eugene forced himself to think of something else.

He was glad that his father had taught him well. It had become like second nature to him, to always be alert. It was a natural thing for him to listen to the tiniest of sounds. In the woods, he could even distinguish the sound of human footsteps from that of animals'.

Even though he did like his learned abilities, sometimes he wondered.... He wondered what it would've been like for his father to have taught him normal things. What would it have been like to've thrown a baseball, or played a game of basketball?

Eugene was nearing the edge of the woodland when he felt something, an intimation of danger. Something was wrong. Automatically, his footsteps became quieter, more stealth.

The moon protruded from the darkening blue-gray sky. It was magnificent, a luminous, pearl-white globe, splendid relievo against the dull sheet of sky.

Darkness was just beginning to descend, so it was still light enough for Eugene to see his car fairly well. The car was parked a few feet from the road on a grassy path.

On the side of the car opposite him, Eugene could see the silhouette of a man. The doors were locked and the windows were rolled up. But that didn't stop the guy from trying to get in. He was forcing something between the top of the window and the top of the door.

The trespasser looked up suddenly. His gaze went directly to Eugene. To Eugene's amazement, the man paused only for a moment, then continued his task! Such coarse bravado caused Eugene to hesitate. Either the guy was on some kind of drug, or he was a lunatic. Either state meant that a confrontation was imminent, a serious one. Eugene let his hunting gear fall.

He was, by nature, a quiet person who avoided trouble. But at times in his life, he would let anger get the best of him. It was scary. To him, it was like another person taking over his body, a mean one. The boldness of what the man was doing at his car brought that person to the surface.

Adrenaline rush made Eugene tremble; his voice quaked with anger. "Hey, what are you doing? Get away from my car!"

The guy looked up again. Eugene was close enough now to see his eyes; his eyes were cold like a beast. The voice that arose from the guy's throat wasn't much different from the look in his eyes. "Kid…if I were you, I'd turn around and get!"

Eugene kept coming. The man's eyes showed a momentary surprise. Stepping away from the car, he grunted.

Eugene's steps were cautious as he went to the same side of the car as the culprit. His heart thumped madly. His hands tightened into fists. The palms of his hands were hot and moist with sweat. Again, the mean side had taken over, the deadly side. He paused a few feet away from the crook, fixing him with an icy stare. An equally unwavering stare emanated from the eyes of the would-be thief.

The tool the man had been using clunked to the ground. Through gritted teeth, he spit out deep-throated words. "If I don't see you turn and run in about five seconds, you're gonna find your guts in your hands, boy. Now get!"

Anger washed over Eugene, deep, powerful rage, something not much different from what he'd felt in the past. It was how he'd felt that time in the ninth grade. He remembered how he'd lost control, how two bullies got hurt really bad.

As an answer to the man's command, Eugene shook his head. Slowly he shifted his feet and his body into a fighting position.

His opposer's eyes narrowed. The man reached for the back of his waistband. In an instant his hand came forward. The silver blade of a long hunting knife glinted in the moonlight.

Eugene swallowed hard, rapid motions making his Adams apple bob up and down. His body tensed. The man lunged, knife outthrust. Eugene's hand shot out in a blur of motion. His grip clamped down hard on the guy's wrist. Simultaneously, he slid one foot forward quickly and gave the man's wrist a hard jerk. The actions caused the guy to slam into Eugene's hip. Eugene rolled his hip at the moment of impact.

The end result of Eugene's expertly executed moves was that the man found himself sailing through the air. He crashed to the ground. A loud whoosh burst from his lungs. He lay stunned.

In his fall, the man had dropped the knife. It lay not far from his hand.

He sat up groggily, giving his head a vicious shake. It did not take him long to spot the knife. Surprisingly, in an instant, he was on his feet again with the knife in his hand. The man's eyes glinted, steely with rage.

Under his breath, Eugene cursed. His anger seemed to reach another level. This is crazy! he thought. What sense did it make for one human being to be so determined at wronging another? This time he didn't wait for the man to attack. He saw the man rush toward him, but he was already charging too.

The man made a wide swing with the knife for Eugene's face. Eugene ducked smoothly. Even while ducking, he caught the man's outstretched wrist. In the same instant he curled the fingers of his free hand, leaving the palm exposed. Snatching the guy forward, he slammed his palm up under the edge of the guy's chin.

A grunt of pain escaped the guy's lips; his head snapped back. His eyes fluttered rapidly, and he was no longer able to keep his balance. He began falling backward, toppling slowly like a felled tree. But even before the fall could reach an end, Eugene was still in action. While keeping a hold on the guy's wrist, he quickly stepped around behind him. In a matter of seconds, his free arm was in a strong chokehold across the man's neck. And with his other hand, he held the guy's hand in such a position that the knife was pointed at the attacker's body.

The man, almost unconscious, felt the point of the knife poke through his clothes. He was beginning to realize that death was only inches away. He struggled against the force that Eugene was exerting to drive the knife in.

For a moment, Eugene was engulfed in the insanity of rage. He didn't even realize that he was slowly forcing the knife through the man's clothes and skin.

Eugene's breaths were heavy. He could hear the sounds of it being sucked in and then rushing out. His voice, too, was heavy when he gritted words into the struggling man's ear. "How's it feel, huh? How's it feel to know you're about to die, scum?"

Although Eugene was tightening his arm against the guy's neck, the man managed a few strangled words. "Pl…please? D…don't ki…kill me."

Somehow the words penetrated through Eugene's fog of anger. He blinked rapidly and suddenly let the man fall to the ground. Instantly the guy clambered to his feet. He turned as swiftly as he could, swayed and took a few hurried steps backwards. He kept his eyes pinned on Eugene, but especially the knife Eugene now held.

Chests heaving, the two stood staring at each other across the dark clearing. Fear, and the speed with which everything had happened, held the man in temporary immobility. Eugene, too, was not moving except for the tremble running through his body and the heave of his chest.

Suddenly he stepped toward the man. The guy's eyes remained glued to the knife; they widened when Eugene moved. The force that had held the attacker had broken. He exhaled some sounds that could have been words, words rendered incoherent by trepidation. Within the next second, he was running away, blindly crashing into the nearby foliage.

Eugene remained standing in the same spot for a while after the guy had run. He could not believe he had lost control again. Once more, he remembered when he was in the ninth grade, two people had almost lost their lives. He wondered if the things his father had taught him were a blessing or a curse.

By the time he dropped the knife and turned to leave, his breathing was returning to normal. He retrieved his hunting accessories.

Shortly, he was driving along the road leading back into the city limits. He prided himself in his aptitude with the crossbow. Most always he'd hit the bull's eye on the target. When he didn't, he was rarely more than a few centimeters off. Of all the things his father'd taught him, he felt that the crossbow was the least likely to be of any real use. He knew he'd never use it to hunt and kill animals. But he'd become adjusted to practicing with it anyway.

As he drove, a picture of Sandy painted itself in his mind's eye. He dearly anticipated seeing her. The silky, waist-long, ebon hair, those large, dark eyes. He dismissed the thoughts, feeling a twinge of guilt. Sandy was Brad's girlfriend. But it seemed that almost everyone knew Brad was unfaithful.

It was not a good feeling to have a crush on someone involved in a relationship. But at times he felt that Sandy liked him too. He'd often seen her watching him in class. Everyone knew that he was the smartest person in class. People often admired intelligence. But he thought that he'd caught glimpses of more than admiration in her eyes. He wondered.

Eugene pulled up in front of Sandy's house. He parked the car and then reached toward the ignition switch. His hand poised over the key, he looked at the driveway. Sandy's parents' car was there. Eugene realized that he'd partially blocked the driveway. Putting the car in reverse, he backed it up a few feet.

His moving the car proved to be prudent, for just as he got out and headed for the steps, the front door opened. Sandy's parents stepped out. Their attire made it obvious that they were headed out for a night on the town.

Sandy's father looked up, catching sight of Eugene heading for the steps. A genuine smile spread across his face; it showed in his eyes. Eugene returned the smile, his too, was genuine. He'd come to like Sandy's father within the times he'd visited.

Sandy's mother was a chatty woman. At the moment, she was talking so much that she didn't notice Eugene until Sandy's father gestured toward him. "Well, look who's here again, Mable."

He stuck his hand out to Eugene. Eugene took the proffered hand and gave it a sincere shake. "How are you, Mr. Fields?"

"Fine, well, at least I will be when I get the circulation back in my hand."

He rubbed the hand Eugene had shaken. "Got yourself a heck of a grip there, son."

They smiled. Eugene turned and stuck his hand out to Mrs. Fields. "How are you, ma'am?"

"Just fine. You?"

"I'm fine, Mrs. Fields. Everything's okay."

"Good," she said, staring at Eugene strangely. He lowered his eyes quickly; his face grew a little warm. Mrs. Fields didn't seem to notice that she'd embarrassed him. She kept talking without diverting her gaze. "You know, you are a lot nicer than that, that…" she glanced at her husband, "what's his name, Alec?"

"Brad," Sandy's father replied. He rolled his eyes heavenward. Eugene noticed; he tried hard not to smile.

Mable went on talking. "Yes, that's it, Brad…Brad something or other." She frowned a little.

"You know, I don't like that boy. Something about him…he looks downright sneaky or something. But…you, you're different. You're an honest, respectful young man. Sandy should've picked…"

Alec reached out quickly; he tugged on his wife's elbow. "Come on, Mable, the boy came to see Sandy, not us."

"Oh, Alec, you're always in such a big rush. And what for? The world's not going any place."

Mable, though voicing mild complaints, allowed herself to be steered away. Eugene watched amusedly.

When Sandy's parents stepped onto the ground, Mable looked back. She spoke as if there'd never been an interruption. "You're a nice looking young man too. But that hair! That hair is a bit long."

Eugene blushed. He saw Sandy's father standing slightly behind her mother. Her father was smiling and shaking his head. He reached for his wife's elbow again.

Mable turned, but she continued talking as she walked away. "I'll tell you, kids nowadays are really something, not at all like when we were growing up. I don't know what in the world…"

"Eugene," Sandy said. She had come to the door without Eugene having noticed. Her voice muffled that of her mother's. She stood in the doorway smiling. Eugene smiled back. For an instant, they both seemed transfixed, staring and smiling at each other.

"Oh, how rude. I haven't invited you in," Sandy said. Her face reddened. She stepped aside, holding the door open for Eugene. "Come on in."

Eugene stepped in just beyond where Sandy was standing. He watched as she closed the door. Her long, shiny hair rippled, flowed with her movements. The ebon sheen was in stark contrast with the red color of her dress. The dress was tight; it showed Sandy's young, supple body in detail, a bit arousing for Eugene.

Sandy moved slowly when she closed the door, giving Eugene ample time to examine the way the tight dress clung to her figure. Eugene was still staring at the way her butt moved under the stretched fabric when she turned suddenly. He averted his eyes, but Sandy had seen him watching her. She started toward him, trying hard not to look at him. And she resisted the urge to smile.

Gesturing toward the couch, she said, "Have a seat. I'll go get my books."

Eugene nodded and hurriedly turned his face away from Sandy. He felt the flush of embarrassment hot against his cheeks.

Sandy was gone from the room only a short time. When she came back, she was carrying a dictionary, a note tablet, and a chemistry book. She sat down, putting the miscellany of items between her and Eugene. Then on impulse, she picked them up quickly and moved them to her lap. She slid over to the spot from where she'd removed the books.

When she slid over, her dress moved up. The movement caused about half of her thighs to show.

Eugene reached for the chemistry book, pretending that he didn't notice how Sandy's dress had moved. "Um, okay...," he stopped and cleared his throat. "Okay, so I guess we'll get started."

He looked at Sandy, awaiting a response. But she seemed distracted. She was staring toward the door. Clearing his throat again, he riffled through the pages of the textbook. "Alright," he said, "first question. What are the differences, if any, between a sulfite, a sulfide and a sulfate?" He frowned when Sandy didn't answer. Eugene noticed that she was still staring toward the door.

"San? San, did you hear the question?"

"Huh? Oh, I'm sorry, Eugene. I...my mind seems to be somewhere else. I just can't seem to focus. Do you think that you can...you know, kinda' do what we did about that last assignment we had?"

She smiled pleadingly. "This time, though, I promise, you won't have to sneak it to me like you did at the game. I was only trying to protect you...what I mean is, I thought that you might have trouble with Brad."

Another quick smile lit up her face. She paused a moment and looked at Eugene askance. He didn't say anything, so she continued.

"I'm not being totally honest with you. I, um, I was a little ashamed to. You know, people at school think that you are...are different. But I…"

"San," Eugene said, interrupting her, "no need to soften the blow, so-to-speak. It's not different…what I mean is, I know that people think that I'm weird, not just different."

She stared at Eugene surprised by his candor. He stared back. Sandy looked away quickly.

A moment of quiet made them both feel a little embarrassment. Temporarily, they were at a loss of the proper things to say. Sandy spoke first, while pulling her dress down. She made more moves and took more time than was necessary. "Eugene, I don't think you're weird. Well, can I be honest with you?"

Eugene nodded. She went on. "At first, I thought like that. But, I know now that you're not weird. You're just, just…"

"Taciturn," Eugene said.

Sandy raised her brows questioningly. "Taciturn?"

"Yeah," Eugene replied. "Taciturn, means not inclined to conversation, quiet. That fits me, at least most of the time anyway."

"You're right," Sandy said, "that does fit you. I think we have something in common."

"We do?" Eugene asked.

"You sound surprised," Sandy replied.

"I am," Eugene said. "I mean, I see you as this really outspoken person. And you seem to always have a lot of friends around you."

"Well, yeah, you're right. But that's just me while I'm at school. Actually, I like being alone a lot. And unless the topic is of interest, I don't really like talking about it. So, you see, we both are taciturn."

Eugene smiled and nodded. Sandy smiled reciprocally. They both stared into each other's eyes. Eugene looked away. "You know, there was a time when I was a little more inclined to talk and mingle with people." He grew quiet, contemplative.

"What happened?" Sandy asked.

Eugene hesitated. "Well, it has been like a secret for a long time. So, if I tell you, you won't tell anyone else, will you?"

Sandy was intrigued; she shook her head.

Eugene went on. "When I was in high school, there was this incident where two bullies were almost killed."

"Really?" Sandy said. She sat up a little straighter. "What happened?"

Eugene sighed heavily. "To make a long story short, do you believe that everyone has a good side and a bad side? A Jekyll and Hyde, so-to-speak?"

Sandy nodded. "Yeah, I do."

"Well," Eugene said, "I think that my bad side is worse than most people's. And these two guys made it come out. I mean, it was scary, like something or someone had taken control of me."

Eugene grew quiet for a moment. Sandy reached out, gently placing a hand on his knee. "How? I mean, you did that to two guys?"

Eugene nodded in answer. "When I was growing up, my father taught me how to fight. He was in the Special Forces."

"Wow!" Sandy said. "That's really cool."

"Well, it has its good points as well as bad ones," Eugene said reflectively. "Like, for instance, I almost hurt a man pretty bad before I came to your house."

"You did?" Sandy asked, her eyes alight with interest. "Tell me about it."

"There's really not too much to tell. I was outside the city limits, in the woods. I had been practicing with my crossbow until it started to get dark. Anyway, when I came back to my car, there was a guy trying to break into it. I disarmed him and almost killed him in the process."

Eugene sighed. "I guess now you've changed your opinion about me, huh?"

"No," Sandy said bluntly. "If anything, I think more highly of you now. You're a very special person, Eugene."

She moved her hand to his face and placed her palm against it. Again, they both stared quietly at each other. Eugene broke the spell. "I...I guess we'd better get started on that test review."

Sandy removed her hand slowly. She stood up, smoothing her dress with her hands.

"No," she said almost in a whisper. "I can't concentrate. You see, I have a secret too." She paused. Eugene thought he saw the shine of tears. But then she turned her head.

Eugene stood up, taking hold of one of her hands. She looked him in the eyes. She seemed to have read his mind, answering the question he was about to ask. "No, Eugene, believe me, you can't help."

She turned her head quickly away and slowly freed her hand from his. Her voice quavered when she spoke. "I need to get out of here for a while, be alone." She spoke so low that Eugene hardly heard her. It seemed that she was talking to herself.

Sandy started for the door. Eugene watched. He felt helpless. He didn't know what to do or say. But, he did know that Sandy was acting very strange. She seemed to have forgotten that he was even there.

For some reason, an echo of Eugene's father's words went through his mind: "That sounds like the description of the woman last seen with Henry Johnson." A warning? Was Sandy somehow connected to the killings? He brushed the thoughts from his mind. Scolding himself, he started after her.

Catching up to her, he asked, "Are you sure there's nothing I can do?"

"Yes. Yes, I'm sure, Eugene." She put her fingertips on her temples and began to make small circles. "Humph, I'd better get some help from somewhere, though. Can you believe that, for a second, I'd forgotten that you were here? God, I need help."

She sighed and reached for the doorknob. Eugene followed her out quietly. He didn't know what else to do.

When they got on the porch, Sandy turned to lock the door. She heard Eugene say, "Oh damn, here comes trouble."

Brad drove up and braked so suddenly that he and Travis were jerked forward. "Come on, Trav. That weirdo made a fool of me one time already. Now he thinks he can sneak around and get fresh with my girl." His words were tinged with anger. And the alcohol he'd consumed worsened the anger.

He got out of his car and slammed the door shut. Brad started forward with long strides, his eyes never leaving Eugene's face.

Eugene stepped down from the last step. His easy manner belied the slow anger building inside. He knew that the time always eventually came when bullies had to be taught a lesson. This was one such time. Hooking the thumbs in the front pockets of his pants, he assumed a stance of nonchalance. But inwardly he was ready.

Everything seemed to happen in a blur. But Eugene quickly examined his status. It didn't escape his notice that Sandy was moving around him so as to intercept Brad. Nor did it escape his notice that Travis didn't follow Brad. Instead, Travis was leaning on the car with a beer in his hand. And his eyes were wide with anticipation or fear. Which? Eugene didn't have time to decide.

Sandy walked quickly in front of Brad when he'd come within a few feet of Eugene. She put both palms firmly against Brad's chest in an attempt to hold him back. "Brad, listen to me."

He quickly brushed her hands down while keeping his eyes on Eugene. Then he stepped around her. Sandy shouted uselessly. "Brad! Brad, don't!"

Even before she'd completed her plea, Brad reached Eugene and threw a wild punch. He lunged with it, grunting in surprise when Eugene easily avoided it. Eugene sidestepped swiftly while keeping his body mere inches from Brad's. Brad's momentum propelled him past. In that split second, Eugene stabbed a perfectly timed elbow into his back near the side. The momentum and the effects of the blow resulted in Brad falling clumsily to the ground.

Before Brad could scramble to his feet, Eugene turned facing him again. His pulse was roaring in his ears. His blood was rushing through his veins, adding strength to his muscles. He heard Sandy saying something, but it seemed unclear, far away.

Eugene waited while Brad straightened up. In an instant, Brad was on his feet again. He started toward Eugene, this time though he proceeded warily.

Travis was the only one to notice Eugene's father drive up. He didn't know Eugene's father, but he could tell that the car was one used by law enforcement agencies. That fact made him nervous. He turned quickly, placing the beer in front of the front tire.

Within the short time that it took to conceal the beer, a lot had transpired. Eugene had knocked Brad to the ground and straddled him. He had just drawn his fist back when Sandy rushed up, grabbing his forearm. At the moment she opened her mouth to plead with him, Eugene's father rushed from the car. He shouted, "No! Son, don't hurt him!"

Eugene turned his head quickly, shocked at seeing his father running toward him. Sandy and Brad too watched in surprise to see the big man running into the yard. Travis was tagging along behind Eugene's father. Eugene, Sandy and Brad remained practically motionless as they watched Eugene's father and Travis approach.

As Travis and Eugene's father neared the trio, Sandy slowly released her grip on Eugene's arm. Eugene dropped his arm heavily to his side. He got up and turned to face his father. Brad stood up behind him, a little to one side.

Eugene's father put his hand on Eugene's shoulder. "Are you alright?"

Eugene nodded to his father's question. Then John Garrison went on in the professional manner to which he was accustomed. "Tell me, what happened here?"

"I'll tell you," Brad blurted out. "I'll tell you where you can go if you don't mind your own business. Who the hell are you supposed to be anyhow?"

John Garrison eyed Brad coldly for an instant, but didn't say anything. Without taking his eyes off Brad, he reached for his wallet. He stepped calmly around Eugene and walked up to Brad.

"I'm Detective John Garrison, Eugene's father," he said, flipping his wallet open. He stuck it up close to Brad's face. Brad's mouth opened slowly, but no sound came out.

John Garrison went on, "I'm also the guy you don't want to piss off. Got that?"

Back straight and rigid, John Garrison turned swiftly on his heels. He left Brad there speechless. He walked over to Eugene again.

"From the description you gave me, I'm supposing that must be Sandy," he said, gesturing toward her.

She was walking across the yard to where Brad was standing. Travis was coming from the other direction.

Responding to his father's statement, Eugene nodded. But he was distracted. His gaze followed Sandy. His father continued talking, but Eugene failed to hear him. He was trying to hear what Brad, Travis and Sandy were saying.

"Son? Son, did you hear me?"

Eugene looked at his father quickly. "Huh? Oh, Dad, I didn't hear you." He flashed an embarrassed smile. His father reached out, laying one hand on his shoulder. "That's okay. I'm here to talk to Sandy."

"Okay," Eugene replied, casting a glance at Sandy. He noticed that Sandy and Brad had moved a few feet away from Travis. He could tell by their hand gestures and facial expressions that they were arguing. But they were keeping their voices too low to be heard.

Reluctantly, Eugene headed for his car. He wanted to stay, but he knew that if he did, he'd likely worsen the situation. Eugene was still several yards from his car when he heard fast-approaching footsteps. Half turning, he saw Brad and Travis coming directly toward him. His body tensed, readying itself for quick action. But at the last moment, Brad and Travis veered. Travis stepped around Eugene, leaving a distance of about two feet between them. But Brad hardly missed brushing against his shoulder. As he passed Eugene, Brad paused very briefly. Looking Eugene in the eye, he said, "It's not over, freak."

Eugene stood watching for a moment after Travis and Brad passed. He took several deep breaths, attempting to suppress the anger welling up inside him.

"Eugene." Eugene looked up at the sound of Sandy's voice. "Call me later?"

He nodded and then proceeded, once again, toward his car. He saw that his father had approached Sandy and was showing her his identification badge.

"My name is John Garrison," Eugene's father said while putting his badge away. "As you can see, I'm a detective with Bartenfield Homicide Division."

He paused, noting how Sandy's eyes had widened. John Garrison could not tell if the reaction stemmed from admiration or guilt, perhaps.

Reaching for his shirt pocket, he took out a small note pad and pen.

"I need to tell you that you are under no obligation to answer any of my questions. However, if you're not opposed, I'll need to proceed."

For a moment, Sandy only stared. Then, as if emerging from a daze, she nodded reticently.

"Oh, Mr. Gar…, I meant Detective Garrison, forgive my lack of manners," she said, gesturing toward her house. "I guess I should invite you in?"

John Garrison shook his head. "No, that's alright, thank you. We'll only be a minute. And…call me John." He smiled broadly. "Your full name?"

"Sandy Kay Fields," Sandy responded. John Garrison's easy manner was making her feel a little less tense.

He went on. "Miss Fields, do you know any of the following names?" He looked at his note pad and read the names of the latest homicide victims.

John Garrison watched Sandy's eyes as she answered no in response to each name. His years of experience working with people helped him realize the truth of the age-old adage: The eyes never lie.

"What about Henry Johnson? Ever heard of him?" He watched Sandy's eyes intently. For an instant, he thought he detected something. A flicker of recognition perhaps? He couldn't be sure.

Sandy shook her head as she answered, "No."

John Garrison sighed. "Well, that's the last of the names. Henry Johnson was the last one killed. The coroner's report said that the time of death occurred approximately between the hours of 10 p.m. and 1:30 a.m. on the fourteenth. Can you remember what you were doing them?"

"Sure," Sandy responded quickly. But then she paused, seeming to have temporarily forgotten what she wanted to say. "I…uh, I studied with Eugene that night." Then as an afterthought, she added, "We were up till about 1:15."

He studied Sandy's eyes momentarily. Something was there, but what, he couldn't pinpoint it. He felt, though, that she was lying.

Sandy shifted her weight, a sign of restlessness. John Garrison saw it, but pretended not to. He cleared his throat. "Uh, Miss Fields, I only have a couple more questions. I hope I'm not taking up too much of your time." He glanced at his wristwatch. Then glanced up at the sky. "Humph, 9:30 and not very dark. It's amazing how much light the moon sometimes reflects, isn't it?"

Though he'd asked a question, he went on before Sandy could respond. "You know, they say that the full moon influences peoples' behaviors. Me, personally, I'm a bit of a skeptic when it comes to…"

"Excuse me," Sandy interrupted, "but you were going to ask me two more questions, right?" She didn't bother hiding the irritation that crept into her voice.

A thin, quick smile split John Garrison's wide face. Sandy shifted her weight again. She failed to see any humor in his prolonging her questioning.

"Oh, sorry, Miss Fields. Sometimes I tend to get a little prolix.

Well, another thing I wanted to ask is, have you ever…you know, had any trouble with the law?"

Sandy sighed. "Well, when I was about fifteen, I did get picked up for shoplifting. That was only done because of a dare…I swear it," she added defensively.

John Garrison nodded and made another note.

"One final thing," he said. "Do you happen to have a recent photo, a wallet-size, maybe?"

Sandy shifted her weight again. She scowled, and crossing her arms, she stared defiantly into the detective's eyes. "I don't believe this! I just don't believe it. You think I know something about these murders," she said. Her voice was hardly below a shout. "I've never done anything more serious than…than taking that stupid dare, and here you are…"

"Miss Fields, please, calm down. This is only procedural."

Sandy threw both hands up and shouted, "Calm down? You want me to calm down? No. I'll tell you what; I'm going to get that freaking picture you asked for! And then I want you to leave!"

She turned quickly on her heels. John Garrison called to her, but she refused to look back. "Miss Fields? Miss Fields, I…"

Within a few minutes, Sandy came back carrying a picture of herself. She shoved it roughly in his direction. John Garrison took the picture, ignoring the cold stare Sandy leveled at him. He could understand how she might feel. But, in his job, he also understood that sympathy could impair one's judgment.

He turned and said, over his shoulder, "Thank you for your time, Miss Fields."

As he walked to his car, he could feel Sandy's eyes upon him like an invisible grip. It made him just a little tense, a little uneasy.

John Garrison's thoughts were about his job as he drove off. Just one misdemeanor, when she was fifteen. Humph, that hardly qualifies her as a murderess. But, I'm sure she lied to me about a few things. Why? It would be horrible to find such a nice looking kid guilty of something so animalistic. But, God, I don't even have another suspect, not even anyone to consider. Wait a minute. What was it that caller said?

John Garrison frowned in concentration. "Sorry…I'm so sorry." Yeah, that was it. That was what she'd said. And she'd said that she'd had to. Had to what? And what was it she was sorry for? He took in a deep breath, then expelled it in a long sigh. "This is going to be tough."

Somewhere in the back of his mind, the caller's voice echoed. He grappled with the fact that the voice had sounded like his wife Margaret's. If it had indeed been Margaret, that would explain how the caller had known his name and number. But what about the drunken slur in the caller's voice? Margaret had never drank, never touched the stuff.

John Garrison took one hand off the steering wheel. He placed it behind his neck and began to massage it powerfully. His thoughts seemed loud inside his head. No way it could have been Margaret. Just couldn't have been.

Sandy stood in the yard a while, staring at nothing in particular. She took one step then stopped. God, she thought, forgot my keys. I must be losing my mind. I've got to talk to someone, tell somebody who'll understand.

When she turned back toward the house her steps were languid. It seemed she hardly had the energy to place one foot in front of the other. The warm, liquid feel of tears moistened her eyes slowly as she walked.

Sandy found her keys and returned to the outside. Her tears had become a pair of tepid trickles. She got into her car, biting down on her lip to still its tremble.

Eugene awakened with a start. Something was wrong. He sat up slowly, scanning the perimeter of his room. Had something brushed him? Or was something intangible, some innate prod from his subconscious, the disturbance?

In the dark, his sleep-dulled gaze went to the red numbers on the clock beside his bed. It was 1:30. What the devil had awoken him at this hour?

His eyes searched the room again. They were beginning to adjust to the gloom. He could now make out the dark shapes of furniture, shadows of substance.

What drew his eyes to the window, he did not know, but he got up and headed to it. Eugene leaned on the windowsill and looked down on the street. He started a powerful stretch and then went stiff. A car sat right in front of the mailbox. It wasn't his father's because he'd always used the driveway. And Eugene had parked his own in the garage.

The last vestiges of sleep were slowly melting from his mind when he realized that he recognized the car. "Mom?" he whispered. "Mom?"

Spinning on his heels, he turned quickly from the window and raced for the stairs. Heart hammering, pulse pounding, he took the steps two at a time. He had so many questions racing through his mind that he couldn't pin down any one in particular.

Eugene hardly noticed that the light was on in the den as he bounded over the last two steps. But he did catch a glimpse of his father sitting, slumped over on the couch. John Garrison's head hung down, his chin nearly resting on his chest. He was fast asleep. A few pages of scribbled notes were still in the grasp of one hand. Other notes lay on the small table in front of the couch.

"Dad!" Eugene shouted as he headed to the door. "Mom's outside!"

John Garrison's eyes snapped open. "Wha, who?" he mumbled groggily.

Eugene flung the door open. He ran down the steps. "Mom!" he shouted.

At the sound of his voice, his mother's head came up sharply. Her cheeks were shining with tears. A nervous hand went out quickly to the ignition switch. In an instant the car was racing away.

Eugene yelled again; this time his voice quaked with emotion. "Mom, wait! Mom." His steps came to a halt quickly. His shoulders slumped. He watched helplessly as the car slowed. The brake lights winked briefly. Then the car turned at the corner.

His father's steps sounded softly as he approached. Eugene dropped his head. He did not notice that he was crying until one teardrop fell soundlessly on the concrete at his feet. The little dark spot spread slowly. Another fell beside it, imitating with a similar pattern.

John Garrison stood behind his son looking in the direction the car had taken. He put one hand firmly on Eugene's shoulders. Without turning, Eugene asked, "Why, Dad? Why didn't she stay?"

"I don't know, Son, but I wish I did. I really wish I did."

John Garrison turned slowly then paused. "You going to be alright?"

"Yeah, Dad, sure, I'll be okay. I'll be in there in a second."

Eugene took one more look, wiped his face and turned slowly toward the house. When he entered, his father was busy assembling his scattered notes. He plopped down beside his father.

John Garrison paused. Looking over at Eugene he asked, "Sure you're alright?"

"Yeah, Dad, fine. But I know you must be pretty tired yourself. You've been examining the progress of your case all night, huh?"

A broad smile lit up John Garrison's face. "What progress? I don't call nodding off every ten minutes progress, do you?"

Eugene shook his head. He smiled a little. He felt sure that his father, like himself, was purposely not talking about his mother.

For an instant only the shuffling of paper could be heard. It seemed neither Eugene nor his father knew exactly what to say.

John Garrison stopped busying himself with his notes. "Sleepy?"

"No," Eugene answered.

"Well," his father said, "want to hear some official police business? Between you and me now, this is strictly esoteric. It's not to be discussed outside of this room, okay?" He winked at Eugene and let a thin smile come to his lips. Eugene nodded and smiled reciprocally.

After pursing his lips briefly, John Garrison continued. "I've come up with some pretty disturbing, uh, things to be considered. Only one week after your mother left, the killings…" He let his voice descend to a whisper. "It's some weird coincidence, I'm sure. But as a detective, I have to use keen observation, and even when it deals with the improbable."

Eugene's mouth hung agape for a moment before he said anything. His eyes were a bit wide, incredulous. "Dad, are you saying that…that Mom…?"

"No, no son," John Garrison said, shaking his head vigorously. "But, I have got to find her. I've got to find out if she knows anything about…about… But that's impossible. What am I saying? Margaret could never…" He let the words trail off unfinished.

Eugene watched as his father stood up quickly. John Garrison placed one hand on his chin. He began to rub it slowly and pace back and forth at a short distance from the couch.

"If I could just talk to your mother, I'm sure she'd explain why, but then again… God, I'm confused. Why did she leave?"

He stopped pacing suddenly and walked to the couch again. The last question he'd asked remained unanswered, not that he really expected one.

"Your friend, Sandy, how well do you know her?" he asked. He felt glad, not really to change the subject, but at least take it in another direction.

Eugene hesitated before replying. "I…I really don't, to be honest." He hesitated again, dreading the answer to the question he was about to ask. "Why, Dad, do you think that she may be somehow involved?"

"Honestly, son, I truly don't know. But the description of the woman last seen with Henry Johnson seems to match. And I really don't think she was completely honest during my questioning." Then, as if changing the subject, he asked, "Do you remember where you were the night Henry Johnson was killed? Sorry, that sounds a little like I'm questioning you as a suspect." He blushed a little, then went on. "What I mean is, did you study with Sandy that night?"

Eugene frowned in concentration. "I can't remember, Dad."

John Garrison looked at his son thoughtfully. "It was on the fourteenth. Remember anything at all about that night?"

Eugene repeated the date. "The fourteenth?" He frowned again in concentration. His eyes lit up suddenly. "Oh, wait! Now I remember. Yeah, Dad, we did study, but Sandy said she felt like she couldn't concentrate, just like tonight. So I left there at about 9:30. I don't…"

"Nine-thirty!" his father interjected. "Are you sure, son? She told me you all studied until around 1 o'clock."

They both looked at one another quietly; no words were necessary. Each felt what the other must've been thinking.

Eugene shook his head slowly, his eyes dazed. "But Dad, there has to be some...some reason for her to just lie, some logical explanation."

There was another brief spell of silence. "Dad," Eugene said, "you're not going to arrest her, are you?"

"I would hate for it to come to that, son. She seems like a nice girl. Still, she lied as to her whereabouts on the night of the last murder. Right now, though, I don't think a lie is enough to arrest someone for such a serious charge as murder. But, I'm most definitely going to have another talk with Miss Fields. I hope that this time she is honest with me. If not...I'll have to take some further measures."

John Garrison stood up, stretched and yawned. Noticing the troubled look on his son's face, he stuck out his hand and tousled Eugene's hair. "Don't look so down, son. It'll be alright. Some gut feeling tells me she's not the culprit. But I'll have to talk to her some more." He yawned again, glanced at his watch and said, "Whew, way past bedtime. I'm turning in."

"Good night, Dad," Eugene said. "See you in the morning."

After his father left, Eugene glanced over at the pile of notes on the table. At the top of one page, Eugene saw the heading: Possible Suspects. Under the heading: Sandy Fields! He sucked in a giant but intense breath. Sandy, a murder suspect!

Eugene blinked rapidly and leaned closer as if he couldn't believe his eyes.

There were scribbled notes below the name, but Eugene's eyes roamed over the words so quickly that he didn't read much of it. His gaze stopped about halfway down the page on another name: Margaret Garrison. Mom! he thought.

A sense of unreality surrounded him; it seemed that his mind had gone numb. He stared at the name for what seemed a long time. His eyes widened when he realized that nothing was scribbled under his mother's name. A pent up breath rushed from his lungs. He felt a little relief that his father had written nothing under his mother's name. But still....

Quickly, he reached for some of the other pages of notes. His mind was in a swirl; he didn't focus long enough on any page to read many of the words. Okay, calm down. Think, think, he admonished himself. There's got to be something that I can do, got to be something I can come up with.

His breath was coming fast as he scanned one page after another. He willed himself to slow down. He went through the rest of his father's notes, but he didn't see anything that he thought would be helpful as a clue to him. Still, he felt deep down that something was there, something that could point to a real suspect. He told himself that it had to be. He was not willing to believe, even for a moment, that either Sandy or his mother was guilty of murder….

He had no recollection of how much time had passed when he awoke with one page still clutched in his hand. He'd dozed, and awakened by the sound of a noise; what it was, he didn't know. But his heart leaped at the thought of his mother. Had she come back for the second time that night? Was the noise he'd heard her car pulling up?

He got up fairly quick for someone barely awake. Eugene rushed to the door and flung it open. He was disappointed. His mother's car was nowhere to be seen. Still, he stood there, numb, looking out but focusing on nothing. Finally he turned and closed the door softly. He paused long enough to switch the light off, and then headed for the stairs. A heavy sense of defeat weighed him down. His steps were slow and without much energy.

When Eugene got to his room, he plopped down on the bed. He put his hands behind his head and began to perpend over the notes of his father. There has to be something there, he thought. I'll find it too, I know I will….

The next day, after school was over, Eugene was headed for his car when he heard Sandy's voice behind him. Turning, he stopped and waited for her to catch up.

"Eugene," she said, "are you alright? You seemed so distracted today in class. Anything wrong?"

"Yeah," Eugene answered. "I mean that in reply to both questions. I am alright, but something is wrong. There's something that I've got to tell you. It's about…damn!" he said, glancing past Sandy.

Sandy half turned. She swore under her breath. Brad and three of his football buddies were headed to where she was standing with Eugene. She felt herself tense. Turning quickly to Eugene again, she said, "He's itching for trouble. You'd better go. You can call me about 8 o'clock."

Eugene shook his head. He had a stubborn look in his eyes. It was evident that he was ready for a confrontation.

Sandy's heart beat faster. With a quick, nervous look, she saw that Brad and his comrades were now almost at the spot where she and Eugene stood. "Please, Eugene, go!"

It was obvious that Eugene wasn't listening, so she started in quick steps toward Brad. "Brad Richardson, don't do this!" she shouted.

The other three guys hung back a little as Brad tried several times to step around Sandy. He wouldn't look at her; his gaze was pinned on Eugene.

A crowd of eager, expectant students were making an assemblage around the commotion.

Sandy held her books tightly against her breasts with one hand. With the other, she kept pushing against Brad's chest. "Stop this…this nonsense. What'd you want? He's already made a fool of you twice."

"Twice?" someone in the crowd said. "Dang, Brad, I think instead of you being captain of the football team, you ought to be captain of the foolsball team."

The crowd roared with laughter. Brad's face reddened. He looked around quickly, his temper flaring. Turning back to Sandy, he shoved her hard. "San, get the hell out of the way!"

Sandy stumbled. Eugene tensed. He let his book bag drop from his shoulders. Some in the crowd oohed loudly.

Sandy regained her balance. In a flash of motion, she lashed out, slapping Brad firmly across the face. Brad's eyes showed the pain and shock. His lips moved, forming a silent word. His hand went slowly to the spot Sandy had hit. Suddenly, Brad swung a stinging backhand. Sandy yelped in pain. The blow knocked her around so that she fell. Her stomach landed on her books still clutched in her hand. Eugene yelled, "You low down son of a…." Then he took two long, swift steps and leaped. He moved so quickly that it caught everyone entirely off guard, including Brad.

Eugene sliced through the air like a ninja. One leg was drawn up neatly while the other stuck almost straight out. One instant he was slicing through the air, the next, his foot made a solid smack against Brad's forehead.

"Whoa!" someone shouted. "You see that?"

Brad hit the parking lot hard. The crowd went into an uproar. Amid the roar, one of the guys who'd come to help Brad shouted angrily at someone in the crowd. "No, I'm not going to help him! Anyone who'd hit a girl deserves whatever he gets."

Brad struggled to his feet. He looked quickly at the three guys he'd brought along with him. Each one looked away and stepped back a little, becoming part of the crowd.

Eugene waited. His observant eyes had taken in everything around him in a matter of seconds. He'd seen someone help Sandy up and noticed that she was grimacing in pain. She was obviously badly hurt. He'd also seen Brad's three buddies' reactions.

Brad was slow about getting up. Eugene watched. He wanted to draw the fight out, humiliate Brad, and make him suffer.

Brad straightened and moved toward Eugene. He pressed his teeth together hard. He moved in a circle around Eugene. Eugene watched his opponent. His feet shifted, following the route of Brad's movements.

Hands outstretched like claws, Brad made a sudden lunge. Timing Brad's sudden move, Eugene leaped high. He twisted in mid-air. His movements were well coordinated, graceful, smooth like ballet. For a fraction of a second, his back was toward Brad. Then his head came around quickly. He sighted his target. His legs whipped around. The side of one foot slammed hard against Brad's jaw. Upon the impact, Brad's head snapped to one side. His eyelids fluttered rapidly. His eyes rolled back.

Eugene landed on his feet with cat-like grace. The crowd went into an uproar again.

Brad's legs buckled. He began falling slowly. There was a brief hesitation. Eugene moved swiftly. He grabbed Brad's collar in one hand.

Staring hatefully at Eugene through dazed eyes, Brad clawed weakly at the grip on his collar.

Brad's legs wobbled badly, but he didn't fall. Eugene's strong grip was partially keeping him up. Eugene tightened his grip on Brad's collar. He made a tight fist with his other hand. As if concentrating all energy into that one hand, he drew his fist back slowly. At the very instant he chose to smash his fist into Brad's face, Sandy called to him. Her voice was very weak. If the crowd had not quieted, he would not have been able to hear her. He looked at her. Sandy shook her head. Eugene noticed that two girls were helping her remain on her feet. He looked at Brad again, felt some of the tension drain, then pushed him away in disgust.

Brad crumpled to the ground. The crowd of students gathered around him. Some sneered; others giggled and made disparaging comments.

Two of Brad's buddies, who had come with him, reached down to help him up. Brad brushed their hands off angrily. "Get off me, cowards! I can get up by myself." He got clumsily to his feet, watching as Eugene put his arm around Sandy.

Most of the students had started crowding around Sandy, Eugene and the two girls who'd helped Sandy. Some patted Eugene on the back, others were asking a lot of questions. Slowly, the rest of the students gravitated to where Eugene, Sandy and the two girls stood. Someone brought Eugene's book bag to him and one of the girls picked up Sandy's books.

"Oh no," someone said, "here comes that mean fart."

"Dean Braswell," someone else said. "I've got to go. I'm really not in the mood to face that scumbag."

As if on cue, a majority of the crowd headed for their cars. A few waited, though, giggling and whispering among themselves.

The dean strode across the lawn, a short, black, balding man. He was fat, virtually rotund. His face was clean-shaven, except for a conspicuously small moustache. It was cut far too small and short to fit his wide lips and fat face.

Dean Braswell hurried across the lawn, huffing, waving his fat arms. "Hold it! Just hold it right there!" he wheezed. "No one's going anywhere until I get some answers."

A few grumbled protests were heard, but slowly, the students came back. The fat dean waited until the grumbling stopped. He eyed the crowd distastefully. His gaze stopped on Sandy who was leaning heavily on Eugene. She had one hand around his waist, the other she held against her stomach. Her forehead was creased in pain. Little beads of sweat shined on her skin.

The dean stared at her a moment, then his gaze flickered to Eugene's face. "Mister uh...," he paused, holding his fat chin between his thumb and forefinger, "...Garrison, right?"

Eugene nodded. The dean went on. "I believe that you can tell me what's going on here, Mr. Garrison." He looked pointedly at Eugene, emphasizing his statement.

Everyone grew extremely quiet. All eyes were watching Eugene in anticipation. Eugene felt tense. He forced himself to think quickly, something that sounded believable.

Eugene looked at Sandy. "I was walking her to her car when, all of a sudden, she said she didn't feel too good." Eugene paused. "I mean, look at her, Dean Braswell, don't you think she needs to see the nurse?"

The fat man stared at Sandy for a moment and then he nodded slowly. "Yes sir, I believe you're right, Mr. Garrison. Get her over to see the nurse right away."

Turning, the dean said over his shoulder, "The rest of you all are dismissed." He stopped in mid-stride; his gaze rested on Brad and his three buddies. "Now, tell me gentlemen, why are you four way over here, and the rest of the crowd over there?"

All the guys looked at one another, each hoping that the other would volunteer to explain.

The dean crossed his fat arms. His brows arched in a commixture of amusement and impatience. Suddenly, he threw his hands up. "Okay then, refuse to communicate, huh? Well...I'll see all four of you in my office in not more than five minutes."

The guys started to complain. The dean threw his hands up again, this time in a gesture to silence them. "Five minutes," he repeated.

They all watched as the fat man shuffled away. Then Brad turned to see Eugene heading for the infirmary. Sandy was leaning heavily on Eugene, one hand firmly around his waist. The girl who'd picked up Sandy's books followed closely behind them. Sandy's fellow cheerleaders followed also. And other curious students tagged along, whispering and crowding, attempting to get a good look at Sandy.

Brad watched for a moment. His eyes squinted in anger. He spoke in a low, hard voice. "Sooner or later, I'm going to hurt that creep...really bad."

"You mean, just like you did a minute ago?" one of the guys jeered.

Brad turned on him quickly. "Shut up! I didn't see you doing anything, you coward."

"Brad," someone said loudly. It was Travis. He was running across the lawn to where the guys were standing.

Travis approached. "Where've you been?" Brad asked.

"Oh, Miss Beavis asked me to stay and help her a little. Man, what happened to your face?" Travis queried.

One of the guys snickered. "I'll bet you Egg can tell you."

Brad looked sharply at him. The guy turned, ignoring Brad's hot stare. He looked towards the infirmary. "Look," he said, pointing in the direction Eugene, Sandy and the others had taken. They were at the steps of the infirmary.

All the guys turned to look. They could see that Sandy was bending over as if she were throwing up.

The guy who had pointed spoke. "Brad, you shouldn't have hit her like that."

Brad's jaw locked stubbornly, then he replied, "Oh, but it's okay for her to hit..."

"You hit her?" Travis interrupted. He stared at Brad incredulously.

Brad stared back. His nostrils flared in anger. "Hey, what the hell is this...a freakin' courtroom? Jesus Christ!"

"I'm going to see how she is," Travis said. Brad opened his mouth to reply, but Travis turned quickly. His manner made it obvious that he was angry. Brad stared after Travis as he jogged toward the infirmary. One of his buddies tapped him on the shoulder. "I think we'd better be headed to Braswell's office. It's been about five minutes." Travis jogged over to the steps of the infirmary. Eugene eyed him contemptuously as he approached. At the sound of the footsteps, Sandy straightened.

The girl who was with Sandy spoke suddenly. "Do you see what your buddy did?" Her voice was sharp with anger. It caught Travis off guard. For a moment, he was at a loss for words. The girl didn't give him time to get his thoughts together. "If I were you, I'd find me another kind of friend," she said. She reached her hands out to help Sandy. "Come on, Sandy. We'd better get you inside to see the nurse."

Travis watched mutely as they headed up the steps. He seemed not to notice that Eugene was still watching him coldly.

A few of the students followed Sandy and the other girl up the steps. The rest of them hung back, talking amongst themselves. They watched Travis and Eugene like scavengers. They were eager to see another confrontation.

Travis took a step toward the infirmary. Eugene stepped directly in front of him. The two eyed each other momentarily. Travis looked away. He sighed, throwing his hands up in a helpless gesture. "Look, man…I can understand that you're angry. But Egg…I mean Eugene, I just want to see how she's doing. I mean, you can't blame me for something Brad did. Shoot, I'm angry too. I don't believe that girls should be hit."

Travis could tell that what he'd said had not dissuaded Eugene. Eugene just stood there, like a statue, continuing to stare at him. Then he simply turned his back and headed up the steps.

Swearing, Travis brushed his hair back in frustration. "Okay, okay, wait a minute…."

Eugene stopped on the top step. He turned slowly.

Travis stuck both hands in his pockets for lack of anything better. He felt very uncomfortable about what he was about to divulge. "I, uh…I'm worried about Sandy because…well, because I kind of like her…."

He shifted his feet uncomfortably, took his hands out of his pockets, and dropped his head.

Eugene felt surprise, but he didn't say anything right away.

Travis went on. "I … I know that this all sounds kind of, of…."

"You don't have to explain," Eugene said. "I understand. Come on."

Travis didn't move at first; he was shocked. Then a smile lit up his gaunt face. He hurried to the steps.

When they entered, a nurse was coming from the back. Her expression made it evident that something was wrong. She looked from Travis and Eugene to the girl who'd come in with Sandy. She glanced at some of the other students too. "Are all of you with Miss Fields?" she asked.

Some of them nodded, others said yes.

The nurse glanced around again. She pressed her lips together firmly, then continued. "I regret being the bearer of bad news. But, at the moment, Miss Fields is…she's not doing so well. She will have to…."

"What's wrong with her?" Eugene interjected, his voice high with emotion. "I don't…I don't understand…."

The nurse held up one hand, silencing him. "At this point, it doesn't appear to be life-threatening. However, she will need to be transported to a facility that is better equipped to address her condition. I've already phoned Bartenfield General Hospital. Someone will be here shortly."

"Wait a minute...hospital? Condition? What the devil is going on?" someone asked. "All she did was fall."

"Yeah," Travis said, "what are you talking about?" He couldn't keep the tremor and the anger from his voice.

Eugene felt the same; he wanted answers too. But now, he only stared at the nurse expectantly. He was sure she'd explain, given the chance.

The nurse pressed her lips together again. "I'm afraid that I can't tell you anything more. Any further information would be a violation of patient confidentiality. I'm sorry."

She turned to go. She paused suddenly and turned around. "Why don't you all meet her at the hospital? It'll be strictly up to her, though, if she volunteers to impart any further information."

Immediately after the nurse left, a noisy chatter began. Eugene took control of the situation.

"Wait a minute. Calm down," he said. "This won't do us a bit of good. I suggest we get going to the hospital."

He scanned the small group. "Anyone here need a ride?" No one did. They filed out the door.

The girl who'd helped Sandy made no effort toward the door. That caught Eugene's attention.

"Sharon, do you have a car?" he asked.

"No, she said," but my parents are coming to pick me up. They should be here at any minute." All the other students had left, so she was speaking to only Eugene and Travis. "You guys go on. I'll see you when I get there."

Later, at Bartenfield General Hospital, Sharon, Eugene and Travis sat in the waiting area. They were restless. They waited while Sandy's parents were in Sandy's room. The other students who had been concerned had already visited and gone.

When Sandy's parents finally came out, Mrs. Fields was leaning heavily on her husband. Her walk was a bit unsteady. And she kept dabbing at her eyes with a large handkerchief. The two stopped in front of Eugene, Travis and Sharon. The three of them stood up. They cast quick, worried looks among themselves.

Sandy's mother kept her head practically buried against her husband's shoulder.

Alec Fields addressed the three. "I...I've been informed by the nurse that Sandy's going to be okay." He cleared his throat and went on. "She told us that in all probability, they'll let her come home tomorrow...."

His voice quavered and diminished to a level that could barely be heard. "I, uh...I guess you all can go back there to see her."

He steered his wife gently toward the door, hesitated and then spoke. "Oh, Eugene, she said to tell you to come last."

"Alright," Eugene said. Eugene paused. "I'm sorry about what happened."

Travis and Sharon expressed their condolences too. Alec Fields hesitated again. "Thank you," he said, "thank you all."

Sharon started in the direction Sandy's parents had come from. She glanced over her shoulder and noticed that Travis was still standing next to Eugene.

"You coming?" she asked.

"Yeah, go ahead though, I'll catch up in a minute."

Travis turned to face Eugene. The hesitance he felt showed clearly on his face. "Eugene…, I, uh, I want to apologize for what Brad did and for…well, you know how most of us have been treating you at school."

They both remained silent for a brief time. Then Eugene allowed himself a slight smile. "Well, I'm no one to hold a grudge. And anyway, I've never had anything against you personally. Apology accepted."

He stuck his hand out to Travis. Travis gave it a firm shake.

"Well, I guess I'd better go see how Sandy is doing," Travis said. He turned, then paused. "Hey, man, you think you can teach me some of those kung fu moves sometime?"

Eugene smiled broadly. "No…not a chance."

Travis laughed. "Well, I'll tell you what, after seeing your skills, this is one guy who's not gonna disagree with you about anything."

"Uh, oh," Eugene responded, "my dad always said watch out when people start to flatter you. He says it's a sign that they want something."

Travis chuckled. "Man, what an amazing family. You're the kung fu kid, and your dad, he's a psychic, huh?"

"Well, actually, he's a homicide detective," Eugene told him.

Travis' eyes lit up. "Cool! Man, that's really cool. You know, your dad was right about why people use flattery. I do want something. Well…at least, in a way."

There was an awkward quiet while Travis searched for the right way to phrase his request. Eugene eyed him quizzically.

"Eugene, what I'm saying is, you know, if some days you don't have anything to do, maybe we can sort'a hang out or something."

"I guess that there's nothing wrong with that," Eugene said.

"Really?" Travis said. Realizing he'd spoken too loud, he looked around the waiting room. Some of the people waiting frowned at him. Travis' face turned red with embarrassment. With effort, he ignored the stares and lowered his voice. "I guess we can exchange phone numbers then."

He patted his pockets. "Humph, nothing to write with."

"Come on," Eugene said. "There's something over there." He pointed to a long counter in one corner. Two hospital personnel were busying themselves behind the counter.

Eugene and Travis walked to the counter. They asked to borrow pen and paper. The two exchanged numbers. Travis walked away, buoyant like a kid with a new toy.

Eugene watched as Travis left. He shook his head a little. If Travis' admiration of him was any indication, he was going to have a lot of fans at school. Yes, school was going to be a lot different.

About thirty minutes passed before Travis and Sharon came back. They stopped briefly to chat with Eugene, and then they departed.

When Eugene entered Sandy's room, he felt somewhat hesitant. It was a puzzle to him why she'd asked the nurse to have him come alone.

Sandy's eyes were closed, but she opened them slowly when she heard his footsteps. She managed to smile, although her eyes were drooping heavily. "Come on over here. I promise I won't bite you, okay?"

Eugene flashed a quick, lucent smile. He walked to a chair near the bed she lay on. He sat down and instinctively reached for her hand. Inches from her hand, he stopped his own.

She giggled, noticing his reticence. "Aw, go on, you can touch it. My fingers won't bite either."

Eugene smiled again. The humor helped him to relax. He reached for her hand again; this time, he cradled it gently. It felt soft, moist and warm against his palm. A wonderful, peaceful feeling. He wondered, did such a feeling mean that someone was falling in love? For some reason, he wondered was that the way his mother and father had felt at one time.

"Hey," Sandy said, smiling, "you're kind of quiet. What are you thinking?"

Caught off guard, Eugene's speech faltered. "Oh, I uh, I was just…it, it's not very important." He blushed. "Anyway, I want to talk about you, not me. What did they say is wrong?"

She looked directly at him. He could see that her eyes had begun to water.

Sandy didn't answer immediately. Eugene squeezed her hand gently, a silent statement that said, "It's okay."

Her throat moved, swallowing an immaterial lump. Her voice trembled emotionally. "Remember when we used to study, and I could never really concentrate?"

Sandy continued, "And remember that I told you I had a secret?"

"Yes, I remember," Eugene answered in a low voice.

"Well," she sniffed quietly, "I was…I was pregnant. When Brad hit me and I fell on my stomach, it caused me to…to…"

"Curse him! Eugene said. "I…I'll kill that, that…."

"No, Eugene. It really wouldn't serve any purpose," Sandy said. "But, I promise, he won't get away with what he did…." She paused, wiping gently at the warm tears on her face.

"San, I'm so sorry," he said, his voice near a whisper. "Please, let me know if there is anything I can do, I mean anything at all?"

She sniffed again and managed a smile. "Yes, there is something. I'd like for you to remain my friend."

"Done," Eugene replied. He returned the smile. "You know, I think I'm changing. Within the last few weeks, I feel myself becoming a little less withdrawn."

"Yes, I think you are," Sandy said. "I think that…wait a minute, I've just remembered something. Didn't you have something to tell me at school?"

"Oh yeah, you mean right before the fight?"

"That wasn't a fight," Sandy giggled. "That was an embarrassment."

Eugene laughed too. It felt good to see a smile on Sandy's face. But his face suddenly turned a little serious. "San, I hate to tell you what I wanted to mention at school, especially now. You've already been through so much."

Sandy's forehead wrinkled in concern and quizzicality. She took a deep breath and exhaled it slowly. "I'll be fine. Go ahead. I guess it can't be worse that losing a…a baby."

"Well, what I was going to tell you is that my dad will be questioning you again. He knows that some of your answers were…were not true."

Eugene stopped talking. He looked into her eyes.

"Man!" Sandy said in a low exhalation, "I should've just told the truth. But, I was so…I was under so much pressure. I couldn't even think straight. I was scared for anyone to find out that I was pregnant. You've got to believe me, Eugene, please?"

"I do believe you. Trouble is, we'll have to find some way to convince my dad."

Sandy smiled at him. "Oh, Eugene, you don't know how much that means to me."

Her hand trembled a little when she reached up to wipe at fresh tears. "God," she said, "I was going through so much. I used to just get in the car some nights, just ride, and get away from everybody. I just felt so confused. I thought, at the time, that it was a sort of escape."

Eugene nodded, showing that he understood. Sandy continued. Afterward, a couple hours passed in which they both became engrossed in desultory conversation.

It was well into the evening when Eugene left the hospital and headed for home. He felt sad for what Sandy had experienced. But he was glad that he'd found out why she'd lied to his father, glad that it had nothing to do with murder.

Unwanted thoughts about his mother entered his mind. He hoped that she'd come back some day to explain why she'd left. Eugene couldn't help but recall that soon after his mother had left the murders had begun. In his mind, though, it was unfathomable that his mother could be responsible for such heinous acts. And yet, there was no fathomable reason why she'd just up and left....

His mind formed an image of his mother. He realized that she did, in some respects, fit the description of the woman last seen with the last murder victim. His father had mentioned that the suspect bore a likeness to Sandy. But, purposely, he and his father had neglected to mention that his mother also had similarities to the suspect. Though her eyes were not large, they were dark, like the suspect's. And her skin was smooth and white...a stark white. His mother's hair was waist-long too, like the suspect's. It was dark brown, though, not black. But if it wasn't looked at closely, it could be mistaken for black. Despite the similarities, Eugene felt that there was an explicable reason for his mother's sudden disappearance. There had to be....

John Garrison opened the door to his house. He paused in the doorway long enough to flip the light switch on.

He carried his briefcase loosely in his hand. His shoulders sagged in fatigue. He expelled a long sigh and headed for the couch.

When he reached the couch, he let his briefcase fall heavily on it. His gun was holstered on his side. He reached for it, intending to take it off and deposit it beside the briefcase. But the jangle of the phone stopped him.

"Hello, Detective John Garrison here. Can I help you?"

"Yeah, detective, this is Mack, you know, one of the bartenders at Jimmy's." The guy was talking rapidly. It was obvious that he was pretty excited.

He went on. "When you were here before, you left your card. You said to call you if that lady showed up. You're in luck; she just walked in not more than five..."

"Are you sure?" John Garrison asked excitedly.

"Yeah, it's her," the bartender answered.

"Okay," John Garrison said hurriedly, "Then, whatever you do, don't let her leave."

The bartender tried to say something else. “What am I supposed to....”

John Garrison interrupted. “Think of something...anything. Just don’t let her leave. I’m on my way, right now!”

When he arrived at Jimmy’s, he was unable to still the light flutter in his stomach. He tried to ignore the feeling, got out and headed for the bar in quick strides. It irritated him that after years in the Special Forces and investigating murders, he still got a little nervous at times.

He entered the dimly lit bar. Lazy smoke drifted near the ceiling. The dim lighting and smoke commingled giving the air a bluish hue.

A few noisy patrons gave him quick, indifferent glances as he entered. John Garrison returned the looks with the same air of indifference.

With expert scrutiny, he scanned the faces quickly. He couldn’t spot the woman the bartender had told him was there. Perhaps she was near the back, concealed by the dimness and smoke.

He blinked. The smoke made his eyes water. The pungent aroma made him cough and wrinkle his nose.

He started toward the bar while scanning the crowd furtively without seeming to do so. Because the place was so crowded, he sidled up to the counter. Only one of the two bartenders was behind the counter. It was not Mack, the one he’d spoken to over the phone. The man finished serving a customer, glanced at John Garrison, and headed in his direction.

“Anything for you?” the bartender asked.

John Garrison shook his head. “No thanks, I’m here to see Mack.”

“Oh,” the guy said. “He’s back there.” He motioned with his thumb toward the back of the place. “But if I were you, I’d be prepared to wait awhile. Right now, his face is hung over the commode.”

The bartender leaned over a little closer. He had a humorous look on his face. “Mack likes to test what we’re supposed to be selling.”

John Garrison smiled. “Yeah, I understand. Listen, maybe you can help me then. Have you seen a lady in here with long black hair, big dark eyes and....”

“Sure have,” the man interjected. “Can’t miss one like that. Go all the way back. She’s at the last table in the corner, probably still surrounded by a bunch of slavering hopefuls.”

“Thanks,” John Garrison said, as he turned and weaved his way through the noisy crowd.

It didn’t take him long to spot who he was looking for. True to the bartender’s assumption, she was practically surrounded by guys. Her giggles reached his ears, shrill, yet melodious, sensuous. He smiled inwardly at the stir he felt on the inside. You’ve been without companionship too long, old man, he thought.

Strangely, the woman looked up just as he was nearing the table. It was uncanny. She looked straight into his eyes.

John Garrison approached the table. "Excuse me, fellows, I have to talk to the lady for a minute."

One of the four guys sitting there opened his mouth to protest. "Now you wait just one..."

John Garrison put one hand up as if quieting a child. "I'm tired tonight, and I don't really feel like being hassled."

Knowing he had the man's attention, he moved his hand to his holster. Looking the guy in the eyes, he left his hand there and patted his holster gently.

The guy's eyes showed comprehension. He slid his chair back from the table and walked away without another word.

Two of the men left at the table had only glanced at John Garrison and then continued talking to the lady.

The third man's eyes kept going from John Garrison's face to the holstered gun. He leaned over and whispered something to the others.

"So what," one of the guys said, "let him wait." However, the other two stood up rather quickly. They slowly integrated into the crowd.

Some in the crowd were now paying attention to what would likely develop into a confrontation.

The last man at the table sat with his back to John Garrison. He was completely ignoring him. The woman, however, divided her attention between the two of them. Every few seconds she let her gaze flicker to John Garrison then back to the guy at the table. The corners of her full, ruby lips were slightly upturned in a smile. John Garrison could not tell whether the smile was fomented by contempt, amusement, or some other sentiment.

Being ignored so blatantly gnawed at his patience. Placing one hand on the guy's shoulder roughly, he said, "Okay, fellow, time's up. Due to your obvious disregard for the law, you're about to find yourself in troub..." The man pushed his chair away from the table suddenly. Even amid the din in the bar, the scrape of the chair legs could be heard. Standing, the guy turned quickly.

John Garrison was, himself, a large and tall man, but when the guy stood up, he virtually dwarfed him.

As always, in times of conflict and tension, things moved at a speed seemingly impossible.

The big man pointed his finger, nearly touching John Garrison's face. His eyes were a bit red from boozing. But John Garrison could tell that the guy was not inebriated. He was sober enough to become a problem.

"Law or not, I'm not done talking to this lady here. And anyway,

I didn't see any identification."

John Garrison reached for his wallet. He brought it out quickly, opened it, and shoved it close to the guy's face.

"Aw, you could've gotten that at any old toy store," the guy sneered.

The woman had stood up. She peered around the big man, the same trace of a smile on her lips.

"Okay," John Garrison said, feeling his patience penetrated, "no more playing around." He stepped to go around the troublemaker. The guy, though, clamped one hand down hard upon his shoulder.

John Garrison exploded into action just as the guy started to protest. "Hold on, you..."

He brought up the arm that was toward the big man. With lightning force, he slammed the outer edge of his forearm against the bigger man's forearm. The move effectively dislodged the man's grip. In action now, he continued in quick, fluid motion. While the guy's hand was still falling, the detective's hand shot out. He clamped a steely grip onto the guy's wrist. A hard, quick jerk on the guy's wrist brought him forward. At the same moment, John Garrison brought his knee up sharply into the man's stomach.

A loud oomph rushed from the guy's parted lips. From the impact to his stomach, the man began to bend slowly.

A well-executed elbow to the man's chest straightened him up again. Without a noticeable pause, John Garrison, with his elbow still buried in the guy's chest, slammed a backhanded blow into the big man's face. The guy's mouth opened in silent shock. His eyes slowly rolled back. He toppled, crashing heavily into the table behind him.

After the man fell, John Garrison watched him long enough to know that he was out cold. Suddenly he looked up. The woman was gone! He turned quickly, scanning the noisy crowd. The woman was nowhere to be seen. He headed for the front door, pushing his way through the tumultuous assemblage.

Chest heaving in heavy breaths, John Garrison rushed into the parking lot. Some of the people followed, but stopped just outside the door. John Garrison kept running for a few steps while his eyes scanned the surroundings wildly.

"Damn!" he exclaimed as he skidded to a halt.

"Hey, man," someone yelled, "look!"

Jerking his head around quickly, he looked at the person who'd yelled. They were pointing to a darkened corner of the parking lot. Turning his head just in time, he caught a glimpse of the woman running into a dark alley between two long, short buildings.

"Hey!" he yelled futilely and sprinted toward the alley. Entering the mouth of the alley, he drew his gun. Flattening his back against one of the buildings, he hurried his way along. The alley was stygian, so dark and gloomy it seemed to create an almost tactile atmosphere.

The sound of his heavy breathing created a steady rhythm in his ears as he moved along. The rustle of refuse, the skitter of a scrambling animal and a cat's sudden loud meow, he heard distinctly.

By the time he made it to the end of the alley, his breathing was normal. The alley ended in a bifurcation: One alley stretched off to his left, another to his right. Both alleys appeared to be empty.

"Curse my freakin' luck!" he said. He stood with his head cocked, listening for any sounds. Nothing. He cursed under his breath, turned slowly, and headed back up the alley. He'd taken only a few steps when a peculiar feeling caused him to stop. It was a feeling not unknown to him: the weight of a predator's gaze. Someone was watching.

Frowning a little, he turned slightly. The heft of the gun was heavy in his hand, a symbol of readiness. He looked over one shoulder, then looked over the other. All that he could make out in the direction he'd come from was darkness. So, turning, he continued up the alley. Still, the feeling of being watched enwound itself about him; clung like an invisible wrap.

When he exited the alley, a few of the curious onlookers were still loitering outside. He ignored them while heading to his car.

Explanation escaped his grasp. He knew he'd reached the alley very quickly, and after entering, had moved along at a fast pace. So, where had the woman gone?

John Garrison drove slowly out of the parking lot. The question still nagged at him. For an answer, all he had to do was look back and let his gaze travel to the top of one of the buildings. Atop one of the buildings, a lone figure watched. It was the woman he'd chased, yet; it was not. Her whole body seemed to take on the property of liquid. It seemed to ripple, almost melting into the surrounding dark. Then, suddenly, there was no one standing there at all. A large bat rode the air just above where the woman had stood. Its huge, red eyes shined like hot coals, cutting two holes in the darkness. Two sharp fangs protruded out of its partly opened mouth. Saliva dripped from the glistening protrusions, silvery amid the gloom.

With its giant wings, the creature propelled itself forward. The predator had a prey to follow.

John Garrison drove his sedan into the driveway. He turned the ignition switch off. He sighed, frustrated that the woman had somehow eluded him. But he considered the night not a total loss. For now, he felt sure that neither Sandy nor his wife had anything to do with the murders. Yet two seemingly unanswerable questions stuck in his mind: Why had the girl, Sandy Fields, lied? And was it coincidental that his wife had left a short time before the murders had begun?

Tiredly, he reached for the car door. Opening it, he put one leg out then stopped. Something was wrong. His mind was screaming a warning. While in the Special Forces, he learned to trust such instincts. Without looking, his hand went to the snap that secured his gun in the holster. His eyes scanned what he could see of his house and the immediate vicinity. Still sitting in the car, he scanned the street behind him.

"Humph," he said mentally, reached for his briefcase and got out. Intentionally, he appeared not to be alert as he headed for the steps. But his hand remained near his gun. And he strained to hear any unusual sound. There were no sounds. His steps were slow on purpose. Something was going to happen; he felt it.

Suddenly loud, shrill, twitters and the flap of huge wings shattered the night.

In an instant, John Garrison turned sharply. His briefcase fell to the concrete driveway. At the same moment, he brought his gun out swiftly. His eyes bulged at the horror he saw. The sheet of dark sky was no longer a uniform stretch. For the huge bat suddenly exploded from the curtain of darkness. Its red eyes shined. Its mouth hung open in hungry anticipation.

Not taking much time to aim, John Garrison whipped the gun up and fired. The bat screamed in agony as the bullet pierced its body. The shriek tore through the night. It was so penetrating that, instinctively, John Garrison felt the need to cringe and cover his ears.

The impact of the bullet caused the creature to jerk almost completely around. It flapped its wings clumsily as it fell toward the ground. Mere feet from colliding with the ground, it managed to regain its balance.

John Garrison tried to align his gun for another shot. But the bat was too swift. It flapped its wings frenetically and disappeared into the night sky.

With his gun hanging loosely, and his mouth slightly agape, he stood watching the sky in the direction the bat had taken. He was in awe. There was not a species of bats that grew that large. The thing had been at least two feet long! But that wasn't where the oddities stopped. Somehow, strangely, the creature's face had reflected human qualities….

He searched the sky briefly before he turned, stooped, and picked up his briefcase. He'd taken only a few steps when he heard Eugene yell from his bedroom window. "Dad, what's going on? Are you alright?"

"Sure son, I'm fine. I'll tell you about it when I…."

A car pulled up slowly. It braked near the edge of the driveway.

John Garrison turned. He recognized the car instantly. It was his wife!

"Mom!" Eugene yelled from his window. In a burst of speed, he headed for the stairs, hoping that, this time, his mother wouldn't leave. He felt moisture coat his eyes as he bounded down the stairs and rushed through the living room. His heart leaped in joy and hope when he flung the door open. He was so overwhelmed by emotion that he only stood there watching.

Margaret and John Garrison walked toward each other slowly, their steps awkward and hesitant. When the two approached, neither one said a word at first. Words didn't seem immediately necessary. Still without words, they reached out and embraced. Each released a breath that they'd not realized had been held in. And suddenly, they both commenced trying to talk at the same time.

Finally, though, John Garrison paused long enough to let his wife speak. "John, I…I have to tell you something. I have to tell you why I…."

"Mom!" Eugene shouted suddenly. He bounded down the steps and raced to where his parents stood, still embracing.

"George!" His mother said, loudly. She stepped toward Eugene, her hands outstretched for a warm embrace.

John Garrison stood with his arms crossed. As he watched the two of them, a smile lit up his face. They were trying to talk at the same time just as he and she had done.

"'Scuse me, but, if two chatter boxes can stand a cup of coffee, I'll put some on."

Neither Eugene nor his mother heard the offer for coffee. They continued talking like two excited children.

John Garrison considered voicing his offer again. Instead, he shook his head, smiled, and decided to go ahead and make coffee anyway.

Eugene and his mother were so busy chattering that they did not notice when he headed for the steps.

When Eugene and his mother realized that his father had left, they went into the house also. Upon entering, they saw that he was coming from the kitchen. He carried an oval platter on which had been placed three cups of coffee along with powdered donuts.

They all sat down upon the couch. For a time they felt like a family again. Chatter went on well into the night.

Purposely, no one brought up the subject of Margaret having left without explanation. Finally, though, Margaret brought the subject up. "John…I have a confession to make…."

Her voice became shaky and barely audible. Her eyes agleam with moisture, she paused, searching deep inside herself for the strength to continue.

Taking a deep breath, she exhaled slowly before going on. "I've started drinking...heavily. It was me who called you that night, saying that I had to. What I wanted to say was, I had to leave, I had to get away. I didn't know how to tell you two that...that, I have cancer. I think I'm dying, John...."

Margaret Garrison was no longer able to restrain her tears. They flowed freely. She dropped her head into her palms and groaned, "Oh, John...."

Eugene sat immobile, paralyzed by the sheer gravity of what he'd just heard. His mind fought to reject it, to believe that he had not heard correctly. He watched as if from afar, as if in a dream-sphere. John Garrison put his arms around his wife.

Eugene heard his father talking to his mother in a comforting tone. But his own thoughts were so loud that he didn't understand what his father was saying.

When Eugene's thoughts quieted a little, he heard his mother saying, "...going to New York early in the morning. Doctor Thurguild recommended a specialist there. He's sure that the specialist there is better equipped to do the testing. He seems to think that there is some hope. Because, as he puts it, 'things are often not as bad as they seem.'"

When Eugene went up the stairs to his bedroom, his mother's words repeated themselves inside his head. "He seems to think that there is some hope...."

At school the next day, he could tell that he'd slept fitfully. His attention span was very short. To make matters worse, Sandy had called him before he left for school. She'd told him that she was feeling depressed, but she didn't accept his offer to visit her. Worse still, he wondered what news his mother would have upon visiting the doctor in New York.

The teacher had noticed that he'd not been paying attention. When he looked her way, she beckoned to him. Eugene went with her into the hallway. He divulged what the problems were. The teacher told him that she'd send him to the dean with a note from her so that he could be excused.

Eugene went back into the classroom to gather his belongings. As he readied his things, he kept glancing at Sandy's empty desk. It was strange not seeing her sitting there.

Leaving the parking lot, he decided on a pastime that he hoped would prove to be a pleasant distraction. He drove home, gathered his archery apparatus, and headed for his favorite practice spot.

Night came, a quiet, omnipresent descent. It found Brad talking on the telephone. Travis' familiar knock sounded on the front door.

Brad cupped the receiver with one hand. "Come on in, Trav," he said loudly.

Travis came in with a serious look on his face. He carried a thin, wide book. He sat down across from Brad.

Brad shifted his weight on the couch. He frowned at Travis' facial expression. Then he continued talking on the phone. "Listen, Jessey, my buddy just came in. Nine-thirty, right? Oh, can you give me that address one more time? I want to make sure I remember it."

He scribbled the address down on a sheet of paper. "Okay," he said, "I'll see you in a little while."

After putting the phone down, Brad looked at Travis who was staring directly at him. "Alright, Trav, I can tell something's wrong. So you might as well get straight to it. I've got a date." He glanced at his wristwatch. "If you can, make it snappy."

Travis shook his head. "I can't believe you, man. You're one cold dude. I called Sandy. She said that she hasn't even seen or heard from you. And I'm sure you know what...."

"Whoa, Trav," Brad said, his voice a little sharp with irritation. "If you came all the way over here to preach to me, you wasted your time. I'm not in the mood to hear that crap."

Quiet, ponderous tension permeated the room. Brad stood up suddenly and walked to the window. He sighed loudly and ran one hand through his hair.

Travis watched quietly, his gaunt face taut in anger. Though he'd grown up with Brad, he couldn't believe that his friend could be so cold. How could a man be responsible for aborting his own baby and seemingly not feel a thing?

Brad held the curtain apart with one hand. He peered out into the night sky. His voice disrupted the discomfortable quiet. "Listen, Trav, the truth is, I feel kind'a bad about the baby. But everyone knew that I didn't have any special feelings for Sandy. Even she knew that, man. Shoot, I'm the captain of the football team. And plenty of girls are naturally a part of the territory. Faithfulness is just not a...."

"You don't have to explain yourself to me," Travis interrupted. There was no attempt to conceal his anger.

The tension thickened the air. Sighing again, Brad turned, leveling a hot gaze at his friend. Travis stared back and then turned his head.

Taking a few steps toward him, Brad's gaze flickered to the book Travis held. He approached Travis. Taking the opportunity to change the subject, he stuck his hand out and asked, "What've you got there?"

Travis gave him the book but didn't answer immediately. When he did speak, he hesitated. "A book I got from the library. I went there, today, hoping to find something I could show you. But I didn't expect to be that lucky. That…"

"Lucky?" Brad interrupted. He read the title. *The Truth About Vampires*, by Dirk Von Vlad." He laughed. "Trav, you've got a hell of an imagination."

Travis just looked at his friend. He didn't say anything, but he felt that he would be wasting his time trying to convince Brad. But he'd try….

Brad went on, "So, according to this guy, what is the truth about vampires?" He had a trace of humor in his voice. The question had not been asked out of sincerity. It was meant only as a diversion. He wanted to get around arguing with Travis.

Travis watched as Brad went back to the couch with the book. He sat and began to rifle through the pages disinterestedly.

"I'll tell you, but I know it won't do any good," Travis said. "The truth is, vampires really exist. The author…"

Brad giggled loudly. Travis ignored him and continued. "…himself, was a vampire. But he never believed in killing humans for blood. He would always get his blood from animals. Time after time, he tried to get the others to see his point of view. They laughed at him. So, in time, he defected. Dirk wrote a journal that revealed secrets about vampires. He feared for the human race, mainly because of what a particular family was working on.

"The Nedloh family had many generations of scientists. Each generation continued the work of the one prior to it. Their goal was to create a drug that would make them immune to sunlight so that they could live among humans secretly.

"Well, somehow, Dirk gained a lot of human followers. They launched a campaign to eradicate the vampires. The campaign was working. But, the trouble came when the vampires launched a retaliatory campaign of their own. In one of the vampire attacks, Dirk was injured near the heart. But since he wasn't injured directly in it, he lived long enough to hear something he'd hoped for. His group had almost completely wiped out the vampire population. A couple escaped. That was bad. But what's worse was, the two that escaped were Nedloh's, a father and daughter. Eventually, the vampire hunters found the body of the father in a cave. The girl had disappeared. They found partially burned notes in the cave, proof that…."

"Wait a minute," Brad interjected. He laughed. "I think I know where this is headed. You're thinking that Jessey is the girl that escaped, right?"

Travis nodded. "I know how you tried to explain before, but something's not right about her. I just know it."

Brad studied Travis a moment, his lips turned up in a half-smile. "Listen to yourself, Trav. First you want to chew me out, then you want to protect me from some vampire woman. Boy, I'll tell you, you're acting just like an old hen or something. Do you actually believe..."

"Okay, Brad, I'll admit; I wanted to lay into you about Sandy. But we've been friends way too long. And, right now, my main concern is your life, man."

For a moment, Brad considered what Travis had said. It was almost as if he'd taken Travis seriously. But when he spoke, his voice carried a hint of jocularity. "I'll tell you what. To keep you from worrying your head off, I'll go get my dad's cellular phone. I'll give you the number and put the phone in my pocket. And another thing, Jessey told me where she lives. It's only ten to fifteen minutes outside the city limits. Furthermore...Mother, I'll call you if I get into anything I can't tame, alright?"

Travis laughed, despite how he felt. "Humph, you wish your mother was this pretty."

"Yeah, right," Brad said. They both laughed. Brad had a smile on his face when he headed for his father's room. He came back holding the phone up so that Travis could see it. Then he stuck it in his back pocket.

Stopping where he'd left the paper with the address on it, he picked it up and handed it to Travis. He then told Travis his father's cellular phone number.

"Better write it up there with that address. I might forget it," Travis said.

Brad hesitated. "Okay. Never can be too careful when it comes to night creatures that bite people, huh, Mother?" he joked.

Travis' only response was a half-hearted smile. He was worried. He even thought about calling the police. But, then, what could he tell them, that his best friend went to see a vampire? He took the paper from Brad and put it in his pocket.

The two headed for their individual cars. Neither spoke for a few paces.

"So," Brad said, "what are you going to get into while I'm at Jessey's house?"

"Well, I have somebody coming over who promised to watch the game with me." He avoided telling Brad that it was Eugene who was coming.

"I'll be playing a game of my own," Brad said. He emitted a boastful laugh. "Jessey said we were going to sit around, drink expensive wine, and get to know each other. Then she said she had a special surprise for me. I can't wait," he said, rubbing his palms together.

Travis paused at his car door. He looked Brad in the eyes. "Brad, be careful, man, alright?"

"Yeah, sure, Trav," he answered indifferently. "See you when I get back."

Brad didn't hear Travis whisper, "I hope so."

Eugene met Travis at his house like he'd promised. They sat in front of the television awaiting the start of the ball game. Eugene had been telling Travis about his life growing up as the child of an ex-Special Forces soldier.

"Man," Travis said, "I sure wish that had been me. I'll bet that was a lot of fun, huh?"

Eugene did not reply immediately. For a moment, he seemed not to have heard. His gaze was distant, his appearance pensive. "Yeah, I guess you could say that. But…, sometimes I wish I'd grown up like other kids. I think being taught so much violence has really affected my temper. When I fight, I actually get a kick out of it. And the crazy thing is, I don't want to be that way…."

"I think I understand that," Travis said. "But, still, I think your fighting skills are really cool. And really, you shouldn't feel bad about it."

"Thanks," Eugene responded. Again, his gaze grew distant.

Brad stared across the table at Jessey as he talked. He couldn't seem to keep his gaze from flickering to the low cut in the front of her black dress.

They each had a tall, slender glass of wine in front of them. Brad reached for his. It was his third glassful. He took a sip and smiled. "Whew, this stuff really has kick to it. What vintage year did you say this was?"

She smiled at him. "Expensive." Her sweet, melodious chuckle filled the air. Brad laughed too. "For the last twenty minutes or so, I've been doing all the talking. So, now, tell me a little about yourself."

Jessey stared at him. She had a look in her eyes that said, "I want you." She picked up her wineglass. Moving it toward her lips, she kept her gaze on Brad. Her tongue snaked out slowly; it ran leisurely across the length of her top lip. The erotic gesture made Brad shift his weight in his chair. At the same time, too, he felt a stir of arousal.

Jessey ignored his question. "You know, I like reading about vampires."

Brad frowned. What the devil…, he thought. How'd she get on that subject?

He was distracted by his thoughts. Jessey had to call to him twice before he heard her.

"Brad, Brad, are you listening?"

"Yeah, sure. Go on."

"Are you feeling okay?" she asked.

Brad had just taken a mouthful of wine, so he nodded his response. It went down in a hard gulp. He was beginning to feel rather nervous. Something was very strange about Jessey…. The stare she was leveling at him made him feel as though she knew what he was thinking.

"You think I'm strange?" she asked.

The question took Brad aback. It was as if she'd actually read his mind! He tried to remain calm, but despite his efforts, his chest began to rise and fall at a quickened pace.

Brad started to reach for his glass, noticed that his hand shook, and quickly laid it flat on the table. When he looked up at Jessey, he saw the trace of a smile on her lips. Had she seen his nervousness?

It was only a matter of seconds before he answered her question. But to him, it seemed much longer. "No, not at…at all," he lied.

She went on. "I guess I'm suppose to be telling you something about myself, right?"

Brad nodded. He swallowed dryly. The weight of her eyes was horribly uncomfortable.

"Well," she said, "my kind, we like fine things…."

My kind, Brad's thoughts echoed. Jessey's eyes never wavered from his face. She eyed him like a predator, a ravenous raptor.

"We love sex," she continued. "I mean not in the sense of the average person. We are actually obsessed with the act. We have heightened…"

Brad interrupted in a shaky voice. "When…when you say my kind and we, what do you…"

Jessey held up her hand, stopping him. She watched him hungrily, licked her lips again, and then continued. Again, though, she ignored his question.

"My family's name is Nedloh. We…"

Brad had just taken in a mouthful of wine. It spewed out in a violent burst. He leaned forward, pounding his chest, coughing loudly and gagging for breath. The name, Nedloh, repeated itself in his mind. Nedloh was the name of the girl in the book that Travis had!

Jessey got up quickly. She went around behind Brad's chair. While Brad struggled for breath, she patted his back, and spoke to him consolingly.

Shortly, Brad began to get himself under control. But he still coughed sporadically and wheezed.

"I've got to go…."

"Go?" Jessey questioned. Suddenly both hands were on Brad's shoulders. The grip was iron-like. He had made a move to stand up, but

Jessey's sudden action had said no, more intensely than mere words.

Brad felt the nervousness turn to cold fear. He managed to quake out the completion of his sentence. "...get some water. I need a swallow of water."

For the moment, the woman's iron-like grip did not relent. Slowly, though, she released her grip.

Brad stood up with fear-spawned alacrity. His father's cellular phone clattered to the floor. He turned. His heart leapt when he saw that the woman was already picking it up. His hand shook when he reached for the phone. For a tense moment, Jessey made no move to give it to him. A skeptical look was clear on her face. She eyed him strangely while slowly extending the phone toward him.

A frigid smile spread across her lips as she watched him. She pointed. "The kitchen's through there."

Brad turned quickly, stiff with fear. The thud of his heart felt like something attempting to escape from his chest. He walked quickly toward the kitchen, barely able to keep himself from running. His mind raced, snatching at threads of rationalization. Maybe the name Nedloh was just a coincidence. Maybe the fear he was feeling was due to imagination and the amount of wine that he'd drank. But, the strength! He rubbed one of his shoulders where Jessey had gripped it. It actually ached. No woman could be that strong....

Brad rushed through the kitchen doorway. He glanced back quickly. Good, the woman had not followed him. Quick, long steps brought him to the back door of the kitchen. His knees grew weak when he shook the doorknob. Locked! He was trapped!

Suddenly, he was aware of the weight of the phone in his hand. The police? No, they were too far away. Trav? His sweaty hand punched Travis' number on the cellular phone.

Travis had gone to the bathroom. When the phone rang on the end table near where Eugene was sitting, he looked in the direction Travis had gone.

The phone rang again. Eugene looked again and saw that Travis wasn't coming, so he picked the phone up. "Hello."

A whispery voice spoke to him. Eugene could detect the distinct sound of fear in the voice. He could tell, too, that it was Brad.

"Trav," Brad said, "you've got to get help. I'm in serious trouble."

The dislike Eugene felt for Brad caused him to frown. He felt the urge to hang up. But there was something innate that wouldn't let him.

"Travis is in the bathroom," Eugene said, somewhat flatly. "I'll tell him...."

"Is that...is this Eugene?" Brad asked.

"Yeah, it is...." Eugene hesitated. "What do you want me to tell...."

Brad interrupted. Eugene could actually feel the fear now. "Pl...please forgive me, man. I'm sorry for what I did. I'm asking, please, tell Trav to send some help. I'm at ...." Click.

Eugene held the phone away from his ear. He was staring at it when Travis entered the room.

"Who was that?" Travis queried.

"That was Brad," Eugene answered. "He said something about needing some help. He started to say more, but..."

"Oh, God!" Travis shouted. "I knew it! I knew the...that lady...the killer, she, she's about to kill..."

"Travis, calm down," Eugene said. "Explain to me what's going..."

"I can't now. We don't have the time. I'll tell you in the car." No sooner had Travis spoken than he ran for the door. Wild-eyed, he paused at the door, noticing that Eugene wasn't behind him.

Eugene had been caught off guard. He had not had time to evaluate the whole situation.

Travis shouted from the doorway. "Come on, man! Please, I can't do this alone."

In a moment they were running to Travis' car. Eugene stopped. He stared at Travis' Ford Escort. "If you need speed, we'd better take my car."

As they ran for Eugene's car, Travis asked, "Anything in there that we could use for a weapon?"

They reached for the doors. Eugene spoke across the top of the car. "Weapon?"

"Yeah. We're really going to need one. Trust me," Travis said.

"The only thing I have is an archery set," Eugene replied.

"God, that's not going to work. It's not enough. It's just not...."

"Where're we headed?" Eugene interrupted.

Travis fumbled for the paper Brad had given him. His hand shook as he read the address. "Oh, God, I don't even know where that...."

"I do," Eugene said.

The tires squalled as Eugene raced away. Smoke drifted softly on the quiet, night breeze. It curled away from the tires, slowly dissipated in a dance unique to smoke.

Eugene didn't know what to make of the whole chain of events. He'd heard the fear in Brad's voice. He'd seen the same in Travis' eyes. Yet, pivotal pieces were missing from the overall puzzle.

Travis filled in details as they sped along. It was about vampires, blood-sucking creatures. The very concept seemed ridiculous to Eugene.

But, yet, a part of his mind seemed to accept so fantastical an idea.

They were less than five minutes away from their destination when Eugene glanced at Travis. Travis' mouth was a tight line. He had grown quiet.

"Suppose this…this thing is real, what good can a bow and arrow do us?" Eugene asked suddenly.

Travis looked at him. His eyes widened, then narrowed. "You have to aim for the heart…." He paused. "Can you…can you shoot that thing and hit what you aim at?"

Eugene smiled a little. A swell of confidence sounded in his voice when he spoke. "Yeah, almost always."

Travis' mouth opened to verbalize a question. But, instead, it only sounded in his mind. Almost…almost?

Brad had not heard Jessey enter the kitchen. He had no idea how much she'd overheard. As a nervous reaction, he'd depressed the hang-up button on the cellular phone. He watched as the woman moved toward him, unnaturally gracile. Her every movement was stealth, seeming to better fit something in the animal kingdom, a stalker.

Brad's mouth was partly agape as he watched her approach. It seemed that all his muscles were incapable of functioning.

The woman let a slow strange smile come to her lips. She reached for the phone held loosely in Brad's hand. He relinquished it. She laid the phone on the kitchen counter and, taking his hand she led him back to the dining room.

The command to wrench his hand away from the woman and run was issued by his brain. But fear had rendered his will impotent. Thus, he followed the woman like one hypnotized.

She led Brad near the table. Without taking her eyes off him, she let his hand fall to his side. It fell against Brad's thigh, but he barely felt the touch of it. Fear coursed through his body, his mind, numbing him like a drug.

"Sit down. Finish your wine," Jessey said. The voice was still sweet and melodious. Yet, the tone of command was intense.

Brad obediently moved toward the chair he'd formerly occupied. His mind continued to urge him to run. He just couldn't. His thoughts were fuddled; never before had he experienced such helplessness and icy terror.

Jessey smiled when Brad sat down. "Brad, I'll be blunt with you. My name is Henrietta Van Nedloh. My kind goes back thousands of years. We are like you people, yet different in some ways. We're quick healers, stronger, and of course, we're malicious."

She rolled her eyes slightly, in reflection. "Me personally, I'm a bit sick too…mentally. You see, I have this oddity. I don't just kill my victims, I like to talk to them, watch the terror in their eyes…" she giggled, "…like that in yours right now.

For a moment, things were almost quiet, but for the roaring of Brad's pulse in his ears.

Henrietta Nedloh had remained standing after Brad sat down. She turned her back. In deliberate slow steps, she moved toward the chair she'd sat in earlier. It angered Brad that she was toying with him. The potent mélange of fear and anger became a force of compulsion.

When the vampire reached for her wineglass, Brad reacted. His hands tightened upon the chair. He leaped up suddenly. Grabbing the chair in both hands, he flung it with all his strength. He didn't wait to see whether or not it would hit its target.

Brad turned quickly. He sprinted desperately toward the door. One fearful glance back told him what had happened to the chair. The vampire held it in one hand. It was evident what'd happened. She'd actually caught the chair while it was still in the air!

His breath rushed out in raspy exhalations. His legs pumped frantically. His hand was only inches from the doorknob when he heard a terrifying sound. The sound was an atrocious commixture. It shattered the air like the hiss of a maddened cougar, the roar of a lion, and a woman's piercing scream.

The vampire leaped over the entire table. Saliva trailed from its gaping mouth, strung back by the force of its leap. Its pointy fangs shined with saliva. The red eyes narrowed when Brad's hand closed on the doorknob.

Brad had managed to open the door only a fraction before the knob was forced out of his grip. The vampire had slammed the door shut from behind him. The creature was fast.

For an instant, Brad was paralyzed by a sense of doom. Hot breath caressed the back of his neck. It prickled his nerves. The vampire's breathing seemed labored, asthmatic almost. The wheezing, rattling sound made a sickening rhythm in his ears.

Brad rammed his elbow into the creature's stomach. And in a move he would've used on the football field, he twisted quickly, ducking around the vampire. He ran, all the while his eyes searched for a weapon. One of the chairs! He could break a leg off and brandish it as a club.

He'd almost reached one of the chairs when he felt the familiar iron grip on his wrist. The creature jerked him around with pure brute force. Before he could react, the vampire unleashed a stinging backhanded blow. The force literally lifted Brad off his feet. He felt his back land across the table. His feet dangled off the floor. The gloomy depths of unconsciousness pulled at his mind. He struggled to maintain consciousness. But the pull was too powerful. His mind was shrouded in total darkness when he felt the fangs pierce the skin on his neck.

The creature had gotten on the table. She had straddled Brad, one knee on each side of his hips. It was so intent on feeding that the sound of Eugene's car racing into the driveway was not detected immediately.

Hearing the car slide to a halt, the vampire leaped off the table. It landed lithely, much like a cat. Its heavy asthma-like breathing resonated through the room.

Travis' footsteps sounded upon the porch. The vampire moved like a wraith. It stationed itself beside the door, back pressed against the wall.

Eugene rushed to the trunk of his car. His heart pounded with excitement as his hand closed on the bow and one of the arrows. He sprinted toward the door, noticing that Travis was already rushing into the house. Man, this is stupid. There's no such thing as vampires, he thought.

Travis' mouth gaped widely when he skidded through the doorway. His eyes bulged at the sight he saw. Brad lay sprawled upon the table. A shiny, dark spot spread out slowly from his head.

The vampire bared its teeth. A sudden lunge carried it near Travis. Before Travis could react, the vampire snatched him up like a toy. Travis emitted a strangled cry of shock. For an instant, the vampire held him above her head. Then, with strength belying her size, the creature threw him. He landed on the table near Brad. The table crashed to the floor, taking both him and Brad with it. It was now a pile of broken wood.

Loud, erratic breathing bouncing off the walls, eyes alight with murderous intent, the vampire started toward the two.

Eugene stood in the doorway, rendered useless by what he'd just witnessed. His mind screamed, Impossible!

Still in a state of disbelief, he managed to will himself to move. He put the arrow in place. Travis' earlier words came to him in a potent echo. "Aim for the heart…."

"Hey!" Eugene yelled.

The creature turned sharply. A split second later, Eugene let the arrow fly.

The arrow sliced the air with ease, whistling toward its target. But the impossible happened. The vampire whipped one hand up in a blur. It caught the arrow mere inches from its chest.

Smiling at the look of disbelief on Eugene's face, it turned the arrow sideward to him. Then, with the arrow held tightly in its fist, it moved its thumb slowly. Placing the thumb against the shaft, it snapped the arrow in two.

"Oh, Jesus," Eugene exhaled, "help us…."

The vampire laughed a loud raspy laugh. Then it smiled. "I'm afraid he's probably not concerned with your plight. But, I'll gladly entertain you…before I kill you, that is."

Without hesitation, the thing leaped long and high. It seemed that gravity was temporarily in submission.

Eugene went into action a mere second after the creature leaped. He stepped into the room quickly. With hardly a pause, he turned swiftly on the ball of one foot. His opposite leg cut through the air like the blade of a pendulum. The timing was perfect. Eugene's heel cracked against the side of the vampire's face.

A loud, pained grunt exploded from the creature's mouth. It fell to the floor heavily. But, with incredible speed, it sprang to its feet.

Eugene's eyes widened. That kick would have put the strongest man out cold! He felt the chill hand of fear. How could he hope to win against something so strong…so fast?

The creature had backed away a half step, while Eugene took a fighting stance. It eyed him with something like curiosity and shock. It ran the back of its hand across its mouth and smiled. Between raspy breaths, it said, "So, we want to play, do we?"

In the brief instant that the vampire started toward him, Eugene glimpsed Travis getting to his feet shakily. He saw Travis' hand close upon a piece of broken table leg. The wood had broken in such a way that one end was a jagged point.

In rapid succession, Eugene threw three swift punches. The vampire ducked all three.

Eugene backed up a step. Again, he caught a glimpse of Travis. The vampire didn't seem to hear Travis approaching. It laughed. "Something's wrong with your aim. You missed me."

Travis raised the makeshift wooden stake. There was a sickening thud when he rammed the stake through the vampire's back.

"I didn't!" Travis shouted vehemently.

The vampire's breath rushed out loudly. Its red eyes watered in shock and pain. Taking a few stumbling steps backward, it clutched at the bloodied point sticking through its chest.

Eugene gritted his teeth. He felt the battle lust he'd told Travis about. He stepped forward quickly, pivoted smoothly on one foot. His other leg swung around in a beautiful kick that landed solidly near the staggering creature's temple.

In a clumsy heap, the vampire crumpled to the floor onto its back. A nerve-wracking crunch sounded as the wood was forced further through the creature's chest. The creature screamed, arched its back, and then fell back.

A burst of maniacal laughter filled the room suddenly. It diverted Travis and Eugene's attention away from the creature on the floor.

Their hearts ached when they looked near one corner of the

room. Brad sat cross-legged, Indian-style. His eyes roamed wildly about. His hair stuck out in all directions. Froth bubbled over his trembling lips. One hand was pressed against the puncture in the side of his neck. Blood seeped through his fingers. Slick, shiny, carmine trails.

He rocked back and forth in a steady rhythm. "Watch out now!" he said, laughed, then repeated the statement. "Watch out now!"

"Come on," Travis said. He hurried to where Brad was sitting. "We've got to get him to a hospital." Eugene took another quick look at the vampire then followed Travis. Their backs were to the creature as they walked, so they didn't see the body when it twitched.

The vampire's back arched slightly. Its lips trembled. And then, there was a sound like a long, growling exhalation.

Eugene and Travis jerked their bodies around in shock. But to their relief, the creature had ceased to move. It had exhaled its last breath.

Brad's insane laughter cut through the quiet. "Watch out, now! Watch out for her. Watch out for Jessey Lee Baker."

END

www.ingramcontent.com/pod-product-compliance
Ingram Content Group UK Ltd.
Pitfield, Milton Keynes, MK11 3LW, UK
UKHW021052270726
13967UKWH00012B/629